Rise

of

Alpha

The Prodian Journey, Book 1

What a fantastic series opener!

The queen of the unexpected twist is back, and this time, Font is taking her storytelling skills to the next level. From the first page, *Rise of Alpha* unfolds like a movie, sucking you into an elaborately crafted world filled with vivid imagery and characters who are real, engaging, and flawed.

Amidst an action-filled tale of teenagers and royalty, fantastical weaponry and other worlds, is an endearing story of young love and heartache. For a brilliantly executed roller-coaster ride of emotions packed with everything from laughter to despair, I can't recommend this book enough.

R.E. Hargrave- International Best Selling Author

Books by Lorenz Font

The Gates Legacy

Hunted

Tormented

Ascension

Reckoning

Redemption – Coming soon

Indivisible Line

Feather Light

Pieces of Broken Time

Rise
of Alpha

The Prodian Journey, Book 1

By
Lorenz Font

Paperback ISBN – 978-0-9973858-0-9
E-book ISBN –978-0-9973858-1-6

Cover Design - Claudia Trapp/Phantasy Graphic Design
www.phantasygraphicdesign.com

Interior Design - Jennifer McGuire | JEMBookDesigns.com

http://www.lorenzfont.com/

With love to Eric Banaag for twenty-three years of friendship. I'll keep counting.

Acknowledgment

This endeavor wouldn't have been possible without the support of the following people.

Mom—Thanks for constantly picking me up when I'm down. I'm truly blessed.

Trenda and Patrik Lundin—Your tireless critiquing and listening to me ramble on and on about every aspect of this story has been much appreciated. I couldn't have a better husband and wife team (or friends) in my corner.

Wendy Depperschmidt—Through hell and high water, we've been through it all. Thanks for sticking by me all these years. Love you more!

Mavvy Vasquez—Sensei, you're amazing. Thanks for taking on this project.

Judith Somera—Thanks for being the steady hand and the guiding voice in all my journeys.

Bunny, Noots, Mickey, and Kevinsky—Love, love you guys!

Claudia—The Trident rocks!

Rachel Hargrave—You're simply the best. I can't say it enough.

Finally, to the gals in my street team, namely Cynthia, Kitty (Paula), Melissa, Lori, Wyndy, and RE. You ladies are awesome.

Table of Contents

The Wheel of Fortune

Normal people rang doorbells. However, my best friend insisted on throwing rocks at my bedroom window instead. He'd even cracked the glass once, but he had yet to learn his lesson.

"Brian," he called, just seconds before more pebbles rattled the pane.

Groaning, I hurried to stop him. I stuck my head out the second-story window and hoped my father wouldn't hear us.

"What the hell! Dude, if you break it again, I'm going to make you pay for it."

He flipped me the bird. "Get your ass down here. I have two hours before my parents come home."

I sighed and shook my head when he sauntered back to his car. Mark Stanton was the quintessential jock, but for some reason, he liked me. Maybe it was because of our mutual addiction to video games, or maybe it was that I'd won him over with my charming wit and magnetic personality. The latter reason was, of course, a running joke between us.

After sliding the window shut, I snagged my favorite cap from the top of the bureau. I took the stairs two at a time, hoping to slip out of the house unnoticed. My parents weren't as strict as Mark's, but since my social calendar tended to be empty, they were bound to ask a million questions. I'd also heard them talking earlier about my dad's latest client—a popular athlete who needed a nose job after a bar fight in Beverly Hills—and didn't want to interrupt them if the same topic was still on tap.

"Baby boy, aren't you going to have dinner?" my mother called from the kitchen.

I cringed at the nickname. Caught, I changed my route and headed to the kitchen to peek through the doorway.

"I'm not hungry and I'm running late." I glanced at my watch to prove my point.

My father looked over the rim of his reading glasses and regarded me with mild amusement. "Not so fast, young man. Your mother wants to tell you something." He looked at her, urging her to speak with a jerk of his head. "Cynthia, go on."

She folded the dinner napkin on her lap and took a deep breath, her kind blue eyes peeking through a curtain of long, dark lashes. I had to admit she was pretty and still looked young, but she couldn't hide her emotions. I knew she was going to tell me something I wasn't going to like.

"Dr. Singer called today. There's a new medication he wants you to try, but he needs to see you in his office first. Are you available after school on Monday?"

"Well, let me check my social calendar." No one laughed when I pretended to spread out an imaginary scroll. My parents refused to skirt around my disease, and if there was anything they loathed, it was my sarcasm and constant self-mockery. "There's nothing going on that day, Mom. I'm good."

Before she could launch into an hour-long lecture on how hard I was on myself, I gave her a quick peck on the cheek to distract her. She didn't understand that either I made fun of myself, or other kids would. My choice was easier to live with.

Hurrying to escape, I called over my shoulder, "I'll see you guys in a few."

I heard my father asking, "What is up with that child of yours?" just as the door slammed shut behind me.

I hated running out of the house like that, but I was sick of going to doctors, trying different medications without any luck. Kids my age should be worried about dating, hanging out with friends, and school. Instead, I was faced with an insurmountable dilemma—how to control my damn tics.

The night air was stifling, thanks to the heat wave that had been tormenting Southern California for several days now.

"Fuck!" I blurted out when I slid across the front passenger seat.

Mark snickered. In the back, the third member of our Three Stooges act laughed but didn't look up. Darryl was engrossed in his brand new cell phone.

Darryl Martin and Mark Stanton had been my best friends since middle school, when my family relocated here from Minnesota. My father had promised it was the last move we'd ever make. A prominent plastic surgeon, he'd never been able to turn down a good opportunity, so the first years of my life had been spent living out of a suitcase. The illustrious career of Dr. Gerald Morrison took us to ten different cities in three states before the Los Angeles partnership came along. I was lucky to meet Mark and Darryl, the only kids who were willing to be friends with the "freak with a tic".

"Ready, tic-boy?" Mark asked, already pulling out of my circular driveway.

I flicked my middle finger before fastening my seatbelt. "Yeah, sure. Where to?" I asked.

Darryl leaned forward to slap me on the shoulder, his usual greeting. "Madame Elizabeth, here we come."

"Are you guys serious?" I had a long list of items I could spend my money on—video games and a new laptop came to mind—but a tarot card reader on Hollywood Boulevard was not one of them. Then again, we'd been doing a lot of crazy stuff lately, and we supported each other. The trip to Madam Elizabeth's was going to happen whether I liked it or not.

Darryl hooted from the backseat. "Yeah, I feel lucky tonight."

"Just in case you didn't know, psychics can't predict lottery numbers," I said, hoping he'd change his mind.

He scoffed. "I'm not trying to win the lottery, Talon."

I rolled my eyes. Talon was my favorite character in the online game *League of Legends*. It was one of the geeky things we enjoyed doing on weekends or when our parents thought we were doing our homework. Mark liked the marksman, Varus, and Darryl preferred Garen. We had gotten into the habit of calling each other by those names.

"Madame Elizabeth better come through for us. She's supposed to be good," Mark said, turning the car onto the busy street.

Darryl rubbed his palms together. "I heard she's bea-uuuu-tiful."

That wasn't good news. In my experience, beautiful people were mean or would have nothing to do with me.

"Fuck!" My shoulder gave an involuntary twitch.

For seventeen years, I had endured the embarrassment and the stares that came along with Tourette's Syndrome. It was a curse—the kind of punishment you wouldn't wish on your worst enemy. My waking hours were plagued with ceaseless jerking. The vocal tics were even more embarrassing, coming out regardless of time or place. It destroyed my confidence, so I hid behind a wall few people could overcome. Although my parents had been steadfast in their support, they sometimes became the target of my frustrations. There were good days mixed in with the bad, but I was still holding out hope that I would outgrow my symptoms like my doctor said I might.

In the meantime, I had just two "real" friends. Everyone else was either embarrassed to be seen with someone who had no power over his episodes, or too put off by the onslaught of verbal profanity. Well, it was only the one word. Of course, it *had* to be a term not acceptable in most social situations.

Mark and Darryl had grown thick skins. Most of the time, they just jumped in during my verbal attacks, making light of the outburst and taking the focus away from me.

I thanked my lucky stars for them, but I still wished I didn't have to wake up to another day of these stupid episodes. Seventeen freaking years marred with shame and loneliness. I should be an active teenager, teeming with enthusiasm and lust for life. Instead, I spent my time hiding inside my shell, safe within the fortress I'd created to preserve my fragile ego. I was resigned to living my life in a Tourette's jail.

"Yo, what's the matter?" Mark turned to look at me from the driver's seat. As much as he tried, he couldn't understand what it was like to be in my shoes. After all, he was popular at school. Aside from being an athlete, Mark had legions of girls vying for his attention because of his green eyes and wild chestnut hair.

"Nothing." I dismissed his question with a wave of a hand.

How could I keep on explaining my discomfort at being around new people? Even *I* was getting tired of hearing my lame excuses. My friends understood my dilemma to a certain degree, but they weren't the ones who shouted obscenities at the most inopportune moments. Why couldn't I have gotten stuck with a word like *marvelous, jockstrap,* or even *bastard*? Why did it have to be *fuck*?

"Dude, whatever you're thinking, screw it. You're not getting out of this one. This is payback for when you dragged my ass out to take pictures of birds! I had to wake up early and take pictures of . . . some sparrows!" Darryl shook his head at the memory. It was obvious the expedition still bothered him. His problem, not mine.

Darryl was sort of in-between me and Mark in the appearance department. He was a few inches shorter than me but lanky, with gunmetal gray eyes and flat black hair, courtesy of a cheap bottle of supermarket-brand hair dye. We dressed in similar styles sometimes, depending on how dark my mood was, but Darryl was the one people called *goth.* He was into piercings. So far, he had three in his right ear, two in the left, and one in his right nipple. It remained a mystery how the three of us got along so well, considering our differences.

"They're called Graceful Hedge Sparrows," I corrected, "and they're quite interesting."

"Whatever. We sat there for hours. Hours! I followed you around while you took pictures of those dumb birds. We could've been attacked by a mountain lion, for crying out loud." Darryl's voice squawked while he jammed his fingers through his faux-hawk.

"Sure, whatever," I retorted. "I'm in the car already, so it doesn't look like I have much of a choice."

Mark parked the car in a paid parking lot, and we strolled a few blocks to a dilapidated building that housed several businesses and souvenir shops. I felt for the phone in my pocket and switched it to vibrate, just in case Mom decided to call to check on me. God knew she had the tendency to coddle, and at my age, it had gotten downright embarrassing.

VOYANT's purple neon sign welcomed us when we walked into the dark, rather dingy room. The scent of burning incense was heavy, and I faltered, not digging the eerie atmosphere. The black walls were lined with wall hangings of different tarot card characters, which seemed to be smirking at anyone dumb enough to buy their bogus predictions. Mark glanced over his shoulder at me with an unspoken challenge, leaving me no choice but to follow him to the counter.

The girl behind the counter looked up, her expression one of boredom. I recognized her immediately and stopped in my tracks, my mouth gaping open.

Shannon McKesson?

Whoa! Shannon was the epitome of popularity. She was pretty in that girl-next-door type of way. Her blond hair bounced on her shoulders like girls' did in television commercials. Her eyes were bluer than my mother's, and she had that mature persona most teenagers would die for. I had been watching her all these years, unable to take my eyes off her whenever she drove her yellow Beetle into the school parking lot or walked through the campus with the sure kind of grace only confident people possessed.

Darryl shifted next to me and pushed my chin up, closing my mouth. I coughed, realizing I'd already made my first blunder of

7

the night. And it didn't even have anything to do with my tics.

"Hi, Shannon. We're here for a tarot reading. I called earlier to make an appointment," Mark said, sounding like a real tarot junkie.

"Oh, yeah. Larry, Curly, and Moe." She hopped off the barstool and checked off our names in the appointment book.

Mark and Darryl quickly pointed at me. "He's Curly!"

Of all the things these bastards could do, they had to put me in the spotlight. They knew I hated the attention. I felt my face burning from embarrassment but decided to play along, shuffling my feet for maximum effect. What came next was a reward for my efforts. Shannon laughed, the sound a sweet mix of tolling bells.

Darryl continued laughing, but Mark leaned forward on the counter, about to unleash his killer moves on Shannon.

"Hey, gorgeous. How are you?" Mark said in his most effective man-voice.

"Cut it out, Stanton," Shannon answered with a roll of her eyes.

It was obvious from Shannon's reply that she was familiar with Mark. As much as I hated what I was feeling at that moment, I wanted to sock Mark and tell him to lay off. We all knew he was seeing Brittney, his flavor of the month.

Shannon drew back the shimmery black divider that blocked the entrance to another room. She whispered something to someone before she looked at our group and waved at me.

"Curly, you're up first." She held the curtain open for me while I made my way around the counter.

"Thanks," I muttered under my breath. In the brief moment when I walked past her, I caught the scent of jasmine and inhaled deep. My whole body hummed at her proximity, and I felt like I had woken after a long sleep.

"Madame Elizabeth will take good care of you," Shannon said in a mocking tone.

She drew the curtain closed, and I found myself trapped with Madame Elizabeth for the next God-only-knew-how-long. I glanced at the woman sitting behind the round table in the center of the room that was covered with a velvet cloth. Atop sat a stack of harmless-looking cards.

"Hello, young man." She bowed her head in welcome. With an elaborate wave of her hand, she gestured to the chair opposite hers. "Have a seat."

I returned her greeting with a tight smile, and then, with great reluctance, sank into the chair. I had no idea what the heck this tarot and psychic crap was all about to begin with, except somehow predicting the future. Remaining silent, I rested my clammy palms on my thighs.

Madam Elizabeth pushed three yellow velvet bags across the table. "Each bag contains a deck of cards. Pick one, then shuffle that deck," she said.

Wary, I glanced at her before choosing the bag in the middle. I pulled the drawstring, took out the cards, and began to shuffle them. Her keen eyes watched me and she smiled when I handed her the deck.

"Is this your first time receiving a tarot reading?"

The small talk was unnecessary, but I played along.

"Yeah."

She spread the colorful cards across the table in a single sweep. The cards fanned across the surface like fallen dominoes in a perfect arc. "So, what are you looking to see? Love, adventure . . . perhaps happiness?"

"I do– don't know," I stammered. A jerk shot through my

tight shoulders before I could stop it.

Madame Elizabeth's gaze met mine for a brief moment. Although her eyes were hidden behind red-tinted glasses, it was obvious she saw my discomfort, and it put me on the defensive. The woman was stunning in a disturbing way. It felt like she could see right through me, as if she knew my secrets.

I studied her while she perused the cards. Her hair was tied in a loose bun on top of her head, and she wore a magician's tunic, which reminded me of characters in *League of Legends*. I had the urge to roll my eyes when she began playing the part, momentarily closing her eyes and breathing deep. Hands splayed on the cards, she caressed each one before she collected the stack. Shuffling the cards once, she then laid a few back down on the table with quick and precise movements. With utmost concentration, she studied them, choosing one.

She flipped the card for me to check. "What do you see?"

Considering I had no idea what to look for, I stared at the card then began describing the picture. "I see a circle with four distinct colors on the edges."

Nodding, she dropped the card and looked up at me. This time, her thin, almost invisible brows furrowed. "With every curse comes a blessing," she said.

The moment she uttered those words, the hair at the back of my neck rose.

What the hell?

Freak with A Tic

I stared at Madame Elizabeth, unable to form coherent words. It wasn't as much *what* she said as the expression on her face. I could've sworn that the woman's lips trembled. A violent tic rolled over my shoulders, and the sudden movement shattered the silence of the room. The table rattled when my hands gripped the edges and I tried to suppress the tic.

"Are you okay?" Madame Elizabeth's voice was barely a whisper, despite the calm demeanor she tried to project.

The tics subsided within seconds, but my embarrassment lingered longer. When I opened my mouth to answer, nothing came out.

"Is there anything I can do for you?"

I shook my head. "I . . . explain to me what you just said."

Her statement bothered me, but I wasn't about to admit it. I never believed in superstitions and old wives tales. My mother had come up with the most ridiculous ones over the years. *Sitting too close to the television is bad for your eyes. Chocolate leads to acne.* Sure, tell that to a teenager. And yet, the Madame's proclamation struck me as serious. She lifted her sleeves, and her long, slender arms grazed the table, hovering over the cards as if summoning higher powers.

"All I can see is that you are suffering. You have an affliction. You're angry and frustrated, but as I said, I see a rainbow on the horizon."

"What does that mean?"

"This is the wheel of fortune." She held the card up for me to inspect. "When it appears, it heralds a new phase in the cycle of life. You can associate it with changes in your present situation. It could mean good luck or good fortune—however you want to interpret it. But as it is a turning wheel, it can bring the opposite of luck as well. Obstacles and unpleasant surprises often will be mixed in with the good."

I knew right then that I shouldn't have gone to this tarot reading. There was nothing more disconcerting than being told that there was the possibility I'd go from fucked up to great, and then back to being fucked up again.

Rising to my feet, I offered a tight smile. "Thanks for your time."

"Wait, don't you want to hear the rest?"

I shoved my hands in my pocket and shook my head. "I've wasted enough of your time already as it is. I'll send one of my friends in." I turned and walked away, feeling weird and suddenly out of sorts.

"If you ever change your mind, you know where to find me," she said just as I slid past the curtain that served as the border between profound insanity and reality.

I found Mark and Darryl sitting on the small sofa. Both looked up at me.

"So, how'd it go?" Darryl's fingers were still busy punching text messages on his phone, even though his attention was directed at me.

"It was good," I replied, not willing to divulge how shaken I had been. Mark threw me a doubtful glance before walking into the lion's den. I sat next to Darryl, still smarting from the unusual prediction.

I snuck a glance in Shannon's direction and was surprised to see her staring at me. I squirmed under the close scrutiny and lowered my eyes before pulling out my cell phone as a distraction.

"Hey, Curly," she called out.

Darryl chuckled and nudged me. "Hey, the pretty girl is calling you," he whispered.

I balked. Talking to people, especially strangers, was never an easy thing for me to do. My social graces may have been on par with a caveman's, and yet something inside me wouldn't let me ignore Shannon. I got up and, with hesitant steps, made my way toward the counter. She watched my approach, a slight grin on her face.

"Yeah?" I said, trying to sound nonchalant. I didn't think I succeeded, since my voice came out in a squeak.

"Weren't you in some of my classes last year?"

I nodded, not trusting myself to speak again for fear that I'd remind her why I was so infamous in school.

"If you're friends with Mark, how come I don't see you during the football games?"

Because I'm invisible? I wanted to say.

Instead I said, "Oh, I work right after school," as if my

answer should explain everything. I smacked my head to suppress the tic coming due to the stressful situation, and I hated that my legs were about to collapse from under me.

"Hey, are you okay? You look green." Shannon had a worried look on her face. She reached over the counter and touched my forehead.

If I was looking green before, now I was ready to pass out. A jolt like an electric current coursed through my body at her touch, and it wasn't just from excitement. As embarrassing as it was, she was the first girl to touch me. Or the second, if you counted the girl who kept holding my hand back in first grade.

"I-I'm okay," I stammered. Then as if by some cruel decree of the tic gods, an embarrassing outburst blasted from of my mouth. "F-fuck!" I smacked my head again, another jerk reaction to blurting out my favorite word.

A myriad of expressions crossed Shannon's face. She turned red, maybe out of anger or possible mortification. I would never know, because like the wuss that I was, I fled the scene of the crime without gathering the evidence.

"Brian!" she called to me just as I cleared the exit and joined the pedestrian traffic on Hollywood Boulevard.

I kept running and covered the several blocks from the shop to the parking lot in mere minutes. My legs were aching by the time I stopped at Mark's car to catch my breath. It didn't take long for me to realize what had just transpired in there. I was hyperventilating. How pathetic was that?

Shannon had been how I'd imagined her. Soft hands, beautiful face, and unreachable. She and I could never be. As expected, another round of spasms erupted from my shoulders, followed by a nice round of F-bombs. I braced myself for the barrage of uncontrollable and freakish jerking. It lasted for a few minutes until I was totally spent. I leaned against Mark's car, exhausted and angry, wishing I'd never let Darryl talk me into coming and hoping Shannon would never have to witness my embarrassing display up close.

By the time Monday morning rolled around, I had pushed the whole Friday night disaster to the back of my mind. I refused to dwell on the unfortunate meeting with Shannon. For all I knew, she had forgotten all about it.

I decided to park my car a few blocks from school and walk the rest of the way. As usual, the front of the school was teeming with students swapping stories from their fun and eventful weekend. I ambled past them with my head bent low. I had no stories to share, except the botched tarot reading. School was already hell for me, and the kids were cruel, so I wasn't about make it worse. At least it was my senior year. After it was over, I'd be well on my way to being alone. I preferred it that way— safer, saner, and less stressful.

Since it was our second week back from summer vacation, it was easy to fall into the habit of fading in the background and trying to be invisible. My daily schedule consisted of five AP classes and an elective I'd chosen. Photography had always been my passion, and the class gave me a chance to enhance my skills and be a part of the yearbook team. Otherwise, my club choices and activities were quite limited. After all, there weren't many things a *freak* could do, anyway.

I slipped into my first class and parked my ass in the back of the room, behind the firing line in case my tics sprang into action. Pulling out my notes from Friday's class, I buried my face in them while students piled into the classroom. Lost in my own world of symmetry and composition, I didn't notice that someone had taken the empty seat next to mine until the scent of jasmine wafted through the air. My breath hitched, and I followed my nose to find Shannon staring down at me, smiling.

"Hey, I didn't know you're taking this class, too," she said in that sweet voice of hers.

My mouth hung open while I looked up at her smiling face. What was with that smile, anyway? What had I done to deserve such torture? I stared at her, unsure if she was expecting an answer.

"Curly?" she prompted.

I'd take Curly any damn day over "Tic-boy" or "Freak."

"I-I'm on the yearbook committee," I stammered, sounding like a total dork. "I was advised to ease up on my AP classes, so I had to take this one." I mentally kicked myself when I realized what a show-off I must've sounded like. I added another quick question to wash off the nerdy picture I'd painted. "And you? What are you doing here?"

"Oh, this is exciting. I'm on the yearbook committee, too."

That was where it got weird. Was it my mind playing tricks on me, or did the girl sound interested in talking to me?

"I just came back from visiting my grandmother last Friday," she added. "This is my first week of classes. I hope I didn't miss much."

That must've been the reason why I hadn't seen her on campus the prior week.

"No, I don't think so. You'll be fine," I said.

She flipped the stray strands of hair off her face, and I caught a whiff of that incredible scent again. Oh man, this was going to be a long, long year.

Mr. Peters, a bespectacled man in his late fifties, walked in, preventing any further conversation. His bowtie cradled his sagging chin, and his clothes were pure retro 1960s. The man spoke in a monotone guaranteed to put anyone to sleep. Nonetheless, to us who wanted to learn, he gave the most interesting lectures.

He began his usual attendance, nodding as he checked each row until his eyes rested on Shannon. "Ms. McKesson, welcome to the class. I received the letter from your parents explaining your absence. I hope your grandmother is doing okay."

"She's fine and resting," Shannon replied.

Mr. Peters turned around and picked up a piece of chalk and started scribbling on the board.

For the rest of the hour, being the loser that I was, I immersed myself in everything Shannon. I inhaled hard, greedy to take in all that I could of her scent. Strange enough, my sense of smell had never been this sensitive before, but I wasn't going to complain. I could breathe her in all day. Sneaking glances whenever the opportunity presented itself, I basked in my luck at having the chance to sit next to the prettiest girl in Los Angeles.

"Mr. Morrison?" I looked up at Mr. Peters and realized that he was waiting for me to answer a question. The entire class was watching me. A few classmates snickered while I scrambled to recall what he'd asked. Drawing a blank, I stared at him.

Instead of reprimanding me, he addressed the entire class. "I expect everyone to pay attention during class. This may be an elective, but it still has the same expectations as your required courses. I'm sure you've realized an F wouldn't look good on your transcript."

Several kids snickered, and my face burned. Just like that, I blurted the most dreaded word. "Fuck!"

I tried to mask it by covering my mouth, but it was too late.

Everyone had heard me, including Mr. Peters.

A rumble of laughter spread across the entire classroom, the most prominent being the devil himself, Kevin Masters, who was sitting right in front of me. He was the headmaster of all bullies, the star quarterback of Barrister's football team, and Mr. Good-Looking himself.

"Starting already, Morrison?" Kevin chided.

Ignoring Kevin had worked for me in the past, so I said nothing. Mr. Peters cleared his throat before raising his hand to silence the room. Everyone knew about my problem. Brian Morrison was the freak-boy everyone laughed at. I prayed for the earth to open up and swallow me. Instead, I slid down on my chair and buried my face in a book.

"Guys, I'm going to divide you into pairs. Whoever you're partnered with will be your permanent collaborator for the rest of the year. Look to your right. That's the person who will be stuck with you for the long haul." He began passing out instruction sheets for our upcoming class project.

I looked at the only thing to my right—the window—and wished I could jump out and run away.

"I guess you're stuck with me, Brian." There went that melodious voice again.

I mumbled a quick, "I guess so."

Like the brave person I wanted to appear, I stuck around and suppressed the urge to bolt before the class was over. Once the period bell sounded, though, I gathered my backpack from the floor and sprinted out of the room. There was no point in hanging around. Shannon and I had no business talking as if we were friends. I had one mission. Get out of there, fast.

Slipping out the back exit the way I usually did when things got sticky with other kids, I ran to my car and started the engine.

18

I drove away, creating a safe distance between me and the campus, intent on ditching the rest of my classes. The longer I stayed, the greater the risk of bumping into Shannon, and I wasn't ready for that. I circled around the neighborhood until I found a commercial center and parked in the lot. To kill time, I blasted the radio and tried not to think of Shannon. Mark texted, wanting to know where I was and if I wanted to play *L.O.L.* after school. I didn't bother responding. Besides, I had to meet my mom for my appointment with Dr. Singer.

By the time I pulled into my driveway three hours later, I found my mother inside her car, waiting for me. I got in and gave her the customary peck on the cheek. She smiled and steered the sedan out onto the street. I didn't say a word, eager to bury the memory of my recent incident in class.

"Is everything okay?" she asked while she weaved through the early afternoon exodus on Western Avenue. "You're quieter than usual."

"S'okay." I shrugged and gazed out the windshield.

Beverly Hills was about a thirty-minute drive, depending on the traffic. To block any more questions from my mother, I took out my ear buds, plugged them into my phone, and started the music. One good thing about my mom—she didn't prod. She had always respected my space and was understanding of my need for it. We reached Dr. Singer's office in forty minutes. In the waiting room, we sat next to each other without speaking. Mom engrossed herself in her paperback, while I was busy trying to block the image of Shannon from my thoughts.

After a few minutes' wait, the receptionist called my name, and we were shown to a stark, white room with a view of a little garden outside. I sat on the exam table and focused on the pigeons clucking below the window. Dr. Singer walked in after a minute, a manila folder containing my treatment records tucked under his arm. He smiled and extended a hand to me.

"Brian, it's been ages since I last saw you. You look great."

I returned his handshake as firmly as I could and lifted the corner of my mouth in an attempt to smile. He turned to my mother and enveloped her in a hug. He was my father's best friend and had been his dorm-mate during their undergrad years at Emory University.

"How's Gerry?" he asked while glancing at my records.

"Gerald is buried up to his neck with work, as usual," my mother said. While I was growing up, she'd chosen to stay home while my dad pursued his profession, but once I entered my junior year, she had taken a part-time job as a staff editor for the local paper that allowed her to work from home.

I had a nagging suspicion Mom was keeping tabs on me, even if she never expressed concern about having a child who would never fit in. In her own way, she wanted to be available whenever I needed her. It felt like she wanted to protect me from life itself.

"So, young man. How do you feel? There's a new medication I want to discuss with you and your mother."

I gave him a brave smile, concealing my feelings behind a smirk while under his close scrutiny. He always saw right through me, which was disconcerting, yet I still strived to keep my emotions hidden.

Without hesitation, I looked him straight in the eye and said, "I want to be taken off medication."

Mom jumped out of her chair, her face marked with worry. "Brian, why?" She touched my shoulder.

I didn't look at her when I answered. Instead, I kept my eyes on Dr. Singer. "I want to be taken off. The medicine might be controlling my depression, but the tic isn't going anywhere. I would rather be off it. I'll let you know if I can't handle it."

I'd rather experience sullen moods than pretend that everything was fine. I was sick of shaking, jerking, and cussing. To prove my point, I shuddered as another tic ravaged me.

Dr. Singer studied me, and I returned the favor. After several seconds of tense silence, he spoke. "If that's what you want, we can try it on a trial basis." He glanced at my mother, who appeared ready to cry.

It was understandable. My mother wanted the best for her only child, but there came a point when she had to let go. I hoped this was it.

"Okay, but I want you to be honest with us. Let us know if you need to be back on an antidepressant," she said, pulling me into an awkward hug.

Once we walked out of Dr. Singer's office, I felt like I'd won a small victory. I promised not to give mom a tough time if she hovered. It was a small price to pay for freedom from the medications I'd been on for so long. I was going to take whatever I could get.

Once we got home, I ignored the calls from Mark and Darryl, and another call from a number I didn't recognize. It was probably just a telemarketer again.

The minute I switched off my lamp and darkness descended, I felt a sense of ease course through me.

That night, I dreamed of Shannon.

Dream

In my dream, Shannon was being pursued by an enormous fanged creature that drooled massive amounts of greenish slime and sported claw-like hands. Shannon cried for me to help her. I tried, but when I reached for her hand to pull her to safety, another creature jumped in and wrenched her from my grasp. They said my name. *We're watching you, Brian.*

Distressed, I woke in the middle of the night and couldn't go back to sleep right away. When I finally did, I was launched into yet another nightmare. This one was much clearer, but confusing. In this dream, a woman who worked for a landscape company was bitten by a rattlesnake and was airlifted to a hospital. There were no clues and no indication of the dream's relevance, and the woman was a virtual stranger to me.

I awoke an hour before my alarm clock was set to go off,

confused by the vividness of the dream. Sweating and dazed, it took a few minutes to shake the feeling away. What did it have to do with me? Glancing at the clock one more time, I knew that sleep wasn't possible anymore. Six o'clock. I had an hour before I had to get ready for school, so I decided to get up and go for an early run around the neighborhood.

It wasn't something I did every day, just when time or schedule permitted. I plucked a decent T-shirt and shorts from my drawer and laced up my running shoes. It was still dark outside when I locked the front door behind me. Since the temperature hadn't dropped much overnight, I removed my shirt and threw it on the lawn.

I walked down our driveway and onto the street, quickening my steps until I was moving at a steady jog. Street lamps lit my path, and I kept an even pace, planning to run for thirty minutes.

Turning onto a darker patch of road, I noticed a woman with a limp walking in my direction. Her unsteady gait was alarming, so I hurried toward her in case she stumbled.

To my surprise, the woman touched my outstretched hand and gave me a blinding smile. "With every curse is a blessing," she said.

A flash of panic hit me at the feel of her hand, and I jerked away. I hadn't seen her before, not in our neighborhood. Upon a closer look, I noticed her robe was glittering and fluttering behind her. There was no indication of the unsteadiness I thought I'd seen earlier. I blinked and then blinked again, hoping my eyes weren't playing tricks on me. The woman was not ugly or beautiful—just different, kind of out of this world. My gut feeling told me that nothing about this woman was ordinary.

Taking a step back, I stared at her. I hadn't expected another reminder of Madame Elizabeth's prediction. Just like before, the hair on the back of my neck rose. Freaked out, I moved away from the woman. What the hell was going on?

I sprinted back to my house. There was a faint scratching noise behind me, and I looked over my shoulder to see what it was. Nothing was behind me except the sun peeking over the horizon. I took one last look back before I hurried inside the house.

Once I reached my room, I flicked on the television for a distraction, angry with myself for being such a pussy. My cell phone chimed with a missed call. I picked it up, and the unfamiliar number from the night before showed on my caller ID. Who was this persistent caller? I tossed the phone on the bed and headed to the shower.

At school, I found Mark and Darryl in front of the building waiting for me a few minutes before the bell rang.

"Hey, tic-boy. 'Sup with you?" Mark said when I reached the top steps.

"Had some errands with the parental unit and things got hectic before bedtime. Why, what's up?" I asked and nodded at Darryl.

"Nothing. Just wondering where you've been. You ditched class yesterday and ignored my text." Mark gave me a knowing look.

If there was anyone close to being able to read me like a book, it was Mark. I avoided his questioning eyes and turned to Darryl. He had grown still, so I followed his line of vision and saw Shannon, Brittney and Veronica, three of the most popular girls at Marshall, bounding up the steps. Mark might have no problem, but Darryl and I were on the shy side, so ogling was pretty much all we could do.

My neck muscles tightened, and my shoulders jerked

involuntarily for a brief moment. "Fuccckkkk," I blurted. *Here we go!* The first of many today, I was sure.

I groaned and turned my back while the girls walked by. They giggled, and that was my cue to flush, mutter a quick excuse about forgetting something in the car, and run away.

Embarrassment made me sit out my first period class. I sat inside my car, upset with myself. *Will this ever end?*

By the end of first period, I was feeling a bit better. Good enough to force myself to attend my next class. AP English would be a breeze since it didn't require my full attention. For sure I wasn't going to be able to concentrate if Shannon was in the same class.

Fate must have been playing a cruel joke on me, because Shannon walked in the classroom. Pretending to be busy, I buried my face in my book while she settled in the seat across the room from me. Good. She was as far away as possible. I twisted and turned in my seat trying to control the vibration of my shoulders. One nasty problem with my tics was that they got worse if I got agitated or excited. Shannon was able to make me feel both.

Controlling my twitches had never been an easy thing, let alone keeping the jerky movements at bay for an entire hour. I sat on my hands the whole time to keep my body from jerking while Mrs. Sweeney droned on about our first big project for the year. She'd be pairing students up to analyze *The Glass Menagerie*. With each passing minute, my shoulders were getting sorer from the pressure I was applying to them. Most times, I could pass off the twitches as small muscle spasms, but the more I tried this morning, the more out of control they were. It became unbearable while I counted down the remaining minutes before the end of the period. I was too stressed and terrified of what might come out of my mouth.

Meanwhile, Mrs. Sweeney seemed to be having the time of her life going over the subject matter. Her enthusiasm had no power to rub off on me since my focus was on grinding my teeth together to keep from uttering any F-bombs. Then she started calling the names of students who would be partnered with each other. There were groans and celebratory shrieks as each student was given their assigned partner. I could feel the buildup of unwanted vocal tics that were threatening to spill out.

"Brian Morrison, you're partnered with Shannon McKesson."

What the . . . "Ff-fff-fuckkkk!" The word slipped out, despite my fervent effort to control it. Sure enough, the entire class burst out in laughter. Yep, this was a good time to die, disappear into thin air, or crawl to the nearest exit. Mrs. Sweeney cleared her throat and tried to keep a straight face, but the laughter in her eyes betrayed her. I should be used to the ridiculing by now, but I still felt the sting of being the butt of the joke when I had an unavoidable outburst.

"Class, please, we need to focus on this project. I'm giving you two weeks to work on this. Remember, analyze each line separately, then get back with your partner, compare notes, and use the best combined analysis you have. Your grades will depend on your partner, so make the most out of your interpretations."

Then the bell rang. Thank God. I yanked up my backpack and ran out of the classroom without looking at anyone. The need to disappear was so strong that I almost knocked over several kids in my haste to get away. I ran straight to the restroom, wanting to scream when I found the place filled to capacity. My symptoms were threatening to unleash themselves, and I hurried off to find a quiet place before I exploded in a huge fireball of tics and curses.

Mark was coming out of his class when we bumped into each other. He tapped me on the shoulder.

"Hey, bro. What's the matter?" A worried and all-too-familiar expression of pity crossed his face. This wasn't the first time he'd seen me racing away to avoid people.

My mouth started trembling, a silent warning that more phonic tics were about to break out. "Fuck!"

I grunted and ran out of the building to the basketball court. Here, I could have a little privacy, away from all the watchful stares. To my great relief, there were just a handful of students loitering in the area. I went as far as I could from them before letting one out. I breathed deep and exhaled long enough to ease the pressure in my shoulders.

My facial muscles tightened, followed by a tug at my neck and back as the twitching came hard. One hour was too long to keep the monster at bay. As much as I hated my tics, it was liberating to let them out.

"Ah-ah-ah." My motor-mouth started to unleash its unholy terror. I had ten minutes to get it all out before I was marked late by my third period teacher. My shoulders continued to jerk for several more minutes before my body began to relax.

I sagged against the chain link fence and closed my eyes. There was only one word I wanted to avoid saying, and that was the very word that came out of my mouth during my tic attacks. I could live with the *ah-ah-ah's* or the stammering, but *fuck* was offensive and plain rude. Wishing for my tics to stop was like reaching for the stars. It would come in time, Dr. Singer had reminded me on many occasions, but the million-dollar question remained. When? Shannon must hate me now. Twice today I'd cursed in her presence.

By the time I made my way back to the building, the last bell for the period was chiming. I plastered on a brave mask and reminded myself that I couldn't control the tics any more than I could control the weather. The more I tried, the harder it got. It was stupid to beat myself up about it.

Then I saw Shannon at the far end of the hallway. For a brief moment, our eyes met. There was nothing to say. Apologizing would make me look more pathetic than I already was in her eyes. I looked away and entered my next round of hell.

"Is that you, baby boy?" Mom called from the kitchen as soon as I made it home. I wanted to be left alone, but there was no avoiding her. She'd hound me all the way to my room if I ignored her.

"Yes, Mom," I answered, dropping my backpack on the sofa and heading for the kitchen. She was busy preparing the meatloaf, and the aroma made my mouth water.

"How was your first day without the medication?" she asked, turning around to face me.

I kissed her on the forehead and took a celery stick from the plate on the counter, munching on it before replying. "It was okay," I lied.

She threw me a dubious look. "Are you sure? You know, there's no need to be off it if you're going to be miserable."

Here we go. I knew she would start rambling about how scared she was for me. She meant well, but I wasn't in the mood to hear it. Not today. I grabbed the remote and flicked on the television, not interested in another pep talk. The afternoon news was on, and my mother dropped our conversation in favor of listening to the newscaster. Content that the topic was off the table, I headed to the fridge, humming a tune. Mom shushed me, so I propped myself on the barstool and listened to the tail end of the news report. A few words caught my attention.

When I heard the words "rattlesnake" and "Chino Hills," I swung around to look at the television, but the segment had ended. Mom shook her head and switched her focus back to cooking.

"What was that about?" I felt like I was going to be sick.

"On the news?"

I nodded.

"A landscaping company employee was bitten by a rattlesnake while she was working on a project in Chino Hills."

"How can that be?" I muttered. My shoulders began to twitch. This couldn't be happening.

"Did you say something?" She looked over her shoulder. "Bri? What's wrong? Are you all right?"

"Um . . . yeah. I'm going to my room to do my homework," I said, rising from the chair.

"Okay, but can you toss the garbage first?" she asked, still watching me.

"Sure." I reached under the sink, pulled out the plastic liner, and hauled it to the trash bin at the side of our house.

What were the odds of my nightmare coming true? I shuddered at the thought. It had to be a strange coincidence. What other explanation could there be?

I powered up my laptop once I reached the confines of my bedroom, then toed off my shoes and sat on the bed. Hell, this was more than freaky. I searched the local news station's website for breaking news. The woman's name wasn't mentioned, but everything I'd seen in my dream had happened. She'd been airlifted to a hospital, where she was listed in guarded condition.

My phone rang, and it was the same unknown number again. Muttering angrily, I punched the answer button.

"Piss off! I'm not interested in whatever the hell you're selling."

After hanging up, I glanced back at my laptop and shook my head. What in the hell should I do now? I pressed speed dial to call Mark. Maybe he could help, or at least come up with some convincing explanation for the coincidence.

My call to Mark was directed to voicemail. I had forgotten that he had football practice after school today, and Darryl would be working. The same telemarketing number flashed on my screen while I waited to leave a message, but I ignored it.

I tried to hide the edge from my voice when I heard the beep. "Hey, call me when you get this."

My phone chimed just when I was hanging up. The telemarketer must have left a message. Grudgingly, I decided to listen instead of deleting the crap right away.

"Curly, what's the matter with you? You're beginning to give me a complex. First, you run out on me Friday night. Then you cursed at me today, twice. Now, you're accusing me of selling stuff." The teasing tone was hard to miss, but I also detected a small amount of distress in her voice. "I'm calling because I have your handouts with me from Mr. Peter's class, and I also wanted to find out when we can meet for Sweeney's project. Call me?"

Damn, I'd done it again. I kept piling one blunder on top of another freaking blunder. I listened to her voice message over and over for the next hour, wishing I hadn't been so distracted by the news.

The urge to call her was strong, but what would I talk about?

My stammering might turn her off, and my caveman attitude would just make me look like a fool. Was it too late to drop the classes I had with her? I rested my head on the pillow and closed my eyes. This had to be some kind of punishment for all the *fucks* I'd uttered in my life.

Dead Girl by the River

Another freakish dream made me jump up, drenched in sweat, in the middle of the night. I turned to check the time. It was midnight, and I had fallen asleep still wearing my school clothes. I sat up, but a pounding headache made me slide back down against my pillows.

In the darkness, I tried to recall the dream. It was almost identical to the one I'd had the night before, except it wasn't Shannon who was running away this time. It was a girl my age fleeing a man wielding a baseball bat. There was a body of water in the background, but the rest of the details were hazy. She screamed for help. Although I was there, my role was that of a spectator watching the whole thing unfold. She didn't hear me calling out to her as the man caught up with her. She struggled, and when the first of the blows came, I was dragged away from the nightmare. This was getting downright creepy. What was with the dreams I'd been having? Maybe this was a side effect of the medicine withdrawal. What should I do? Did this mean I was already losing the battle to stay off the drugs?

The growling of my stomach distracted me from my dilemma and made me realize how hungry I was after skipping dinner. I wondered why Mom or Dad hadn't bothered to wake me up. I tapped the mouse pad, and the article I'd been reading the night before came up.

Coincidence. It had to be. That was the one logical explanation I allowed myself to accept.

I got out of bed and winced at the throbbing in my head. Marching to the bathroom, I didn't bother to turn the light on before I rummaged inside the drawer until I found the bottle of ibuprofen. I took three caplets and stepped into the hallway. The hardwood floor creaked under my weight as I made my way toward the staircase to the tune of Dad's loud and even snoring. Despite the closed door, I could hear him loud and clear, and I wondered once more how Mom slept through the racket every night.

In the kitchen, I perused the contents of the refrigerator and settled on a carton of orange juice first. I swallowed the pills down with one long swig straight from the container. I smirked after replacing the cap, knowing mom wouldn't appreciate my drinking straight from the carton. Oh, well. What she didn't know wouldn't hurt her.

Then I began checking every container for something to eat until I found a covered dish filled with leftover meatloaf. I took two slices, spooned gobs of gravy and mashed potatoes on my plate, and stuck it in the microwave. While waiting for my food, I flipped on the television. At this unholy hour, there was nothing but infomercials, so I turned it off again.

Eating in the dark, listening to my chewing and the steady hum of the fridge, my mind wandered back to the odd dream. What did it mean? Coincidence was an easy excuse. But why had I even dreamed of Shannon? Well, it wasn't hard to guess since she'd been on my mind every minute of the day. It'd be interesting to know how she would feel knowing about my growing fascination with her, though I would never admit to it.

After rinsing my plate, I stashed it inside the dishwasher and hurried back to my room to get some homework done. For the next few hours, I worked like a man possessed, intent on getting everything done. It was after two in the morning when my homework was finished. I wasn't even sleepy yet, so I figured one game of *L.O.L.* wouldn't hurt. For the next thirty minutes, the world of strategic thinking and coordinated team-play had me distracted for a while. Then I remembered Shannon's message to call her. Well, it was too late to do that anyway. I'd see her in the morning and figure out how to change partners. The less I talked to her, the better off I figured I'd be.

Several times during the wee hours of the morning, I woke up, sweating and smarting from terrible dreams, disturbing nightmares that felt so real. The next time I opened my eyes, sunshine was streaming through the slats of the blinds. I looked around, disoriented, and glanced at the clock on my nightstand.

What the hell?

How in the hell did I sleep through the alarm? According to the clock, it was well into the third period already. Even if I moved fast, it'd be close to the lunch hour by the time I was ready and out of the house. When I shot out of bed, a crippling pain in my head made me slump back down. Feeling woozy, I stayed still until the throbbing eased up. I took a greedy gulp of water from the glass on my nightstand and felt a bit better after a moment. Despite the spinning sensation in my head, I dialed Mom's number. Good thing she picked up on the first ring.

"Why didn't you wake me up?

"I tried several times, but you were sound asleep. When I felt your forehead, you were burning up."

"I do feel kinda sick." That was an understatement. I felt like my eyes were two huge fireballs and my body was a lump of coal.

"That's why I left you to sleep. Stay home today. I'm just running some errands for your dad. I'll be back in time for dinner. I left you some pills to keep the fever down and a sandwich for lunch."

I lifted my lids to check the nightstand. "Yeah. I see it."

"Keep drinking water and juice. I'll make chicken soup for you once I get home."

After we said goodbye, I turned on some music then squirmed underneath the sheet and pulled it up to my chin. My eyes were watery and my body achy. With nothing to do, my thoughts wandered back to Shannon. She wanted me to call her. My stomach churned at the thought. It would be nice to hear her voice and to be able to talk to her every day and not worry about anything else. Not what other kids would think if we were seen together, or what business I had hanging out with such a beautiful girl. Heck, I could even drive her to school if she'd let me.

Hey, freak. You're a goddamn joke, the voice in my head taunted. Yeah, what was I thinking?

The sound of the buzzer hauled me from yet another dream, and I stumbled out of bed in a total daze, not sure where the noise was coming from. First I pounded the alarm clock, but another buzz came. Scrambling down the hallway, I gripped my head while I attempted to swallow. My throat was dry and parched like it had been sandpapered. Another persistent buzzing followed before I reached the front door. If my guess was correct, it had to be around four in the afternoon from the angle of the sun. I wrenched the door open.

"Mark, what the hell! My head is split—"

Shannon stood outside, balancing books in one hand, and what do you know, a bottle of orange juice with the other, looking so feminine, so pretty. Her hair was pulled in a nice ponytail this time, showing off her bare neck. I had the sudden urge to trail my fingers along her ivory skin.

"Are you always this grumpy?" she asked, her face breaking into a wide grin.

"What . . . " My voice trailed off. I was still in total shock at finding her on my doorstep. "What are you doing here?"

"Are you just going to stand there and scowl, or are you going to let me in?" She shifted from one leg to the other.

In an instant, I was self-conscious, because I was standing in front of Shannon, shirtless, with my hair sticking in every direction and my mouth hanging open. The best I could do was to open the door wider and step aside to let her in. A breeze swept in as she came inside. Her scent was nothing like how she'd smelled before, and I heard the scratching noise again. Weird. Last I remembered, she had the scent of jasmine, not some funky odor that made me wrinkle my nose.

Shannon gave me a bright smile as she walked past me into the foyer. I watched her glance around in appreciation before turning around to face me.

"I got you OJ. Mark told me you stayed home sick."

Okay. It was obvious she loved to talk, and I didn't mind listening to her, but at this point, I knew I had to say something.

However, before I had the chance to utter a word, my shoulder scrunched in a tight loop and a twitch rolled through me. I felt my face redden with humiliation. It was different when she was up close in broad daylight. I closed the door and faced her. What was the point of hiding who I was? She'd have to know what being around me involved—constant embarrassment and a possible heart attack.

"Yeah, I'm sick." I walked to the kitchen, not sure if I should show her back to the door or to give her full disclosure. It wasn't a surprise to find her following me, her shoes creating a soft echo on the kitchen tile. Shannon, I was beginning to learn, could be very persistent and was not easily deterred. "I don't know if it's a good idea for you to be around me."

"Why not?" She placed her hands on her hips, tapped her foot on the floor, and waited for me to answer.

Honesty would come in handy now, but I was at a loss for words. I glanced over my shoulder, half-relieved to see she remained unfazed. *Great. Now what am I supposed to do with a girl inside my house?*

Shannon put the bottle of juice and the books on the counter and faced me. "Look, I don't know why you're acting all weird. If you don't like being around me, you can say so. We can ask to switch partners. I'm sure Sweeney and Peters won't mind. But it's just plain rude to be ignoring my calls."

All I could do was stare at her. Did she think that I didn't want to be around her? I made the decision to come clean and to hell with everything else. "Why don't you sit first?"

She obliged, taking the barstool.

"OJ?" I attempted an awkward smile.

She smiled back, and it was a breath of fresh air. It was comforting to know that Shannon was easygoing, not like some

37

of the girls in school who wouldn't want to be caught dead in my company. "But I brought it for you. Aren't you supposed to be in bed?"

I raised an eyebrow and chuckled. "I *was* in bed until the doorbell rang," I reminded her.

She cupped her mouth upon realizing what I had said. "Do you want me to go?" she asked, poised to hop off the stool.

"No!" I caught her hand to stop her. My skin tingled where it touched hers, and I was quick to release her. She didn't seem to mind, so it must have been me imagining things. To hide my discomfort, I went to the cupboard and retrieved two glasses and put them on the counter. When my hands shook, I wrung them together. At least, the trembling wasn't caused by my tics for a change.

"You're burning hot. If you want, I'll get the juice, and we can hang out and talk right there." She gestured at the sofa in the adjoining family room.

"Sure." I'd do whatever she said if it meant having her around for a bit longer. This felt even better than the time I first laid eyes on my brand new car. I could already tell that even the thrill of winning the lottery couldn't compare to having Shannon in my house.

I handed her the glasses, and my skin continued to tingle where her hand brushed mine. She poured our drinks and followed me to the family room, sitting down next to me and making herself comfortable. My mind started running happy scenarios, which I batted away. I had no right to think there was something more to this visit than getting our project done.

"I want to apologize," I said, and took a big drink to hide the awkwardness in my voice. After all, everything happening today was a first. Apart from my buddies, she was the first 'real' guest

38

to visit me at home, let alone a girl.

"What for?"

My instinct told me she understood what I was trying to say, but she didn't want to make a big deal out of it. "First, I'm the biggest nerd on the western seaboard."

I groaned under my breath. What was coming out of my mouth? I'd better lay off Wikipedia for a bit.

Shannon laughed and took a sip from her glass. Watching her mouth, I felt another twitch building up. I squared my shoulders. She was too sweet-looking, and I was having another urge to trace my fingers across her plump lips. Instead, I sat on my hands to keep from reaching out to her.

"I'm sick." As if to support my statement, a spasm shook my shoulders. "Well, I'm running a fever right now, but that's not all." I continued. "I have phonic tics, and I jerk like crazy. I'm sure you knew anyway."

She took a deep breath before speaking. "Well, I kinda guessed you had something going on medically. I saw Kevin making fun of you last year. It made me sick to my stomach."

So Shannon knew who I was. Now I was really embarrassed.

She hesitated and took another drink. If I didn't know any better, I would have said Shannon McKesson was nervous. "Or you swallowed a bagful of Mexican jumping beans."

That broke the ice, and I roared with laughter. It felt good to have someone make light of my disease without making fun of me for a change. Shannon joined me, and our laughter sounded good together, so natural. I had to remind myself that this was temporary, but I'd be a fool not to enjoy the moment. Maybe there was hope for me. This could be my shot at being a normal teenager.

"What's the medical term for your jumping illness?"

I was glad the question came up right away. "It's called Tourette's Syndrome."

"What is that?"

The question plagued me wherever I went, and I had the answer down pat. Explaining it one more time wouldn't kill me. "The sudden and involuntary tics and vocalizations are byproducts of an abnormal metabolism of my brain's neurotransmitters." I shrugged.

"Wow… sounds heavy."

Yep, it was a big issue for a teenager, something I wouldn't ever sign up for. "If my involuntary cursing and jerking doesn't bother you, then I don't have a problem being your partner. I'm just trying to protect you from a possible heart attack. In my experience, people get nervous being around me." I leaned against the cushion, feeling good now that I'd gotten her all prepared. If my fever was making me delirious with happiness, then I wouldn't mind the mercury spiking up a bit more.

"You sound like you've been hiding for much too long, Curly."

It would have sounded better if she used babe or sweetie, but I'd settle for anything. "It comes with the territory, but let's not talk about me anymore. Why don't you tell me what you want to do for our photography project?" This was a ploy to get her talking so I could keep listening to her voice.

Shannon's eyes rolled up to the ceiling. "Um, I like taking portraits rather than moving subjects. I would love it if you would pose for me. You're very interesting, Mexican jumping beans and all." She giggled.

I glared in mock disapproval at her attempt to make light of my situation. "Hell, no. I'm not comfortable in my own skin, let alone with allowing someone to take my picture for everyone to make fun of."

I stood up, but my legs wobbled. Shannon was quick to get up and place her arm around my waist. *Holy smokes, batman. She touched me!*

"You're such a dork! I'm not kidding. Haven't you checked yourself in the mirror?" she asked, helping me back down onto the sofa.

I felt like a total loser and had no idea what to say. Look at myself in the mirror? I'd been doing that for the last seventeen years and never liked what I saw—blond hair, dull blue eyes, and average build. *Interesting* was a word I'd never apply to myself.

Freakish, yeah. Right on.

"Call me whatever you want, but I won't pose for a picture. Now, do you want to hear my ideas?" I slid as far away from her as I could. This touchy-feely stuff might lead us into areas where I lacked expertise.

"We'll see about that. I'm quite persistent, you know. Besides, I have all the time in the world. Now, tell me what you have in mind." She threw me a challenging smile.

I want to kiss you, I wanted to say. Of course, that thought brought on a lot of unwanted twitching and jerking. Shannon watched me, looking helpless while I attempted to control the tics from breaking out. Her hand covered mine, and I let her feel good about being Florence Nightingale.

After the twitches subsided, I let out a frustrated sigh. This whole scene was so pathetic. Here I was, in my family room, alone with a hot babe, and I was twitching to the beat of "Pumped Up Kicks." I avoided meeting her eyes, not eager to see the pity there. Instead, I focused at a painting on the wall and answered her.

"I like to photograph nature. I enjoy capturing the natural

calm and vibrant colors. It's like they're speaking to me, telling me to express in pictures what they can't say for themselves. With their silence, it's like they're giving me the freedom to speak on their behalf." I rammed my fingers through my hair, embarrassed by my confession. Now she'd know what a total bore I could be.

"That's the most beautiful thing I've ever heard someone our age say," she said in a quiet voice.

I looked in disbelief at the expression of awe on her face. Dang, if she could look any prettier, I could die right here. I had no idea what to else to say. Afraid she'd see right through me, I reached for my drink and took another long gulp, then muttered, "Thanks."

The garage door opened and closed, and Mom strode in with bags of groceries. Her eyes twinkled when she caught a glimpse of Shannon, then gave me a disapproving shake of her head.

"Young man, why don't you go put on a shirt?" She gave me the *eye*. "And who is this pretty young lady?"

"Oh, I'm sorry." I had forgotten how I must've looked. "This is Shannon from school. We're talking about the project we're doing for Photography."

I excused myself to get dressed. Just before I reached my bedroom, I heard them engaging in a full-length introduction. Once inside, I flew to the bathroom to brush my teeth and wash my face. I splashed water on my hair in an attempt to tame it. Applying gel would make me look like I was trying too hard. After several tries, I left it looking like it had before. It had a mind of its own and would end up wherever it wanted, no matter what I did.

I hurried to change into the cleanest jeans I could find inside my overstuffed hamper and slid into a cotton shirt. Running back to the kitchen, I found Mom and Shannon seated at the counter watching the news.

I caught the tail end of the report, and the shock hit me so hard, I doubled over. A teenage girl had been found dead along the Merced River, brutally beaten to death with a blunt object.

Both Shannon and my mom shot to their feet and rushed over to me. I raised my hand to stop them and sat on the arm of the couch to recover.

"What's the matter?" Mom asked, frowning.

The girl had been in my dreams just this morning. It didn't make sense, but who would believe me, anyway? Feeling anxious like never before, I wished I was back on medication. This might very well be a side effect of drug withdrawal. Hallucinations could be dangerous if left untreated. Fear gripped me harder. This coincidence was way too bizarre.

"Nothing." I coughed, and my shoulder twitched. To counter the onslaught of tics, I rotated my head and cupped my mouth.

Shannon looked like she wasn't buying my excuse. "Brian?" She tentatively touched my arm.

I closed my eyes for a brief moment, loving the feel of her hand on my skin and hating what I was about to say.

"I don't mean to be rude, but I'm not feeling well. Thanks for the juice. I'll see you at school tomorrow." I turned to walk away.

"I'll call you tonight," she said before I reached the stairs.

Revelation

In my room, I sat on the bed and tried to think. I felt like a douche bag for driving Shannon away. I would've loved to talk more or maybe invite her to stay for dinner, but I was afraid that my tics would get in the way. Even though she'd been warned, the likelihood of my having a full-blown episode was good, since I was nervous as hell around her. The news report had stressed me out even more.

My hands felt cold and clammy. I had no idea if my sudden discomfort had anything to do with my fever or if it had been the shock I'd gotten from the news. Leaning against my headboard, I brought a pillow to my chest, and my mind wrestled with two realities. Shannon. What should I do about her? Was I jumping the gun here? Imagining things? For all I knew, she was just being friendly for the project's sake. Then there was the disturbing coincidence of my dreams turning out to be real. Two incidents couldn't be mere coincidence. The most important question was what triggered these dreams.

Troubled, I picked up the remote control and turned on the television, avoiding the news channel. I flipped straight to a rerun of *Dragonball Z*, just to keep my mind occupied.

The next thing I knew, someone was rapping on my door.

"Brian? Mind if I come in?" Shannon asked.

Great! I must have fallen asleep again without noticing, and I was still trapped in my dream. Should I pinch myself? I'd play along, if that was what it was going to take to wake up. Once I slid out of the warmth of my sheets, the cold draft made me shiver. I rubbed my arms, trying to calm the rising goose bumps.

"Hi, babe. You're still here?" I chirped when I opened the door. Even if it was just a dream, it felt good to have someone to call *babe*. Shannon stood outside my door, holding a tray of food and looking quite amused. To make it even better, I bent down and kissed her on those luscious lips, wondering if this would ever happen in real life.

Sure enough, her mouth was like a cushion of feathers. Soft and warm, it was a taste of heaven. I watched her eyes grow the size of saucers, and she stepped back. I smiled sheepishly.

"Are you bipolar, by any chance? You're going to give me whiplash with your mood swings. One minute, you're dismissing me like I carry the plague, and the next moment, you're kissing me." Shannon's voice seemed to echo in the quiet hallway.

Okay. This sounded awfully real. I shook my head and blinked. "Shannon? Are you really here?" I asked, feeling stupid.

"Um, yeah?" She enunciated every syllable like she was talking to someone who'd gone crazy.

"Crap." I muttered, and a round of quick tremors pounded my body. "I'm such a loser."

"Well, I'm getting tired here. This tray isn't light, you know. Your mom invited me for dinner, and I asked if I could bring your tray up and eat with you."

I closed the door and took the tray from her. After putting it on the desk, I asked the most obvious question. "Why?"

"Why what?" She stared at me.

"Why are you hanging out with me? What's in it for you?"

As someone who'd been used to rejection and humiliation all his life, I had the habit of verbalizing my inner skepticism. I didn't accept kindness easily, since I had learned a long time ago that most kids my age didn't have compassion in their make-up. Anyone different would always be someone to make fun of and humiliate.

The hurt that flashed across her face made me want to take back what I'd said. "Nothing's in it for me. Do I need a reason to want to be friends?" She turned to the door.

I took hold of her arm to stop her, letting go when she turned around to face me. "Shannon, I'm sorry. I'm not used to girls wanting to hang out with me. It's pathetic, I know."

She chewed on her bottom lip as if deliberating if I was worth the trouble, so I went with the puppy eyes I've seen on television. "Please . . . would you stay and join me?" God, even *I* was giving myself whiplash.

"I don't want you kissing me. Despite my popular reputation in school, I'm not easy, you know." She crossed her arms over her chest, waiting for my reply.

"I know, and I'm sorry. I promise I won't ever kiss you again . . . unless you ask me to." What in the hell made me say that? I'd be an old man, and still waiting for that to happen. "Just blame it on the flu or whatever."

Shannon narrowed her eyes before the crook of her mouth

turned up into a smile. "We'll see about that."

"Thanks," I said with relief. "What's for dinner?" I migrated to a safer topic so I could think straight. The fast beating of my heart made it difficult to think clearly.

"Your mom made chicken soup for you and a ham sandwich for me. And of course, I brought more orange juice."

Her smile grew wider when I pulled out the desk chair for her.

"TV or music?"

"Um, do you have Pink's 'Just Give Me a Reason'?"

I stifled a smile. "I didn't know you were into mushy songs." I got my phone from the nightstand and searched for the song.

"Hey, she's amazing. Stop dissing her."

Once I found the song, I put my phone into the docking station and pressed play. I turned around to find Shannon laughing.

"What?"

"You're unbelievable."

"I like Pink. She's a tough chick." I shrugged.

"Yes, she is. In fact, she has a concert here next month. I was hoping Brittney and Veronica would go with me."

"Cool."

Damn, it would be nice if I were the one taking her to the concert. *Dream on, lover boy.*

After I set the volume to an acceptable level, I sat on the edge of the bed, holding my bowl of soup while Shannon took a bite of her sandwich. After she finished chewing, she glanced around the room.

"What's with boys and *Call of Duty*?" she asked when she spotted the numerous posters plastered on the walls.

"Some of us who have nothing better to do like playing

video games. Try *League of Legends* online. It's fun." This was true. I passed the time playing with other kids, mostly when Mark was out on a date and Darryl had to work in his father's gas station.

"Don't tell me you're so anti-social that you'd rather play video games than hang out?" Shannon appeared surprised. It was obvious that she didn't know much about me. My social calendar had been empty even before I realized what a big loser I'd turned out to be.

"Well, let's see. I have two friends. Two. One is popular enough to hang out with the 'in' crowd, and the other one is content to play video games all of his waking hours. I try to minimize getting myself into awkward social situations. As you can see, I don't do well with people, considering my . . . " I shrugged and jerked my shoulder, "you know what." I shoved a spoonful of soup in my mouth and watched her.

"You're exaggerating!" Shannon socked me on the arm.

"Am *not*."

"Whatever." She took another bite and chewed in silence.

I ate, but I couldn't take my eyes off her. Shannon was not what I'd expected. She was easy to talk to, and as I was realizing she wasn't easily discouraged. The short time we'd spent together showed me I'd passed judgment on her the same way other people always did to me. In my mind, popular people would never befriend the unpopular ones.

"I'm curious. What were you doing at the tarot shop the other night? Don't you guys have better things to do?"

Good opening. "It was Darryl's idea. He said Madame Elizabeth is good . . . and pretty," I added as an afterthought.

"Oh . . . " Shannon sounded doubtful.

"My turn to ask questions. Do you work in the shop every

day?" I would have expected her to work at the mall, maybe at the perfume counter or selling fancy handbags, or whatever women called those things.

Shannon seemed reluctant to answer, but after a moment, she dropped her sandwich back on the plate. "I don't talk about myself or my family all that much, but I'm going to tell you since you look like you can keep a secret." She glanced up at me, looking hopeful.

I placed a palm over my heart. "Not a peep."

"My dad travels on business a lot. My mom gets bored, so she took classes on tarot reading. She's one of those . . . um . . . *eccentric* people. When she got her certificate, she talked my dad into getting her a spot in that awful location. And to make things worse, she demanded I helped her out after school." Shannon's mood shifted, and she seemed unhappy.

"Madame Elizabeth is your—"

She didn't even let me finish. "Yep, my mother."

"Does it bother you to be working there with her?"

Shannon nodded. "Sometimes I ask myself why I agreed to it, but I don't have the heart to tell her to look for someone else. It feels weird, because I feel we're just fooling people. But her readings—I'm not sure what to make of them."

I stared at her, stunned.

"Don't look so shocked. I saw your face when you went out of her *office*." She tried to make it sound funny, but I couldn't smile.

"What are you trying to say?" I put down my soup bowl.

"Madame . . . err, my mother said something that scared you. I knew it, because she's done the same thing to me." Shannon picked up her sandwich again, as if debating another bite, but she put it back down without eating more.

This small revelation triggered the warning bells in my head. "Is that why you're here?"

"Yes and no." She got up to walk over to the window, and she stood there for a long moment before turning around. Her eyes misted. "I didn't believe her at first. She told me after you left that you'll be the key to what lies ahead for me."

I stared at her, dumbfounded. "So our being partners in class is falling into a pattern designed by some cruel jokester?" I tried to make sense of it, but I was drawing blank.

"Fools rush in where angels fear to tread. That's what she told me. It scared me, and for days, I didn't talk to her. It felt like she wasn't the same person. I don't know what to say, Brian. Believe me, I'm freaked out, too."

I patted the mattress and urged her to sit beside me. I had no idea what to say to her. It sounded so weird.

Shannon sat down and wrung her hands. "I have no idea why I didn't believe her then, but I do now. My peculiar mother saw something in those cards. When I asked her, she cried and hugged me. She said she has no idea how to help me. When she saw you, she was certain you're the one who could. It's just plain unbelievable!" She shook her head.

"Did she explain why?" The whole thing was too confusing.

Shannon glanced around as if what she was about to tell me was top secret. "Mom wants me to stay as close to you as possible. I got so upset with her because the whole thing was ridiculous, but she insisted. I know it sounds like I'm taking advantage of you, but how else can you explain how we became partners all of a sudden?"

That much was true. Even if it did sound suspicious, there was no other way of explaining how we ended up on *two* projects together. If I were in my right mind, I wouldn't be complaining. Instead, I should get down on my knees and thank my lucky stars for adding some excitement to my life.

"I'm not going to lie. She freaked me out, too. Besides, I don't believe in psychic stuff," I replied, not apologetic in the least.

"She freaks me out every day!" Shannon laughed. Then she glanced at the clock on my nightstand and bolted up. "Shoot, I have to get home. My dad's getting back tonight, and I don't want him to send out a search party."

"Hey," I pulled at her arm again, "Can I call you?"

"Sure. You have my number." The smile she gave me was more than dazzling—it was mind-numbing.

She made me feel like a million dollars. I almost gave back a big grin, but I stopped myself. Instead, I got up, and we walked down the stairs together in silence.

The rest of the house was dark and quiet. My parents must've retreated to their bedroom for the night.

"Drive safe." I had to fight the urge to touch her again. It'd be a mistake if I let myself get used to it.

"Thanks. Get better, okay? We have tons of work to do." She waved before descending the lit pathway to her car.

I waited by the doorway until she gave another wave and drove away. After I closed the door behind me, I gave in and twirled around with happiness. I was still pirouetting when the hallway light turned on, abruptly halting my celebration. I turned to look up and saw my dad shaking his head.

"Brian, are you okay?" he asked.

"Yep!" I answered way too eagerly and took the stairs two at a time. "Night, Dad!"

I returned to my room, and like a greedy dog, inhaled deep to savor Shannon's lingering scent. When all that was left was stale air and the aroma of our leftovers, I crawled into bed. In the darkness, I recalled Madame Elizabeth's words. *Your curse comes with a blessing.* If Shannon was the blessing, then I wouldn't mind shouldering my curse at all.

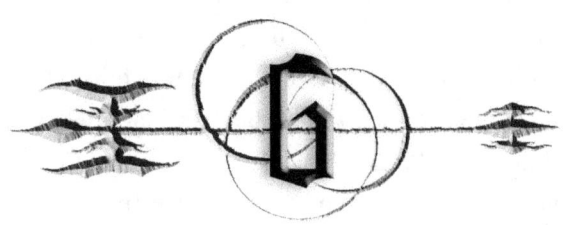

Interpretation

I took another sick day from school. The fever had gone down, but even though I was feeling better enough to attend my classes, it would take crafty maneuvering to convince my mother to let me out of the house so soon. Mark and Darryl called to check on me before class started, and I dozed off after playing a round of video games.

When I woke up, I sent Shannon a text to tell her I'd be missing school again. To my surprise, she responded right away. She even volunteered to come by after school to drop off my homework before she headed to her job.

Even though Shannon didn't stay long and I would have liked to spend more time with her, I wasn't going to complain. It wasn't every day that a fine girl dropped by my house to see me. As usual, I stared at her like she was from another planet. I couldn't get over the fact that she was in my life, no matter in what capacity. Since I didn't have anything else to occupy my mind, I spent most of the day daydreaming about her, still unable to believe my luck in having her come into my life. There was no questioning that a higher force had brought us together.

My plan was to savor the moment and enjoy having a new friend. No matter how thrilled I was with recent developments between us, a nagging feeling that something was about to happen began to plague me. With my sudden recurrent nightmares and what she told me the night before, I felt rather strange and somewhat nervous. Whatever it all meant, it dampened my inexplicable high.

My phone rang, disturbing my inner conflict.

"Talon, we're coming over," Mark said.

"Sure. What time?"

Then the doorbell chimed. "Now." He laughed and hung up.

I opened the door to find him and Darryl with PS4 controllers and a bag of chips. It was typical of them to show up like that.

"Feeling better?" Darryl asked when we reached my bedroom.

"Yeah," I answered absent-mindedly.

We sprawled on my bed, and Mark picked up the remote control for the television and started flipping through the channels.

"Here, let me!" Impatient, I grabbed the remote from him and turned on the auxiliary station right away. "Let's play."

They gave me a questioning look. "I know you're in love with your remote, but what the hell was that about?" Mark opened the bag of chips, and the barbecue scent filled in the air.

"Nothing," I fibbed.

"Nothing, my ass," Darryl said before stuffing his mouth

with a handful of potato chips.

"Bro, you're acting weird today—weirder than usual, anyway. I know you well enough to know something's up, so spill the fava beans!" Mark made that Hannibal Lecter hissing sound from one of our favorite movies.

"Yeah, you ran out of that psychic shop like you'd seen a ghost." Darryl seconded. "Then you got sick and wouldn't answer our calls until this morning. Spill, dude."

I wavered between the truth or a lie about what had happened over the past few days. Telling them would also mean I had to tell them about Shannon. For some selfish reason, I wanted to keep her all to myself. My own little secret.

"We're your best friends, in case you've forgotten. We've shared dirty secrets since middle school," Mark reminded me.

As long as I could remember, these two had been watching my back.

I still hesitated, but the overwhelming need to share my fears with them overcame the urge to keep Shannon to myself.

"Fine. It's weird, and I expect you to keep this on the down-low, a'ight?"

They nodded.

"That night at Madame Elizabeth's, she said something that scared the crap out of me. I know it was bogus, but it freaked me out bad."

"What did she say?" they asked in unison.

I mimicked Shannon's mom. *"With your curse comes a blessing."*

"Really?" Mark narrowed his eyes. "That scared the shit out of you?"

"Yeah." I was sure they'd start making fun of me, but when neither of them said anything, I continued. "She's creepy, bro."

Again, there was silence except for the crunching sound of their chewing, and the music of the forgotten video game's menu screen.

After a moment, Darryl began picking at his ear piercings, a nervous habit of his. "Okay, fine. Madame Elizabeth confused the hell out of me with my reading. I got the man hanging upside down. She said that it symbolized self-sacrifice and adapting to changes. Like there's going to be a pause in my life until I give up something for the greater good. So I asked what it really meant, because my creep-o-meter shot through the roof. She said that my friend would be going through a transition and I needed to be there for him."

Mark and I looked at each other while Darryl resumed his assault on the chips.

"Who is transitioning?" I asked, not sure what it meant.

Mark raised both hands and shook his head with a grin. "Don't look at me. My voice doesn't squeak. I'm circumcised, and all cylinders are a go."

I socked Mark in the arm. "You're stupid."

"What did Madame E tell you?" Darryl asked him.

He was thoughtful for a moment. "Well, mine was kinda freaky, too. She had me pick a card, and I got temperance. She said it meant I had self-control and was able to handle tough situations, but that I had to deal with impatience and conflict. It could also mean angels and guardian spirits were around, but in my case, she said I was it." He sighed and looked over at me. "Go figure what that means. Anyway, now you can tell us whatever it is you're holding back."

Cornered, I knew it was time to tell them about the dreams. I turned my desk chair around and straddled it. "That night, I started having weird dreams. First, this creature was chasing after Shannon McKesson. It was all a blur. I went back to sleep and dreamed something different. This random woman was being bitten by a rattlesnake. It was like I was there watching it happen. Then the next day, there she was in the news."

I stopped to take a deep breath, and my friends stared at me like I'd lost my marbles. "See, I told you it's weird. But that's not all. I dreamed about Shannon and the weird creature again. It woke me up. I went back to sleep, I had another dream. This time, there was a girl running away from a man, and he was holding a bat. I could see everything around them, but I had no idea where they were. The next day, Shannon came over, and she and my mom were watching the—"

"Hold it right there! Shannon was here?" Disbelief was all over Mark's face. Darryl stopped chewing, mirroring Mark's surprise.

My secret was out. "Yeah, she came over when I didn't show up for class yesterday." I tried to make it sound like it wasn't a big deal.

"Why would Shannon care if you showed up in class or not?" Mark asked.

For a brief moment, I felt smug. "We're partners in Sweeney's and Mr. P's classes, so she came by to find out when we're going to start with the projects."

"Bullshit!" Darryl exclaimed. He had a knack for spotting lie from a mile away.

"Fine," I conceded. "According to her, she got a similar reading from Madame Elizabeth—who happens to be her mother."

"They're related?" Mark asked in disbelief. "Are you serious?"

"Yep, and for some reason, she decided to tell Shannon that I was the key to whatever trouble she's about to face."

"What do you have to do with her?" Darryl asked.

"I have no idea, but the coincidences are hard to ignore. First, we were partnered up in two classes." I flashed two fingers. "*Two*," I repeated. "We've shared a lot of classes before, and this is the first time we've been thrown together. After she told me about what her mom said, I was even more freaked out about my dreams." I closed my eyes, still having a tough time believing the story myself.

Mark chuckled and stood up. "Okay, just for argument's sake, what are you going to do if this all turns out to be nothing?" he asked

Darryl leaned forward, and I stood to turn up the volume of the music.

"I don't know, but I'm not going to let her go through whatever this is alone. Funny thing is, I asked Dr. Singer to take me off my antidepressant. So now I wonder if this is like a withdrawal symptom. You know, like I'm hallucinating or something. But it's so real. And how else would you explain Shannon's sudden interest in me if she was lying?"

"Who knows? Maybe she and the girls are planning an early April Fool's prank. I don't know." Mark appeared as baffled as I was.

"Bro, you can say what you like, but I don't think Shannon is making it up. She's all freaked out."

Darryl nodded. "So that's the reason why you went all jumpy with the remote control."

"I don't want to see the news again. It's too crazy."

Mark thought for a long moment, stroking his chin. "Okay, here's what we'll do. We'll take everything seriously for now and keep watching each other's back. Shannon's, too," he said.

"And if you have a freaky dream tonight, tell us in the morning, and we'll search the news or the net for you."

"Thanks, guys," was all I could say.

"Now that that's settled, *Call of Duty* beckons." Darryl chuckled.

We spent the next two hours caught up in a world war with zombies, just like a typical afternoon. I was glad to have a break from all the weirdness and feel normal again.

It was another tough night. I woke up feeling exhausted, despite going to bed early. This time, my dreams were back-to-back. First, I was watching an apartment fire. A few people escaped, but there were two sleeping kids who weren't so lucky. That nightmare was followed by Shannon running away from a pursuer. It ended abruptly when I woke up, all my facial muscles twitching from the dream's intensity.

There were voices outside. Curious, I looked out from my window and saw my mother talking and tending her plants. Mom took her role as a nurturer seriously. She was making hand gestures and looked upset.

I lumbered through my morning ritual, feeling somewhat guilty about my latest vision. By the time I reached Marshall, I was still feeling like I wanted to throw up. As usual, Mark and Darryl were sitting on the brick steps, waiting for me by the front entrance. I didn't have to say anything for them to see something was up. I sat down, the cold concrete surface making me shiver.

"Bro, you look like shit," Darryl commented.

I raked my fingers through my hair. "Gee, thanks. You always say the nicest things."

"Tell us about it." Mark looked around before scooting

closer to me so no one would overhear.

"There's going to be a fire somewhere. Two children die," I said in a flat tone. The possibility made me sick to my stomach.

"Do you know when?" Darryl turned on his phone, ready to search the internet.

"Nope. I have no idea what to think anymore. It's not like I can predict it. I don't even know how all this crap is connected to me."

"Okay, this is what we're going to do. Da-rio and I will look at the news, and we'll let you know. Don't watch TV. We don't want you freaking out on us." Mark got up, and we shook hands. Darryl saluted.

We were at the doors when I heard that sweet voice calling my name. Mark, Darryl, and I all turned around.

Shannon was running up the steps, her backpack bouncing against her back. Brittney and Veronica were trailing behind, and judging by their horrified expressions, they weren't as ecstatic as Shannon was to be seen around me.

"Wait up," Shannon said, flashing a manila folder at me.

I grinned at her, jubilant in the face of Mark and Darryl's obvious disbelief. It seemed like my friends would now have to believe me.

Shannon was breathless by the time she stopped next to me. "Larry, Curly, and Moe!" she said and handed the folder to me.

Mark grinned, and Darryl tried to act cool.

"What is this?" I asked, flipping through the contents. I didn't bother acknowledging her friends, whose dislike was blatant. The folder held a bunch of photos, and I looked them over. "These are pretty good. Did you take them?" The different photos were of people and had been taken in color or black and white, and showed a lot of different emotions. I had to admit, she had an eye for outstanding shots.

Shannon beamed. "Yeah, I put them together last night. I hope they'll convince you that I can do justice to my subjects." She winked, subtly reminding me of her request to photograph me.

That didn't escape everyone else's notice. They all looked at Shannon like she'd lost her mind. I shook my head. Thankfully, Shannon dropped it, but she kept beaming at me. The first bell rang, saving me.

We all scrambled in different directions to get to our classes. Shannon and I walked side by side in the hallway, amid surprised and envious stares. I felt taller, even better looking, with her next to me. It was amazing how beauty could rub off on someone.

We reached our photography class just as Mr. P. was closing the door. He gave us his customary grunt because we were a minute late.

The rest of the day passed in a haze for me. I didn't see Shannon again until the end of third period.

That night, I worked on my homework right after dinner. I'd forgotten about my dream until bedtime when Mark called, sounding breathless.

"Bro, you won't believe this."

I glanced at my clock. Almost midnight. It must be important for him to call at this hour. I had a sinking feeling he was about to give me news I didn't want to hear.

"What is it?"

"There was a fire in Fontana. Two kids died, ages two and seven. The parents weren't home when it happened. The babysitter was able to run to safety with the oldest child. They still don't know what caused the fire."

I closed my eyes, and my racing heart thundered in my ears.

"Oh, man!"

"Brian, dude, this is freaky." Mark's breathing was heavy.

"Tell me about it." My mind was already whirling with morbid thoughts. What if every dream was going to be about dead people or tragedies? Could these visions make some kind of difference?

"Well, I'm going to knock myself out and get some sleep. I scoured the Internet and watched the news. I got the story from the eleven o'clock news." He paused. "You know, there were other fires out of state, one in Arizona and one in Maryland. This is insane!"

I tried to sound calm and cool for his sake. "Marko, go to sleep. Thanks for letting me know."

We hung up, and I sagged against the mattress. Sleep was out of the question. It was going to be a long night. I gave in to an impulse and dialed Shannon's number, hoping she would forgive me for waking her up.

"Hello?" she answered after the third ring, sounding tired.

"Shannon? I'm sorry to call you this late, but I can't sleep." It was better to apologize right away. If she decided to hang up on me, she would already know my reason for bothering her.

"It's okay. I can't sleep either. I've been tossing and turning for the last hour." I heard the sound of the sheets in the background. She must be making herself comfortable.

Like the loser that I was, I imagined holding her in my arms, her head resting on my shoulder. It felt great, even if it was only happening inside my head.

"Why can't you sleep?" she asked.

"I just heard some bad news." I closed my eyes, loving the imaginary feel-good sensation her closeness stirred inside me.

"You want to talk about it?"

"Maybe another time . . . "

"You know my number. You can call me anytime."

That I would do. Listening to the melodic rise and fall of her voice was a drug I wouldn't mind taking over and over. Just like that, I gave in to an embarrassing and spur-of-the-moment impulse.

"Hey, you want to see a movie with me on Friday night?" To let her know that I was a flexible guy, I added, "Anything you want is fine with me."

Shannon didn't respond right away. I wanted to kick myself for assuming she'd go out with me, even if it was only as friends. Who was I kidding? My feelings for her were stronger than that.

"I work Friday night—"

"It's okay." I didn't want to hear any other excuses. It was a big fail for me to consider doing more with her than just being her project partner.

"Don't cut me off," she said. "As I was saying, I work Friday night, but I'd be happy to watch a movie after. Is this a date?"

Duh! Then my idiocy reared its ugly head. "No . . . just friends hanging out."

There was a long pause before she spoke again. "Okay. Sounds good."

Her answer made me warm all over. After we agreed on the time and where to meet, we hung up, and I was left staring at the ceiling and thinking happy thoughts.

Meeting the Tranak Leader

Today was the big day. I had to admit, I wanted it to be a date, but I was too chicken to tell her. Nonetheless, it was enough that Shannon had agreed to see a movie with me. It was strange that she didn't seem to have any movie preference when I asked her in class the day before. I thought she'd go for a chick-flick. Oh well, what do I know about girls, anyway?

I turned onto St. George Street with hopes of finding a parking spot. Since I was thirty minutes early, which was a rarity, I found one right away. I parked my coupe and sat inside to kill time while I waited for Mark and Darryl, who were carpooling together.

I was tinkering with the radio dial, looking for anything besides the usual talk shows, when I heard a rap on my passenger side window. I could see the body, but not the face, of a woman. Her clothes were unusual. Glimmering ribbons were tied around the waistline of her ill-fitting dress, or whatever it was she was wearing. I leaned toward the window to see her face, and she rapped on the glass again.

Good thing I had engaged the locks when I left home. It was something my dad drilled in my head ever since he'd handed me the keys to my brand new car.

When the woman bent down, our eyes locked. It was like an out-of-body experience. My body felt lighter, my breathing slowed down, and I had the odd sensation of time slowing. I fumbled with the door handle, trying to decide whether to flee or stay inside the car.

Then it dawned on me. I had seen this woman before. She was the same limping woman I'd seen on the street several days ago. In an instant, everything around me started blurring, like we'd been enveloped in a cocoon. The woman smiled, and for a moment, I didn't feel the fear I knew I should.

Despite her compelling smile, I was unwilling to let her in. I gripped the steering wheel, electing to drive away while I still could. I pushed the ignition button, but the engine wouldn't start. The radio turned off on its own, and the luminous display on my dashboard dimmed and shut down. Panic began to seep in as I frantically pushed the button to start the car while glancing at the woman outside my window.

With a wave of her hand, she disengaged the locks. In the next moment, she was sitting on the front passenger seat next to me. Her movements were swift, faster than what human eyes could follow, but somehow, I saw every single one as if it were in slow motion. She locked the doors again with a snap of her fingers, and I found myself scooting away from her until my body was pressed against the door.

"Don't be afraid, Brian Morrison," she said. Her voice had

the same wind chime sound as Shannon's. "And don't try to run. We need your help."

"Who are you? What do you want from me?" My voice shook, and my shoulders started jerking. I clamped my mouth in an effort to suppress the harsh words that were guaranteed to make an appearance soon.

"My name is Detherina. I come from another place."

"An alien from another planet?" I blurted out of fear.

She tried to reach out, but I shrank further away. "Don't be afraid, Brian. I'm not an alien. I come from Tranak—a parallel universe." She smiled, showing off a set of perfect, white teeth.

Dether—or whatever her name was—was beautiful, in an ethereal way. Her jet black hair sat coiled in a tight knot on top of her head like a crown. She watched me with crystal eyes that were strange, yet mesmerizing. Her thin lips were dark red, just like the color of blood.

"You're an alien." This wasn't real. This had to be a dream.

She laughed, a melodious sound, and for some reason, I felt she wasn't a threat. All the same, I kept my hand on the door handle, ready to bolt at a moment's notice.

"I wouldn't want to be called an *alien*, but yes, I'm not of this world."

"What do you want from me?" I asked again.

"In our universe, I'm what they call the Totren, or the leader. I'm a bit like the president of your country, except I am filling in for our true supreme ruler. I lead a group of what you would call creatures. We're quiet, disciplined, and self-sufficient." She glanced ahead.

Through the blur of whatever bubble she'd used to surround my car, I could still see people walking by, oblivious to me and my passenger. I gripped the door handle and tried to jerk it open, but it wouldn't budge. Whatever magic she was using, I was beyond freaked out.

She swung her head back in my direction and pleaded. "Please don't run away. I won't hurt you."

"What do you want from me?" I ground the words, wanting the answer she seemed to be reluctant to give me.

"You're the key to my daughter's safety," she said. Her voice quavered, and her eyes brimmed with golden tears.

"Daughter? What are you talking about?" I asked, reeling. *Red alert, red alert. Time to run, Brian.*

Her voice took an eerie tone. "Shannon."

I blinked once and then again, unsure if I'd heard right. It wasn't possible. "No . . . no . . . " *You're a liar.*

"I'm not lying. I am her mother," she reiterated.

"She told me that her mother is Madame Elizabeth!"

"Elizabeth is half-Aarmark, half-human. I am a pure Aarmark—a race thousands of years older than yours. Elizabeth is posing as Shannon's surrogate mother because I am not able to stay here very long. I have people to lead, so her father and I agreed that he'd keep her here until her eighteenth birthday."

"Shannon told me that her father was on a business trip." I still couldn't believe a word she was saying. Detherina nodded, seeming distracted.

I took the opportunity to scream at the passersby. "Help! Help!" I banged on the glass, hoping to catch someone's attention. No one turned, and nobody came to my rescue. I should have known better. Even in my greatest moment of need, I remained invisible to everyone.

"Brian, they can't hear you. I surrounded your car with a mist of obscurity. Whatever we do in here, no one will see or hear. It is the only way we can walk among humans. We must stay hidden."

Despite her words, I didn't stop pounding until my fists were numb and my voice was hoarse. No one spared me a glance. I slumped in my seat, my heart racing, and I felt the next tic coming. "Fuck!" I shook when the word came out.

"Her father, Arthur, died a week ago." Detherina's face took on a sickly pallor, and a steady flow of crazy-colored tears streamed down her cheeks.

"You're freaking me out." My body was shuddering, which heralded more violent tics to come. I gripped the steering wheel and tried to stop them, but they came harder. My shoulder scrunched and jerked while my neck grew tight as I fought to repress the onslaught. Detherina placed a hand on mine, and like magic, the tics ebbed away until they disappeared. I stared at her in disbelief.

"I apologize for getting you involved. When the news of her father's death reached our rivals, they sent Ergans to watch her. If they get hold of my heir, my power will diminish. Being the heir to my throne, Shannon must remain pure. This vulnerability is a curse that was placed on us when our ancestors breached an agreement with Pratrim a century ago." When I gave her a blank stare, she sighed. "It's a long story, which I will explain once you've agreed to help us. But for now, I need your help, Brian Morrison. They can't touch Shannon while she's under the supervision of humans. Now that her father is dead, the gateway of Pratrim is open to wage war with us."

"Why can't Madame Elizabeth help her? Or you, for that matter?"

"She is untouchable when the link between her parents is solid. Once one parent dies, that link is broken, and our enemies are able to weaken our powers. She must make it through her

Aarmark transition so we can safely take her to Tranak with us. The Ergans know this. It is even possible that they caused Arthur's death. Elizabeth is a Binarian, half-human and half-Aarmark. She is just a watcher, a link to us. She does not have the fighting skills we do. As for me, I can destroy the Ergans, but I cannot prevent the havoc they would bring to humans in order to gain access to my daughter. Meanwhile, the leaders from Pratrim are getting ready for an assault."

"I'm the only one who can help her?" Granted this woman was telling the truth, there were millions of people on the planet. Why me? The situation was getting more absurd with each passing minute. I swore to take my medication the moment I got home. My little rebellion against my disease was blowing up in my face. Weird things had been springing up left and right since the day I stopped taking the drugs.

"Yes," she answered with conviction.

"How?"

"It was predicted by what you would call a Shaman that a human boy with his own set of burdens would come into her life the minute her father died. You came to see Elizabeth at the same time Arthur's aura disappeared."

Suuuuuuure. The tic-boy was going to come to Shannon's rescue. The news had trouble written all over it, and I wanted to throw up. I cupped a hand over my mouth and tried to calm my nerves. Once my stomach settled, I launched the first of the countless questions I had.

"Did my meeting with Madame Elizabeth trigger the weird dreams I'm having?"

"When your paths finally crossed, her presence activated the gift you've always possessed. Also, the medication you were taking blocked your ability to see."

"What does that have to do with helping Shannon?"

"You have dreams about her like you did of the snakebite victim and other tragedies that occur around you. Am I right?"

I nodded.

"I can't see everything that you see in those dreams, but I know that you've seen the Ergans running after Shannon."

"Are those the weird-looking creatures?"

"Since you connected with Shannon that day, you're on the Ergans' radar. They're watching you and trying to find ways to take her. You are the only one who can help her. Binarian citizens have been watching over Shannon and her father for years. As I mentioned, Elizabeth is one of them, as well as Gilbert, their butler. Binarians don't fight unless they are of noble blood. Their numbers are dwindling, and we can't afford to send many of them here. With our powers weakened when we cross the gateway into your universe, it is difficult to overthrow our enemies, so humans have become our best defense. I'm afraid our adversaries are going to make their move before Shannon turns eighteen, when she will reach her Aarmark maturity and can live among us."

"Aarmark maturity?" This was getting weirder by the second. I glanced outside the window and sure enough, people continued to go about their business, not noticing me or the strange woman in my car.

"When Binarian Aarmarks reach adulthood, their Aarmark heritage completely manifests itself. This period also ushers in changes that reveal their abilities and modifications to their appearance. This transition also prepares them to travel in safety to our universe. This happens on the eighteenth birthday. If a Binarian doesn't make the Aarmark transition, he or she will remain human and won't be able to change later. This is much more important for those with royal blood. Until their birthday, a royal Binarian is susceptible to acts of violence from our adversaries.

Everything just blew right by me. There was too much stuff to digest. "Shannon is a Binarian, right?"

"Yes."

The thought of losing Shannon to either those ugly-ass Ergans or her mother's universe didn't sit well with me. "Can't she live here on earth forever?"

"Once she learns to defend herself, we can bestow the Wetheiran on her."

"Wither-what?"

"It is a talisman that would allow her to live here in safety."

"Why can't you give it to her now?" I raised my voice in confusion.

Detherina closed her eyes and wiped away more of her colored tears. I wondered if Shannon shed the same colorful tears, too. I watched Detherina contemplate her answer and could see it hurt her.

"It's not time yet. I wish with all my heart that I could protect her here, now. I have been aching to hold her in my arms, but there are things even I can't change."

I had no idea why I believed her. A dreadful ache burned inside me for Shannon. And like the Boy Scout I was, I opened my mouth and swore an oath to help. "I will do whatever I can."

Her relief was obvious. The smile she gave me was so blinding, I had to cover my eyes. A glow emanated from her. It was weird.

"I promise I'll do whatever it takes to keep you both safe, but everything else will depend on you. Shannon has been told that you're the key to what lies ahead for her. That is all she knows. I must warn you not to say anything about her background until the right time. I will be in touch. Elizabeth will find a way to get Shannon to live with you, so—"

She stopped when she saw the grin on my face. Some days I really thought I was bipolar. These mood swings were a tad bit disconcerting.

Detherina exhaled. "It is best if she's with you most of the time. She's safe in school because she's surrounded by other humans, but now that Arthur . . . " she paused, and her sadness rolled off her like a thick fog, "is gone, her home life is threatened."

I asked the obvious question. "Why can't you go to the authorities for help?"

"Do you think anyone would believe us? And if we involved more humans, the stakes increase, and we'll have more blood on our hands. I assure you, our enemies will stop at nothing to get what they want, just as they did in your dream."

"Yeah, not cool. Why do they do this?"

Detherina hesitated and then dragged in a deep breath. "It's a war. I'm afraid you got pulled into it."

I nodded, still not grasping all the details. "I'm not going to lie. All this shit . . . oops, I'm sorry . . . "

"Go on," she urged.

"All this is unbelievable to me. I still can't wrap my mind around it. But for Shannon's sake, I'll do whatever it takes to keep her out of harm's way." It was weird. My whole life was about to change, and I was calm as a clam. This was going to be a long day.

Her smile was gracious. "That's all I needed to hear." Then she vanished, her molecules drifting in every direction,

Just like that, I was alone again. The mist that surrounded

my car disappeared along with Detherina.

Then I saw Mark and Darryl standing by my window. I blinked and tried to compose myself. My radio started playing the same song I was listening to before Detherina materialized inside the car. When I glanced where she had been sitting, I found a little purple bottle on the seat. I grabbed and pocketed it.

"Bro, let's move." Mark pounded on my window.

I checked my watch and was surprised to see that only a few minutes had lapsed. It didn't feel that way, though. I swore I had been talking to Shannon's alien mother for more than half an hour.

"Coming." I unlocked the door and breathed a sigh of relief when everything seemed to be back to normal. The nightmarish episode felt like it never happened, except for the proof I had inside my pocket.

Darryl and Mark kept up their steady chatter while we headed to our class, not commenting on my silence. As was to be expected, the surprise meeting with Shannon's alien mother began taking its toll on me. Shivers started running up and down my spine, and my shoulders twitched hard. Just as we turned down the hallway, I saw Shannon ahead, flanked by her friends. She looked happy, unaware of the devastating news of her father's death that was coming her way. The reality would crush her.

My classes flew by faster than they ever had, even with the nonstop barrage of tics. Instead of heading to my car at the end of the day as was my habit, I hung around the hallway to wait for Shannon. I waved to her the moment she emerged from her Biology class, and her face brightened up when she saw me.

"Now, isn't this cute? The freak-with-a-tic is making a move on my girl." Kevin Masters' annoying voice came from behind me.

From the corner of my eye, I saw Shannon walking faster in my direction. I turned to face him. "Last I heard, she broke up with you," I said, feeling bold for the first time in my life.

Normally, I would have walked away from this type of confrontation. I would watch everything I said around Kevin because he would beat the crap out of me, and I didn't want Mark or Darryl involved in a fight. But not this time—I had to watch over Shannon.

Instead of responding, Kevin launched his fist into my face, and a loud, cracking sound echoed in my ears. "Now you can hear that! Want to hear it again?" Kevin challenged.

I stumbled backward, landing on my butt. Students ran over and formed a tight circle around us. Shannon pushed herself in front, rushing over to me. She tried to help, but I waved her aside. Kevin had gotten away with his attitude in the past, but I wasn't going to let him off the hook this time. I'd had enough of bullies. He was done making my life a living hell.

I cracked my knuckles and was preparing to barrel at him when someone yanked me back.

"Don't even think about it," Mark said from behind. Darryl stood in the middle, his arms outstretched, keeping Kevin and me apart.

"Stanton, tell that freaky friend of yours I'm not finished with him." Kevin spit on the linoleum floor and stalked away.

"Kevin, don't start with me," Mark called out.

"Why don't you tell *him* yourself," I yelled after him.

Just before he cleared the front door, Kevin was approached by the principal. A student must have reported the incident. Mark relaxed his grip, and Darryl picked up my backpack from the floor. I wiped the blood off my nose with the back of my hand before turning to check on Shannon. Her face was red, and she looked like she wanted to kill.

When Shannon caught my eye, she snapped out of her daze and reached into her backpack and produced a tissue. Instead of handing it to me, she dabbed at the blood running down my nose herself, right in front of everyone. I felt like the luckiest man alive, despite the throbbing pain. My nose was already swelling. I'd be sporting an overgrown tomato in the middle of my face for days to come.

"Are you okay?" Shannon asked.

I nodded. "It's nothing." It felt good to sound tough for a change.

"Mr. Morrison, I want to see you in my office," Mr. Delson, the principal, said. The crowd scattered fast, including Mark and Darryl.

"Sir, I saw the whole incident," Shannon volunteered. I shook my head at her. There was no point in getting her involved in the situation.

"You may come, too, Miss McKesson." The principal motioned for us to follow him.

In the end, I was given a warning—for instigating the fight. Not entirely accurate, but at least they didn't call my parents. Since Shannon gave an eyewitness account, I got off easier than I would have otherwise. Kevin was looking at a three-day suspension for throwing a punch. He glared at me the whole time, but I was focused on the boatload of pain I was experiencing.

After we were dismissed, Shannon dragged me to the nurse's office, where I was given a cold pack. I pressed the thing on my nose like it was my redemption. Thank God nothing was broken, although I could barely open my eyes with the swelling.

"I don't think it would be a good idea to watch a movie tonight," Shannon said when we left the nurse's office. She touched my face, maybe trying to find everything else underneath the puffiness.

I leaned into her touch, loving her warmth on my skin, but soon I stepped back.

"Yeah, I don't think I want to be seen with a swollen nose around town. It'll ruin my reputation." I held her car door open for her.

Shannon tried to smile, without success. "I don't want you paying attention to bullies like Kevin. He's not worth the trouble, and he's never going to accept that I broke up with him."

I wasn't sure whether future fights with Kevin could be avoided. He had a well-established habit of threatening me, and he had many friends he could call on if he wanted to hurt me. I would have to be more vigilant to stay clear of him, although I would strike back if he managed to corner me.

"I'll follow you to work, if you don't mind hanging out with 'tomato face'. Then we can watch a movie at my place after. I'll even make grilled cheese sandwiches for dinner." My parents were attending a gala at my dad's office, so either dinner would be take-out or I'd have to make it.

"Cool."

The tarot shop was busy. I barely saw Madame Elizabeth, except in passing. She gave me a knowing look, which confirmed what Detherina had told me.

I kept Shannon company, and we finished our homework together. By the time the shop closed, my empty stomach was growling, but I gathered our backpacks so Shannon could tidy up the magazines in the waiting area.

She laughed. It was obvious she'd heard the embarrassing

noise my stomach had made. "You're just like my dad. His gets loud when he's hungry."

Remembering what her mother had said about her father's death, I responded with a small smile.

"He's coming back this weekend. He's been delayed at work for a few more days. I'm excited to see him."

From the corner of my eye, I saw Elizabeth behind the curtain, watching us. Her face was a mask of grief, and my heart ached for Shannon, too. She had no idea what had happened to her father or what the future held for her.

We convoyed our cars back to my house. On our drive back, I sensed a malevolent vibe that felt threatening. Glancing out my car window, I saw nothing out of the ordinary. Maybe it was the hours I'd been spending playing video games, or my hyperactive imagination was catching up with me. I trailed Shannon's car as close as possible, and I realized that, for the first time in my life, I had a purpose. Just as I'd promised, I would do whatever I could to keep Shannon safe.

Nightmare and Death

"Brian?" Shannon waved her hand in front of my face.

"Huh?" I snapped back to reality and took a quick bite of my grilled cheese sandwich.

"You've been very quiet. Come back to earth, huh?" She laughed.

I snuck a quick glance at her plate. It was empty, even clear of crumbs. I chuckled and said, "Back to earth."

"So why were you staring at me?"

To keep Detherina's secret, I had to make a conscious effort to hide my concern from her.

"Spaced out." I waved off the subject with my hand. "I bet my face is all swollen."

"You look terrible." Shannon reached over and blotted my nose with a tissue. I tried to move away, not wanting her to fuss over me, but it was difficult to say no to her. Her face was almost angelic, and she seemed incapable of doing anything mean. So, like a softie, I allowed her to make my face look better.

"Has my nose gotten big?" I focused on the swollen flesh I could see between my eyes.

"I like plums. I don't mind it." She giggled.

"You're so nice!" I scowled. Even so, Shannon's touch sent warm tingles across my skin, waking another part of my body. I flinched and drew away from her. Although the affected areas were tender and quite painful, I didn't mind the contact, but if she were to stay with us, I had better make sure to keep my hands to myself.

I wondered how Detherina and Elizabeth would come up with an acceptable reason to convince my parents to let Shannon stay with us. Whatever they ended up doing was sure to raise eyebrows.

"Brian, do you know what lies ahead?" Shannon asked out of the blue.

Unsure how to answer her question, I stood up, stacked our plates together, and brought them to the sink. She followed me and began rinsing the plates.

"Why are you so quiet? Have I said anything to offend you?" she asked, her face a mask of confusion.

My eyes were getting watery from the throbbing from my nose, so I took her chin and tilted it up to see her better. "Of course not. Why would you think that?"

"You can be intense or awkward, but I've never seen you like this. You know, like you're keeping a secret."

We'd been hanging out for just a week, not enough time for her to understand all my moods. She must have been observing me closer than I'd realized. If that was the case, then I needed to try harder to hide my emotions until she reached her Aarmark maturity. Whatever that meant.

"I'm still thinking about the fight with Kevin," I lied and let go of her chin.

She wiped her hands on the dish towel. "Then I guess I better head home. You look like you're tired."

I thought I detected a tinge of sadness in her voice, and I spluttered, "Please don't go. We can watch a movie."

"Are you sure?" She looked relieved.

Maybe she didn't want to be alone. I, for one, didn't want her to be. "Positive. What about something scary?" I asked with a grin.

Shannon eagerly rubbed her palms together. "Oooh, I love scary movies."

An hour or so into *Insidious 2*, I felt like a big gob of stupid. My plan had exploded in my face. Rather than jumping in terror and seeking my protective arms, she was sitting up, her back straight, enjoying all the blood and gore.

I sat next to her, hoping to find an excuse to hold her hand. Concentrating on the movie was impossible. Good thing I'd already seen it.

Shannon glanced at me. "You've been squirming like a worm. Is something on your mind?"

"No, nothing," I lied again.

She returned her attention to the movie. After a few minutes, she took my hand and held it. If a man could die from happiness, I was skirting the possibility.

I pressed my palm against hers, and like a balm, the sensation erased the ache in my face. We stayed shoulder to shoulder, leaning against the sofa with our hands entwined. It was after midnight by the time the movie ended. My parents still hadn't come back from their party.

Shannon stood up and gathered her things. "I should be going."

I hated the feeling of not touching her anymore, so I thought of a way to stay with her a bit longer. "Why don't you leave your car here and I'll take you home? Call me in the morning, and I'll drive you wherever you have to go."

Wow, all of a sudden, I felt like Sir Galahad, ready for a quest for the Holy Grail. I stifled a grin and hoped she didn't catch it.

She raised an eyebrow. "Don't you have curfew?"

"I'm turning eighteen soon, so I don't have a curfew anymore," I proudly announced. Slinging her backpack on my shoulder, I bowed. "After you, milady."

Shannon smiled and hooked her arm around mine, and we walked out the door to my car. The early fall air filled my nostrils. The darkness might have been playing tricks with my mind, but I thought I saw two pairs of yellow eyes not far away, watching us. For some insane reason, I felt no fear.

If Shannon saw them, too, she made no mention of it. I hurried to open the car door for her. Once she was safely inside, I walked around to the driver's side. I made sure the doors were locked before I turned on the ignition. "Tell me where to go," I said while I backed my car out of the driveway.

From the rearview mirror, I saw two figures emerge from the bushes. They loped to the middle of the street, but I couldn't make out any details except their glowing eyes. What kind of creatures were we dealing with?

While Shannon gave directions to her house, I casually took her hand and linked our fingers together and continued to glance back to see if we were being followed. Other than the few cars still out, nothing appeared behind us. Driving in silence was comfortable. It felt good to touch Shannon and know I didn't have to worry about carrying on a conversation.

My shoulder twitched once, and she laughed. Her attitude made me feel at ease, without the need to apologize for my tics.

"Are you okay?" She squeezed my hand.

"I feel like Superman." I wasn't kidding this time, and her answering smile was a relief to see.

Her house was not too far from ours. She lived in an affluent and historic neighborhood called Hancock Park. Under normal circumstances, it would take me less than fifteen minutes to make the trip, but with creatures looming around, I took my time. If her mother was not taking any chances, neither would I.

I parked in her driveway. Their house was a quaint Tudor-style mansion, humongous compared to mine.

I looked at the big, sprawling house before me and whistled. "I didn't know you lived in a mansion."

She grimaced. "The place is too big for four people."

Before I got out of the car, I said, "Wait here." I ran around to her side to open the door for her.

"You'd better not spoil me. I might get used to it."

"I'll be forever at your service." I gave a mock bow, bending low at the waist.

"Plum nose, jumping beans, and all?" she said while rummaging inside her backpack for her keys. However, when we reached the top step, the door was opened by a man garbed in a tunic similar to Madame Elizabeth's. He smiled at me.

"Good evening, Miss Shannon," he said in an impeccable English accent. He reminded me of Batman's butler, Alfred. Shannon squeezed my hand, doubtless guessing what I was thinking. I stifled my smile and gave the man a respectful nod.

"Brian, this is Gilbert," Shannon said by way of

introduction.

Gilbert inclined his head and gave me a knowing look. "How do you do?"

So this was the butler Detherina had mentioned. It wasn't hard to tell. The alertness in his eyes gave away his identity, at least to me. This was an instance when I wished I'd paid more attention to Alfred and Bruce Wayne's exchange in the movie. A witty response would've come in handy. I had no idea how to respond to such a formal query, so I just gave him my most dazzling smile. "I'm fine, thanks."

"It's a pleasure meeting you, Sir Brian." Gilbert gestured us in, then took one step outside, surveying the surrounding area. His action made sense, a form of caution.

I followed Shannon past the foyer. It was impressive, to say the least. Elaborate carved wood furnishings were scattered everywhere, and expensive artwork adorned the walls. Whoever her father had been, he'd had an eye for the magnificent and expensive. One particular painting reminded me of Romeo and Juliet, and I studied it for a minute.

"Isn't it pretty?" Shannon asked, standing next to me while I admired the work.

I traced my finger along its intricate frame. "It's mind-blowing." Then for some insane reason, I imagined replacing Romeo's face with mine, and Shannon's for Juliet. That would make the picture much, much better.

"Dad got it during one of his trips," she said, her tone wistful, with pride and adoration in her eyes.

"It's beautiful," I said, and then whispered, "just like you." Shannon rolled her eyes.

"Miss Shannon, your mother is waiting for you in the sitting room," Gilbert said from behind us.

"Mother, I'm home!" Shannon said. She seized my hand and led me to another humongous room with impressive decor. "Brian's with me."

Madame Elizabeth looked deathly pale, and I held my breath, guessing the news she was about to break. I didn't let go of Shannon's hand, holding it tight while we sat down opposite her surrogate mother.

"Hello, Brian," she acknowledged me with a tight smile.

"Good evening, Madame—"

"Please call me Elizabeth."

"Sure . . . "

Elizabeth turned her attention to Shannon. "Honey, there's something I have to tell you."

I felt Shannon stiffen, and her hand gripped mine harder. "Mother, what is it?" she asked, her voice rising.

"It's your Dad."

"What about Dad? Isn't he coming back tomorrow? He promised me." There was the trace of longing in her voice that made me ache to hold her close.

Elizabeth glanced around, as if summoning strength from outside forces to help her. In a moment, I felt a presence around us. My eyes couldn't see, but my entire being sensed company.

"Mother, what is wrong?" Shannon released my hand and went around the coffee table to sit next to Elizabeth. "Tell me, please."

"He's not coming home . . . not anymore." Her voice broke.

"What do you mean? Is business taking longer than usual again?" Shannon's pitch rose higher. She looked ill, and her body began to shake.

"He had a car accident. A hiker found him today. He's gone, honey."

Shannon sagged and began to cry, a shattering wail that penetrated my core and broke my heart. Elizabeth wrapped her arms around her, and they rocked together while they wept.

I sensed despair all around me, not just from the women on the couch, but also from the unseen presence surrounding us. Being an outsider, I held myself back, feeling helpless and wanting to soothe Shannon.

"Dad . . . is gone?" she whimpered.

"Baby, I'm so sorry." Elizabeth looked up at me and urged me to come over.

"Shannon, I'm sorry." I touched her arm.

She turned to me, and I caught a glimpse of her tears. They were the same color as her real mother's. I wondered if other humans had noticed. This confirmed that Detherina had been telling the truth all along. I cradled Shannon, her head resting against my chest.

She cried until her voice turned hoarse and she couldn't cry anymore. I continued to sit with her and comfort her with gentle strokes on her back. There was no way I could leave her, not in this situation. I pulled out my phone and sent a text to my parents.

Shannon's dad passed away. I'm keeping her company. See you in the AM.

I saw a slight movement from behind the curtain, on the veranda. It was Detherina, walking in our direction. Before she reached us, she became invisible, but even though I couldn't see her anymore, I knew that she was there, sharing Shannon's grief.

Elizabeth's cell phone rang, and she left the room to answer it. I heard quiet murmurs in the background, but her voice was too low for me to understand. Still holding Shannon's hand, I saw Detherina from the corner of my eye resting her palm on her daughter's shoulder. Shannon's face began to relax, as if the torment was being sucked out of her. After a long moment, Detherina nodded to me.

"Shannon, do you want me to take you to your room?" I asked, knowing she'd had a long day of school and work before this bombshell.

She nodded, but before I could move, Gilbert appeared in the doorway.

"Mr. Brian, allow me." After I scooted over, he picked up Shannon and cradled her in his arms. "Please follow me," Gilbert said.

We went through a little hallway to a staircase and ascended it in silence. The only sound was Shannon's sobbing. When the butler stopped in front of a door, I pushed it open. The room was fit for a princess, which Shannon was, and it suited her.

Everywhere I looked were pictures of her in various outfits, costumes, and activities hanging on the wall. Propped on her nightstand was a picture of her and her father. Judging by Shannon's apparent age in the photo, it had been taken many years ago.

I pulled back the covers on the bed, and Gilbert laid her down, tucking her in like she was a small child. Then he turned to me. "Will there be anything else?"

"Could you get Shannon a glass of water?" I asked, electing to sit on the chair of the desk at the far side of the room.

He bowed his head and left.

"Can you stay with me tonight?" Shannon's feeble voice was just a whisper.

"Of course. I'll be around for as long as you need me." It was the truth.

"Hold me?"

I lifted the cover and slid in next to her. She turned toward me, and I placed an arm around her and started humming a tune. I'd never felt needed in my whole life before tonight. Shannon was the only thing that mattered. Not my disease, not school, or even my own life. It was an odd feeling.

After a few minutes, Gilbert announced himself and placed the glass on the nightstand, within easy reach. I continued to rock and hum to Shannon until she fell into a troubled sleep. I fought to stay awake, but my eyes drooped several times. Sleep found its way to me.

After an hour or so, I jerked, waking myself up from a dream. The pictures had been so vivid, an explosion of orange fire and thick black smoke rising in a moonless night. Although I replayed my vision over and over, trying to find clues that would interpret what I saw, I drew a blank.

After some time, exhaustion again got the better of me. This time, I dreamed that Shannon was running away, calling my name for help. Two monsters were intent on pursuing her, and they wanted her dead.

Panicked, I screamed, kicked, and splashed liquid at their grotesque faces, and they fizzled into thin air. I felt spasms coming, tics taking over my body. I cursed and cursed until someone called my name.

"Brian. Brian, wake up. You're having a nightmare."

The Prodian

At the crack of dawn, I opened my eyes to find Shannon sound asleep and snuggled against me, her arm wrapped around my chest. When I studied her features, I felt an ache deep in my gut. Her face, even in sleep, still reflected her grief. Although I wanted to keep holding her like this, I had to find Elizabeth, so I slipped out of Shannon's grasp after a few minutes and left her room. Hoping to find Elizabeth in the sitting room, I wandered the hallway, trying to find my way back.

"Mr. Brian, may I help you?" Gilbert appeared at the end of the hallway and eyed me with interest.

"Hey, Gilbert. I'm looking for Elizabeth." I placed my hands inside my pockets.

He pointed to the wall. "This way, please." Before I could ask, he tugged on a low-hanging sconce, and the wall split into two.

Bewildered, I stepped into the darkened room that lay beyond. It felt like something out of a superhero comic, complete with sliding walls leading to secret lairs. We reached the adjoining room, where several people had converged around a table, Detherina and Elizabeth among them.

Everyone looked up at our entrance. The unfamiliar faces regarded me with curiosity. When Detherina beckoned me, I hesitated before moving forward. My hands were cold and clammy inside my pockets.

"Brian, I have no words to offer except thank you," Detherina said in a solemn voice.

"No thanks necessary."

"Sit next to me, please." She pointed to the vacant chair to her right. Once I did, she looked around at the others. "I want you to meet Shannon's Prodian, Brian."

At this, everyone started talking at the same time, giving me a round of welcome in English and another strange language filled the room.

I waved then returned my hand to my pocket. Keeping my shoulders squared helped control my tics. "What is a Prodian?"

Detherina smiled. "A protector."

"Oh."

She pointed to a younger man with a rigid black Mohawk, multiple piercings, and dark eyes. "This is Carionis. He is a Binarian. I have assigned him to pose as a transfer student so he can keep an eye on you and Shannon. He'll be reporting to me."

I smiled at Carionis, who nodded in return.

"And this is Matro." Detherina gestured to another person. The man was muscular and wearing a tunic similar to Gilbert's. "He is family and will be keeping an eye on you, too."

Matro gave me a long once-over before he smiled. His eyes

had that disconcerting crystal hue. Even his teeth glistened. "You got into a nasty fight, my boy?" His voice was strong and quite foreboding. Despite his smile, I knew this guy wouldn't think twice about snapping my neck in two—or anyone else's, for that matter.

"Just a little fight," I admitted.

"Matro and Carionis will give you a lesson or two on fighting once we all get settled," Detherina said.

Me, fighting? More power to both of you.

Matro continued to watch me. Carionis snickered and I had a sneaking suspicion that he knew what I was thinking.

Detherina threw a glare in the younger man's direction and continued. "You've met Gilbert. He's the butler and a Binarian, too. And you've met Elizabeth, of course."

I gave each of them a quick smile.

"The Ergans are going to be aggressive since Arthur is gone. I can feel their wrath spreading, and I want to warn you. They will be hunting Shannon before she reaches her Aarmark maturity." Distress marred Detherina's face.

I nodded and said, "I think I saw two of them last night outside my house. They tried to follow us here, but I lost them."

"They will interfere with your dreams, giving you more information than you're ready for, so you have to be vigilant. It will be a struggle for you since they can manipulate accidents and tragedies around you to keep you distracted and confused. You'll have moments when you will have to choose who you will help."

"I have friends who could give me a hand," I said, thinking of Mark and Darryl. There wasn't a doubt that they'd help. They'd love a good adventure. Besides, they were human, which was a good selling point.

"You have to make them aware of what is in store for them," Matro said. "And I want you to know that, although humans surrounding Shannon are the best defense, the Ergans could find a way to eliminate them. They won't be able to kill humans directly, but they can find ways to stage an accident."

"Like what happened to Shannon's father?" I asked the obvious.

Matro's jaw tightened. "Yes."

Detherina placed both her palms on the table. "So you will have to make sure to keep an eye on them. This is a big load on your shoulders, but you're all we've got. Ergans will play dirty. They'd do anything to incapacitate me."

"How can I keep Shannon safe?" I asked, wondering about living arrangements in particular. Matro coughed, and I realized that he could read my mind.

"The society you live in would not understand Shannon living with you, so I've made arrangements to buy the house next door," Detherina said.

"But that house isn't for sale." I scratched my head, thinking of my neighbors. They'd just moved into the area a year ago.

"It is now," Matro quipped.

"Shannon is awake," Gilbert interrupted and left the room in a hurry.

"Go now and be safe," Detherina said to me. "Try to act normal. You have a good head on those shoulders of yours. Do the right thing and use your best judgment. Maintain normalcy. We'll be in touch." She placed a comforting hand on my arm.

Maintain normalcy? The thought made me laugh. That would be a challenge. I was never *normal*. The idea was ludicrous, but I didn't say anything. Instead, I stood up and bobbed my head in understanding. With my head spinning from all the new information, I walked back through the secret door in the wall.

"Here." Gilbert thrust two glasses of orange juice at me.

"Thanks." Wow, these creatures moved fast.

I tapped on the door before entering the bedroom. Shannon stirred in bed, and when her puffy eyes settled on me, she tried to smile.

"Good morning. I got you OJ," I said in my most cheerful voice.

She sat up and stretched her arms toward the ceiling, stifling a yawn. "You had a nightmare."

I handed a glass to her and sat on the edge of the bed. When her sweet scent floated across the room, my raging teenage hormones made their presence known. I crossed my legs to hide the damning evidence.

"Yeah, I have an overactive imagination."

Shannon sighed, her eyes filled with sadness. I wanted to touch her face, but I kept my hands where they were, wrapped around my glass. I took a quick swig.

"I'm scared," she whispered, her voice quivering.

I had no idea what to say, but I scooted closer. "I know you are, but you have to stay strong. I'm here for you."

Her eyes glistened. "Thanks, Curly."

"Listen, I have to get home before my parents go ape-shit. I'll call you in a bit, okay?" I got up and placed my glass on her nightstand.

She watched me, looking glum.

"Let me know how you're doing." I reached out and squeezed her hand. As usual, electric jolts ran down my spine.

"I will," she paused, "and thank you for keeping me company."

"No worries." The moment I walked out of her room, I got a distinct feeling of loss.

When I got back home and opened the front door, the aroma of bacon and eggs lured me to the kitchen. Classical music was playing in the background, as usual. It was a typical Saturday morning in the Morrison household.

"Hey, guys." I flopped in the chair next to my dad.

"You're just in time for brunch." My mother turned around with a smile, but it soon disappeared when she got a look at my face. She gasped and rushed over to me. "Heavens, Brian! What happened to you?"

My dad looked up from his paper, and his brows furrowed. "Young man, you know how I feel about fighting," he said in a stern tone.

Self-conscious, I tried to cover the evidence with my hand, but when my palm made contact with the bridge of my nose, I flinched from the pain and my eyes watered.

"Explain yourself," Dad ordered while Mom fussed over me, the frying bacon forgotten.

I waved her off. "Mom, I'm okay. It's not broken." Then I turned to my dad. "I didn't start the fight. I'm not suspended from school, but Kevin Masters is."

My explanation seemed to calm my dad down a bit. "That boy is a bully."

My mother huffed. She knew how miserable Kevin had made my life since middle school. "He ought to be expelled."

"Cynthia, it'll take more than one suspension to get the son of a prominent councilman expelled from school," my father reminded her. "I still don't want you fighting, Brian. Avoid him at all costs." We'd had this conversation many times over the years. My father didn't realize the impossibility of what he was asking.

"I know. I'm glad he was suspended. Serves him right."

Mom went back to her bacon while I drummed my fingers on the table. I hadn't realized how hungry I was until I smelled the food.

"How is Shannon?" Dad asked.

I told them about her father's death, omitting all the crazy details.

When I fell silent, Mom asked, "You like her, don't you?"

I'd known it was just a matter of time before she questioned my friendship with Shannon.

"She's a friend," I said, trying to sound casual.

"Well, she's a pretty girl, and such a delight to talk to. I hope she comes out of this tragedy in one piece." Mom shook her head.

"She'll be all right." I kept my expression blank.

"Give her a hug for me," she said.

I'd love to, but since Matro had been designated to keep me in line, I wouldn't dare. I happened to like having my limbs intact.

"Here you are." Mom placed a plateful of food on the table.

I picked up my fork to help myself, but my dad coughed. "Let's say grace first." He took my hand and my mom's to create a little circle. We bowed our heads for a silent prayer.

The moment they released my hands, I dove in. The rest of the meal was spent talking about Dad's new celebrity clients. Thankful that attention had turned away from my swollen nose, I feigned interest to avoid any further discussion about it.

After I helped clear the dishes away, I went to my room and got in the shower. I thought about my nightmare. The explosion meant something had happened, but I didn't know what it was yet or who'd been the sacrificial lamb this time. I hated not knowing.

My cell phone beeped with an incoming text when I was toweling myself dry. It was from Shannon.

Relatives are coming from out of town. Will be busy the entire weekend.

I replied, **Take it easy. I'll miss you,**

Me, too.

Those two words made me feel good, making the prospect of not seeing Shannon more bearable.

With the entire weekend all to myself, I decided to finish my homework right away so I could spend my time hanging out with Mark and Darryl. I flipped my English Lit book open and took out a sheet of paper to outline my analysis. I started skimming, having read *The Glass Menagerie* years ago. For some insane reason, the words "friend" and "tragedy" kept flashing before my eyes while I read.

I tried to concentrate on my outline, but the image of the words kept hounding me. The continuous bombardment exhausted me. I put down my pen and fished out my ear buds, hoping music would distract me. While I waited for inspiration to hit, I leaned against the headboard of my bed and closed my eyes. I must have fallen asleep, because it was dark when I opened them again.

The clock said it was already nine o'clock. I had been asleep for several hours. Why in the hell hadn't Mark and Darryl shown up? I rolled closer to the nightstand and to switch on the lamp, and everything fell into place like a jigsaw puzzle. Matro's words echoed in my head. I jumped up and paced the room while dialing Darryl's number. He didn't pick up, so I tried Mark's number. Thank God, he answered on the second ring.

"Bro, where are you? Where's Darryl?"

"I'm with him. We dropped by your house, but you were sleeping. Then his Dad called him to fill in at the gas station tonight."

"Are you there yet?" I shouted, feeling the ringing in my ears. It now made so much sense.

"Yeah, we got here two hours ago. What's going on?"

"Get out! Get out now!"

"What the hell are you talking about?" Mark sounded alarmed.

"Get out of the gas station. Run as fast as you can. Do it now!" I yelled across the line. "I'm not kidding. Now!"

I pictured the massive explosion, the darkness of the night lit with bright orange flames and filled with suffocating black smoke. The words from *The Glass Menagerie*—friend and tragedy. It had been a warning all along. Now I remembered Matro's advice. The Ergans would stop at nothing.

Mark didn't respond, and the call was dropped. "What the hell?" I redialed but got a busy signal. My heart was pounding hard against my chest. I ran out of the house, car keys and phone in hand, barefoot and still in just my pajama bottoms.

Please, please, don't let this happen. Please!

A cloud of dust was left in my wake when I hit the accelerator hard, hoping I wouldn't be too late for my friends.

The war had begun.

Aarmark versus Ergans

With no plan in mind, I wove in and out of late night traffic, trying to reach Mark and Darryl. There was no way I would let them fend for themselves since I was responsible for endangering them. Without their knowledge, they had been dragged into a war just because of their association with me.

I tailgated and cut in front of cars to get ahead, receiving a lot of angry honks while I snaked through every gap I could find.

Matro appeared in the passenger seat next to me without warning.

"You scared me," I hollered, flooring the gas again.

"Sorry," he said, intently watching the road.

We were still a few blocks away when the ground shook and massive flames shot into the night sky. The intense light burned in the darkness.

"Oh, hell!" I pounded the steering wheel with my fist.

Inch by inch, I worked through the sudden jumble of cars that had stopped in the middle of the street. I took a hard left onto a side street and found a parking spot. We took to the street on foot, Matro running next to me. I threw a quick glance at him, and he was already armed with weapons strapped across his chest. His scabbard made jingling noises while we covered the first block.

Several sirens blared in the distance. Matro stopped running, but I kept on, ignoring the way the rough pavement scraped my feet and each little pebble punched into my skin. When he caught up, he was holding his shoes out to me.

"Stop and wear these." He handed me the big-ass pair of combat boots.

I followed his orders even though I'd look like a clown in my PJ bottoms, T-shirt, and boots. Who would care, anyway? I slipped on the oversized shoes and wasted no time continuing my sprint.

When we cleared the corner, several fire trucks had already trained their hoses on the burning structure. Clouds of smoke were billowing up while they battled the raging inferno. I scanned the crowd, hoping to see Darryl and Mark somewhere. My heart pounded against my chest.

"Sir, you can't move any closer." A cop eyed me with detachment.

I glanced at Matro and realized the cop couldn't see him, so I stepped back.

"Ha-have you seen two teenage boys anywhere?" I stammered, unable to get the words out of my mouth. My tics were trying to manifest themselves, but I suppressed them, rotating my neck to ease the tension in my muscles.

The distracted cop shook his head, and I had no choice but to move to another location. The onlookers multiplied by the minute, gawking at the tower of brilliant flames. There was movement not too far away from us, and I saw two Ergans back away.

"I'll be right back." Matro palmed his scabbard and left in pursuit.

Jesus. What a mess. I cupped my palm to my mouth and called out for Mark and Darryl as loud as I could. My voice had to compete with the noise surrounding me. I walked back and forth, but there were too many people. Just when I was starting to think I had lost them, I spotted Mark and Darryl leaning against a squad car, talking to an officer. I ran toward them as fast as my legs would take me.

Their expressions when they saw me were terrified but relieved. I barreled in their direction, heedless of the cop interviewing them. We hugged like we'd never done before.

After a few minutes, Mark pulled away, looking uncomfortable, and then glanced around. "Did you dream about this?"

I nodded, sparing a glance toward the cop who seemed intent on finishing up the investigation. Darryl spoke up. "Officer, we need a minute here."

The officer huffed. "Fine, but hurry up. I don't have all night." Then he walked away.

Once we had a little privacy, I urged them to sit down on the sidewalk. "I'm glad you guys are okay," I whispered.

Mark could only nod his head.

"I wish I had known this was going to involve you guys."

Darryl released a shaky sigh. "Tell us what's going on."

Before I could speak, Mark found his tongue. "Right after you said to get out, I heard rumbling from the front, like an earthquake, so I pulled Darryl out towards the back exit. We heard the explosion when we were running away."

"Damn. You guys could've been killed." I felt sick to my stomach.

"I'm glad you called." Darryl glanced around, shaking his head.

"I should've warned you guys right away, but everything that's going on is just too unbelievable. It took me some time to figure out the signs, but I'm glad it wasn't too late."

The cop came back and interrupted our quiet conversation, studying me with interest. "Time's up. I need to get back to the station. Who is this?"

"He's a friend of ours," Darryl said.

"Well, let's wrap this up, and you can fool around later." He gestured for Mark and Darryl to follow him.

Fooling around? Cop or no cop, the guy deserved a punch in the face.

I stayed within earshot. No one mentioned anything about my phone call, which was good. I doubted that they would have believed us anyway. The blaze continued to rage, and soon Darryl's parents arrived.

Mark and I stepped back and watched the teary reunion. After being reassured that their son was unhurt, they switched their attention to the cop.

We stepped away and continued our conversation. "Did you call your parents?" I asked Mark.

"Yeah. They're catching the first flight they can find." He still sounded shaken.

A loud crackling from the burning structure distracted us. The extreme heat from the fire fanned across our faces. Nothing had been spared.

Darryl checked over his shoulder to make sure no one was paying attention to us. "So what do we do know?"

We leaned against a squad car, and I launched into a brief explanation, beginning with the death of Shannon's father. Then I told them about my introduction to the Aarmark creatures and how the Ergans were manipulating events.

"You mean that's who did this to us?" Mark asked in disbelief, his eyes wide with terror.

I stood up and tried to shake off the oncoming twitches. "Yes. It's my fault for getting you guys involved."

"Damn." Darryl shot to his feet. "I don't know about you guys, but I ain't taking this sitting down." All those hours of playing video games had given him confidence, but he needed to remember that this wasn't a game.

"Calm down, you knucklehead. We're dealing with aliens here. Aren't you afraid you might end up dead?" It looked like Mark, for a change, was going to be the voice of reason.

Kicking a pebble with his foot, Darryl nodded. "Of course I am, but I'm not going to sit around and wait for those bastards to kill us."

Mark looked unconvinced. He began to pace. "What do you think, Talon?"

"Well, I'm chin-deep already since I promised Shannon's mother I would help. But you guys don't have to be involved in this."

Mark stroked his chin while Darryl started muttering. "This is so not freakin' happening,"

"The hell it isn't," Darryl chimed in. "Just think, we can combine our mad skills from *Call of Duty* and *League of Legends*."

This made me smile, but I shook my head. We were talking

about real danger, and my bonehead friend was treating it like a game.

Mark grinned. "I still get to be Varus."

Darryl clapped his hands. "And I'm going to be Garen. Booyah!" He pumped his fist in the air.

"Epic." *And really dumb*, I thought to myself while we high-fived each other.

A movement from the corner of my eye alerted me to Matro's return. He was wiping the blade of his weapon on his pants.

Mark shook his fist. "This is war!"

"Damn right!" Darryl seconded.

"I think if we're going to do this, it's time to introduce you to Matro, a fighter from the land of Tranak."

Mark and Darryl whipped their heads in the direction I pointed, and they both stumbled backwards, eyes bulging out of their sockets, when Matro became visible to them.

"What the hell?" Mark said.

"He . . . he . . . is the alien?" Darryl continued backing away.

"Hey, guys. This is not a joke. He's real, and we're the only ones who can see him," I said, grabbing Darryl by his shirt and dragging him back.

Matro saluted and moved closer. The man walked like a predator, fierce and determined. "Let's get one thing straight. I'm *not* an alien. I'm from another universe, understood?" My friends nodded with a mix of awe and intimidation. "Then if we're on the same page, I suggest you kids keep your voices down. People might think you're crazy."

"Uh, um . . . " Mark cleared his throat. "Can I touch your weapons?"

Matro chuckled. "Can I touch your nose?"

Mark was clearly out of his element, and Darryl's mouth gaped open.

Matro took this as an opportunity to explain himself. "First rule in my book. A weapon is a part of your body. It is sacred. It could mean life or death."

This made sense, and we all nodded in understanding. "Are you going to teach us?" I asked.

Matro hesitated. "Well, I know Detherina ordered Car to teach you some tricks, but I guess these two can join in."

This seemed to light a spark in my friends, who jumped up, rubbing their palms together. "We're ready!" Darryl said.

"You think you're so slick," Mark told him.

Just then, Darryl's father called for him. Mark and I waited while they talked, and then Darryl came back. "We're going home now. I'll call you guys in a bit."

"Take care, bro," I said before he turned away.

"Brian, can you give me a lift?" Mark asked.

We left the scene, still shaken from the horrible experience, but also filled with anticipation at the prospect of learning to fight from Matro and Carionis. While we walked to the car, Matro walked alongside us, and Mark kept glancing at him until he nearly stumbled.

"Bro, he's real, if that's what you're wondering about," I said.

"Dude, I've always known you were weird, but this one tops the charts." Mark shook his head in disbelief.

"Thanks! I aim to please." I opened the door, and he took the front passenger seat.

"I won't join you, Brian, but I'll be around." Matro waved and disappeared.

"Weird," Mark repeated and then slumped against the leather

seat.

"Fffuccckkkk." Involuntary tremors and phonic tics assaulted me as soon as I sat in the driver's seat. I didn't fight it this time. In fact, I welcomed the twitches, letting them run their course. All I felt was relief that my friends had made it out alive. After some time, the jerking stopped, and I pushed the car's start button. Mark was so used to my attacks that he didn't even pay attention anymore. His eyes were closed, and I could guess what was running through his mind.

I drove home through the maddening traffic around the explosion and made a silent vow to myself. *I will make an effort to take all clues into consideration.* No other human would be dragged into this. The war between Detherina and those ugly mofos had almost taken the lives of my best friends. The last thing I needed was to have more innocent lives affected by my new bizarre reality.

Sunday was humdrum compared to the chaos of Saturday night. Mark, Darryl and I communicated often, either by text or online chat. We even got in several games of *L.O.L.* to take the edge off. On top of that, I also worked on finishing my English outline and even wrote an extra analysis for Shannon. I figured she'd be too distraught to worry about homework. We exchanged texts when she wasn't occupied with preparations for her dad's funeral service. She and Elizabeth had been busy dealing with out of town relatives.

I told my parents about the explosion before they could find out from the news media. The cause of the explosion had been identified as arson, according to the reports on television. Police authorities and fire officials were still piecing all the clues together, but I had big doubts they'd ever find who was responsible.

Monday came and went without incident. I attended all my classes, regretting the reason for Shannon's absence. The news of her father's death had spread like wildfire around campus, and as far as I could tell, most of the senior class was planning to attend the memorial service.

The service was set for the next day, and with my parents' blessing, I skipped school to attend the funeral. Darryl and Mark did the same. Tuesday morning, we all squeezed inside my coupe and drove together to the chapel.

When we got there, I wasn't surprised to see the place packed to the brim. I spotted Shannon right away, sitting in the front pew with Elizabeth and Gilbert flanking her. We worked our way to the front, as close as we could get to her. Carionis was standing close by, hidden by the columns of the tiny chapel, while Matro and Detherina stood like sentinels next to the urn containing Arthur's ashes. I knew no one could see them except me and my friends. Matro dipped his head in acknowledgement when he saw us, but Detherina was too distressed to notice. I saw her looking at Shannon with sad eyes.

Shannon glanced over her shoulder at me and offered me a weak smile. I wished I could do more for her.

The service started, and for the next thirty minutes, we sat and watched and listened. When Shannon stood at the podium and delivered her eulogy, there wasn't a dry eye in the room.

It had been explained to me that as a part of the Aarmark tradition, Arthur's remains had to be buried in the homeland of his beloved. I had no idea how this would be possible. All I knew was that they'd cremated something for show, for his human family's sake.

Afterwards, I had a brief moment with Shannon in the corner of the chapel. I waited until the room emptied before I took her hand and squeezed it. "You okay?" I asked, noticing the dark patches under her eyes.

"I can't believe he's gone." She dabbed her face with a tissue.

"Be the brave girl that you are. You're going to get through this."

"I know. But I'm going to miss him," she sobbed.

I pulled her into an awkward embrace. "Hang in there," I whispered. A movement nearby made me look up to find Carionis watching us with a blank expression.

Shannon and I stayed huddled together. With my thumb, I traced the trail of her tears and wiped them away. After a few minutes, Gilbert appeared in the doorway and whisked her off to a black limousine for the private family-only memorial.

Carionis spoke from behind me, looking rather out of place with his leathers, Mohawk, and piercings. "Do you want to come? I'm sure you're invited, too."

"Can my friends come?"

He looked at Mark and Darryl, as if calculating their coffin size, before nodding his head. "I guess they can. Follow my motorcycle."

Carionis walked fast, so we ran to my car in a hurry. We saw his motorcycle streak by, and I stepped on the accelerator to follow him.

The burial was a short ceremony, also attended by Arthur's two siblings and his mother. They spoke with Shannon and Elizabeth afterwards, while we hung in the background next to Matro and Detherina. Darryl and Mark kept sneaking peeks at Shannon's gorgeous, intimidating Aarmark mother like they couldn't believe she was real.

Shannon glanced my way several times, and each time, I

offered her a thumb's up. I'd never been a cool guy, so I was running out of ideas about how to act with her.

Mark chuckled. "You're killing me," he said.

"What?" I hissed.

"Your geekiness knows no bounds."

I covertly flashed him the middle finger. "Whatever."

Once the small crowd had dispersed, Shannon came over to us. "I'm going home now. I'll be in class tomorrow." She gave me a gloomy smile.

"I'll call you tonight."

We all watched her walk away with Elizabeth and Gilbert, then Detherina spoke to me. "Thank you. My daughter is very lucky to have you."

"It's my pleasure to be there for Shannon." What a loser thing to say, but somehow, this seemed to please her. Matro also inclined his head in a gesture of appreciation.

"Take good care of yourselves," she said to all of us. "I will keep you informed. Carionis will stay and keep watch. After we bury Arthur, Matro will stay nearby." They disappeared without giving me a chance to respond or tell them goodbye.

"That's so weird," Darryl observed after Detherina and the rest left. "That's Shannon's real mom?"

I nodded.

"Wow." From the corner of my eye, I thought I spied him wiping a little drool from his chin.

We went back to school and finished the rest of the day. The mood was somber, and for the first time, I thought about the impact of losing a loved one. My parents were healthy, and they'd probably be around for a very long time. Even though we drove each other nuts, I couldn't picture life without them.

The last ten days had been a whirlwind. Everything had

happened so fast, and most of it still made me shake my head in amazement. Mark had been right. I might have been weird to begin with, but the recent events had taken things way beyond just "weird."

Mertest

The pungent aroma of pot roast woke me up. I'd fallen asleep on the sofa right after school. I scrubbed my eyes and strained to see the time. Once again, my catnap had turned into a two-hour sleep.

I got up and sluggishly walked to the kitchen to give my mother a kiss. "Hi, Mom."

"How was the funeral service?"

"It was okay, I guess." Really, what did people expect from a funeral? "What time's dinner?" I asked, taking a glass from the cabinet.

"In an hour. Your dad is running late."

I poured myself some orange juice and downed it. Then I said, "I'm going out for a run. I'll be back in time for dinner."

"Take a flashlight," Mom called after me.

In two minutes, I was in my running clothes and out the

door, hot air chafing my face. It was early autumn already, but in Southern California, winter didn't begin until late November or early December. I could do without the heat and preferred the winter. I got in my groove with a brisk walking pace and then broke into a jog for the first quarter mile, picking up speed until I hit my stride. To avoid any encounters with the Ergans, I decided to take the shorter route with well-lit streets. I had my ear buds in place and music blaring, but I stayed alert.

Running had been an outlet for me throughout the years. If I had problems, running was the answer. It helped me forget about the bad stuff. If someone made fun of me at school, I would run to let off steam. This time, I needed to clear my head and get a better handle on what I'd gotten myself into.

If I hadn't been crushing on Shannon, I might have dismissed Detherina's plea for help and told her to buzz off. However, I'd been daydreaming about Shannon since freshman year, so the opportunity to be with her looked like the chance of a lifetime. I wouldn't dream of turning down her mother's request. This was a mission, and I was on board with it all the way. After all, I enjoyed being with Shannon, and her safety had come to mean more to me than anything. I wouldn't have had the balls to stand up to Kevin if it hadn't been for the little talk with Detherina, and to be honest, getting saddled with the title *Prodian* was an ego boost, too.

The lamppost on the corner of our street began flickering as if it were taking its last breath. Aside from the faint light coming from our neighbor's house, the street was blanketed in darkness. I glanced up at the dull half-moon and began to sprint. Out of nowhere, heavy panting rose behind me, loud enough to be heard over my music.

Without looking back, I kept pounding my feet on the

pavement. Ten houses before I reached the safety of my home, two massive mongrels jumped out in front of me. I couldn't see their bodies very well, but their yellow eyes glowed in the darkness. They blocked my path, making it impossible for me to move forward. Their teeth made horrible gnashing sounds like they thought I was their dinner. I took a step back.

Why are you protecting a species you know nothing about? The question floated in the air with no movement from their mouths, which got bigger the closer they got. This optical illusion had to be one of the mind tricks Detherina had warned me they'd use.

"Why are you intent on taking Shannon when she hasn't done anything to you?" I asked, not fazed by their proximity. Detherina had told me that Ergans couldn't kill me themselves, so I had to trust that she was right. It wasn't like running was an option anyway.

Her mother is a whore. She's brought destruction to our people. She must die. The words swirled around me like a brush of wind.

I took another step back when they drew closer. Their teeth were jagged and sharp, and I had a sinking feeling that even if they couldn't kill me, those teeth could do a number on my puny body. Each movement of their claws on the pavement made a horrible scratching noise and they stunk to high heaven.

The glare of headlights came from behind me without warning. An engine revved and accelerated, and a motorcycle came out of nowhere, braking a hairsbreadth from my leg.

I turned to see Carionis.

"Hop on," he shouted above the roar of the engine.

There was no hesitation on my part. I jumped behind him. Startled, the creatures rushed forward, but Carionis took out a bottle and splashed its contents on them. On contact, they fell on the ground, convulsing. The motorcycle spun around, smoke rising up from the rubber, and Carionis spat on the ground.

"Serves you right," he said before we sped away.

It dawned on me that he was driving away from my house. "Where the hell are you taking me?" I asked, hating that I was clinging to him like a damsel in distress.

"You and I need to have a little talk, unless you want to introduce me to your mom and pops right away." He snickered and revved the motor.

We had to be going a hundred miles per hour. The wind dried the sweat on my face, so I couldn't complain. I hung on tight while we made our way toward the darker patch of Griffith Park. Carionis turned off the headlight, and we covered several miles in the darkness. When we stopped, I jumped off before he could even turn off the engine.

I knew the guy had saved my life, but something told me that he wasn't too happy about it.

"I talk, and you listen. *Capisce?*" Carionis leaned against the motorcycle.

I put my hands on my waist and shrugged.

"First, I'm here to look after you and Shannon. Shannon mostly," he added as an afterthought. "I would appreciate it if you didn't stand still and wait for those morons to slaughter you."

My eyes widened. "Detherina said they couldn't kill me. You were there. You heard her!"

"True, but I've seen those beasts at work. They can manipulate the weak-minded into doing the damage themselves."

This information made me shudder. "So how do I protect myself from those . . . dogs?"

"They're not dogs. They're a cross between a gorilla and a bull. They can't run fast, even on all fours. They create an illusion to make you think they can. Their claws hurt like hell, and their fangs can shred you to pieces. So if I were you, I'd carry Mertest everywhere I go."

"Mer-what?"

"M-E-R-T-E-S-T," he spelled it out like he was talking to an idiot. "That bottle the Totren left in your car.

"Totren?" I repeated.

"Detherina, she's a Totren—our ruler. She left a bottle in your car when she first showed herself to you, didn't she?"

I suddenly remembered. "Oh . . . *that* bottle." I'd thought it was some sort of perfume. It was still sitting inside my glove compartment.

"You thought she left you cologne?" Carionis snickered.

If this was the guy who'd be watching my back, I had a feeling that we'd end up killing each other.

"You don't have to like me, Morrison. I can definitely say that I don't fancy being your nanny. But an order is an order. I respect our Totren, and Shannon is—" He shook his head.

"What about Shannon? You dig her, don't you? I saw you watching us this morning."

Carionis clenched his jaw and looked away. "I'm not even going to answer that. Just make my job easier, would you? Run with protection, loose the freakin' earbuds, and stay alert."

Looks like I hit a sore spot. Well, whoop-dee-doo. "What is Mertest, anyway?"

Carionis sighed before answering. "It's a potion we use to subdue the Ergans. It incapacitates them and then turns them into dust."

"Where do you get it?" I asked, remembering the purple

bottle Detherina left with me.

"It's a concoction made by our spiritualist," he said. "Now, if we're done with the twenty questions, I want to know if you understand what I'm telling you. No earbuds while running. Keep your eyes open, and most of all, don't toy with your life."

"Yes, I heard you," I replied, wishing he'd shut up and take me home.

"Whatever suits you. Just make sure you take good care of Shannon, or I'll kill you with my bare hands."

If Carionis meant to threaten me, it hadn't worked. The ride back was quiet, but tense. Neither one of us spoke.

Carionis stopped in front of my house. "I'll drop by tomorrow afternoon. Be prepared to introduce me to your parents," he said before speeding away.

Sure, my parents would buy the idea that I'd made a new friend. *Not*! First of all, I didn't make friends, not by choice. Second, I had always hung out with a pretty boring crowd, like the photography club members. Darryl and Mark were the exceptions. Carionis, with his Mohawk and piercings, would make my parents raise their eyebrows and question my choices.

"Bri-boy, is that you?" Mom called out from the kitchen.

I cleared my throat. "It's me." Before I could head straight to my bedroom, she called out again.

"Set the table, will you?"

"Okay." Reluctant, I turned around and headed to the kitchen.

I turned in early that night so I could wake up a bit earlier. My plan was to wait for Shannon in front of the school so I could talk to her before classes started.

Mark and Darryl showed up a few minutes after I got there, so we hung out until I spotted Shannon. I shooed them away just before she started climbing the steps.

"Hey." I stood up. "How're you doing?"

She gave me a weak smile. "I'm okay. It's just hard, you know, knowing I won't see my dad anymore."

I could just imagine. "I'm sorry. You know I'm here if you need to talk."

We walked toward the building together. The corridor was filled with loitering students, waiting for the bell to ring. When we got to our photography class, we both sat in the back of the room.

"Should we schedule something this weekend?" Shannon asked.

"Schedule what?" I had no clue what she was talking about.

"Our photo session." She showed a hint of a smile.

I remembered now. She wanted me to pose for her. Eager to please, I nodded, even if I hated the whole idea. "Where do you want to do it?"

She thought for a moment. "I want a nice background."

How about my bedroom? I wanted to say, but that wouldn't go over well, so I tried to come up with something else. "Um . . . you want nature as the background?"

"Yeah."

"What about the Huntington Library? They have pretty flowers and plants there." I couldn't believe I was talking about this stuff with a girl. I'd come a long way.

Her eyes lit up. "Oh yes! That'll be perfect. I want to see the Corpse Flower."

Great! She'd be taking my picture next to the *Amorphophallus titanium*, an unattractive plant that smelled

115

like . . . well, it lived up to its name. What a way to boost my ego. I tried to smile anyway.

"Should we go on Friday since it's a holiday?" she asked, looking hopeful.

Being a softie, I had to go with the flow and she was going to drown me with all these ideas I had never tried before. "Sure, I'll pick you up around ten?"

Mr. P walked in the room, halting any further conversation. For the rest of the period, I switched between listening to him and keeping an eye on Shannon. She looked so sad. I wanted to help, but only time would soften the pain.

Just before the bell rang, the door opened, and Carionis walked in with a swagger. Mr. Peters raised an eyebrow.

"I'm a transfer student. Sorry I'm late, but there was a mix-up with my schedule." There was an undeniable arrogance in his voice.

"We're almost done here, so we'll just see you tomorrow." Mr. Peters dismissed him. Carionis glared at me before he turned around to leave, and the bell rang soon after. I sighed. This was going to suck.

Introducing Carionis

Second period was uneventful, thank God. When Ms. Sweeney asked us to produce our first analysis on *The Glass Menagerie*, as I'd predicted, Shannon came up empty. Good thing I'd worked on an extra analysis for her.

"Here, I got you covered." I handed her the paper.

She glanced at it and began skimming. "I can't take this."

"Look, you had no time to write anything. I don't want you to flunk this subject, so I went ahead and wrote it."

"But it's cheating," she protested.

"Only if we're caught. You're not going to say anything, and you know I won't. If you want, you can return the favor," I whispered.

"How?" she asked, looking perplexed.

"You can work on the next scene for us. Think of it this way. I took care of the character analysis, and you have my back on the next one. Then we're even."

She considered my proposal for a moment.

"Is there anything you want to share with us, Brian? Did you want to be first to read your analysis?" Sweeney walked over to our desks, keeping a close eye on Shannon, who still seemed to be deliberating. "Or perhaps Shannon would want to go first."

Startled, Shannon flashed me an 'I'm going to kill you later' look and nodded her head. "Yes, I can go first." She stood up and walked to the front of the classroom.

Before she began reading, she took a deep breath. Thank God I'd printed the damn thing. There was no way she'd have been able to decipher my hieroglyphic handwriting.

"I'm going to discuss Tom Wingfield and his double role in the story." Shannon started off a little shaky, but as she went along, her voice grew stronger. She covered just about everything I'd written, except a few times when she looked up and spoke without reading. I stared at her in disbelief. Despite everything, she had done her reading.

When she finished, Sweeney looked pleased and called for the next student. Shannon walked along the rows of seats and grinned at me just before she sat down.

"Thanks," she whispered.

"I didn't do much. It seems like someone actually did their homework," I whispered back, glancing at Sweeney.

"I had a chance to do a little reading before, you know . . . "

I knew what she meant and nodded. After third period, I didn't see Shannon again until I ran into her in the hallway before the last period. Kevin had her cornered by the lockers, so I picked up my pace and ran in their direction.

Kevin had his back to me and didn't hear my approach. I caught a bit of what he was saying. "How can you be so stupid?

You dumped me for that freak-boy?"

Shannon's eyes blazed with anger. "First of all, I'm not stupid. It was smart to break up with you. And it's none of your business who I hang out with." She tried to move, but Kevin's arms wrapped around her waist.

"Don't you miss this, babe?" He brought down his mouth onto hers in a punishing kiss. She tried to push him away, but he didn't budge.

"Stop it. You're disgusting." Shannon slapped him across the cheek.

My rage now blinded me. I seized Kevin's shoulders and yanked him back. He released Shannon and turned around, and his earlier grimace was replaced by a wicked grin. "Freak-boy wants another bitch-slap, I see." He cracked his knuckles and stepped forward.

"Stop it, Kevin!" Shannon tried to step in between us, but I pulled her aside.

"You're way out of line, Masters," I said, holding my ground and squaring my shoulders.

He stopped a few inches away and looked down at me. Yep, I had no way of getting out of this one without bruises, a broken bone, or a black-eye.

"Why don't you just tic your way out of here, and I'll forget I ever saw your face today?" Kevin snapped his teeth together.

"Why don't you pick on someone your own size?"

Okay. I didn't have to turn to see who had spoken. I'd recognize that arrogant, lazy drawl anywhere.

Kevin pivoted to face Carionis. "Well, well. Who do we have here?" He sized up this new contender. "So, the new guy is freak-boy's babysitter. Ooh, I'm terrified!" Kevin pretended to shudder. Several kids who had gathered around us snickered.

"The name's Car, and I'm going to make you cry for your mama." Carionis hooked his thumbs on his pockets and smacked his chewing gum loudly,

Kevin smirked and covered the distance between them in two giant steps. "So you have a big mouth, too." He threw a punch, but Carionis sidestepped and countered with a sharp jab to Kevin's stomach.

Kevin staggered backward and yelped. Some students clapped and cheered while I moved in Shannon's direction.

"Are you okay?" I inspected her face.

"I'm fine."

Carionis took Kevin's shirt in his fist. "If you want a rematch, I'll be around." Then he dragged the wheezing boy to the principal's office.

It was unheard of that someone would volunteer to go the principal's office, but then, Carionis wasn't a normal character.

I took Shannon's hand. "Let me walk you to your next class."

Shannon didn't move, pulling me back. "I saw him at Dad's funeral. Mother told me he's related to you. Is that true?"

Okay, now the bastard was family. I guess someone forgot to send me the memo. "Yeah, he's a cousin from out of state. He arrived right before the funeral, so I brought him with me. He's a bit odd, as you can see."

Shannon was silent for a moment. Just when I thought she wasn't going to buy my feeble cover-up, she nodded her head. "Does he live with you?"

Hell no! I shook my head. "His parents got him a place somewhere nearby." My lies were piling up by the minute.

The bell rang, saving me. I walked Shannon to her class before running to mine. Jesus, this whole thing was snowballing into one large mess. I wonder how difficult it would be to get in touch with Matro. We needed a little talk.

I came home exhausted. After I dropped my backpack on the chair, I headed to the fridge to hunt for leftovers. There was a container with pot roast. My mom had sliced it up already, so I popped some bread in the toaster and waited. I made myself a sandwich and brought it into the family room. Before I flopped down on the sofa, I doubled back to snag a drink, too.

After I'd downed my meal, I felt a little better. I closed my eyes. I had no idea why I was so tired. This whole Aarmark thing was zapping all of my energy.

I must've fallen asleep. When I woke up, hours later, I heard my mother talking animatedly in the kitchen. Then came Carionis' voice and Mark and Darryl's answering laughter. *What? What the hell did I miss?* I shot out of the sofa and into the kitchen. They all looked up at my abrupt appearance.

"Hi, baby-boy!" Mom smiled. She was wearing her 'I'm the boss in the kitchen' apron and had a spatula in her hand. "Your friends are here. I invited them for dinner. Your dad's running late, as usual." She rolled her eyes.

"Oh, great." I went over to the counter, where they were all seated on the barstools. I threw Mark and Darryl a questioning look, but they shrugged their shoulders in response. When I locked eyes with Carionis, he shrugged, too. He looked strange without his usual dark denim, black shirt, and piercings.

If not for the mohawk, I wouldn't have recognized him. I guess he wanted to make a good impression. Way to go, shit-face!

"I heard Car is a new student in your school. How exciting," Mom said while dishing out hefty portions of pasta. "Did you know that his father is a doctor, too? He runs the OB-GYN department at Cedars."

"Oh, yeah?" I feigned interest. So Carionis had been weaving his story already.

"Take your plates and eat while it's hot." She waved us to the dining room. We picked up a plate each and went to sit at the table. All of us were poised to dig in when my mom signaled us to stop.

"We'll say grace first."

I rolled my eyes when she took my hand and prodded me to take Mark's. Once we were all holding hands, she began to enumerate the things we should be thankful for.

We all muttered amen when she was done and started our race to see who would finish first. It had been a contest for the three us for a long time. The rule was that whoever finished last would help with the dishes. Like pigs that hadn't eaten for days, we devoured dinner as fast as we could.

Unsuspecting, Carionis took his time and finished last. We all laughed when he found himself letting Mom teach him how to load the dishwasher. This gave me a little time to talk to my friends, so we headed upstairs. Once we got to my room, I closed the door.

"What the hell is *he* doing here?" I asked, giving my buddies a venomous glare.

"Bro, we all got here at the same time. I was going to ask you the same thing," Mark answered, turning on the television and PS4.

"He's cool." Darryl pressed the remote to pick his character.

"Whatever." Maybe Carionis was cool, but he was also arrogant. I refused to trust him completely.

"What are you so worked up about? I heard Car saved your ass from another beating from Kevin." Mark chuckled.

"There's nothing funny about it." Great. Now everyone thought I was incapable of fighting my own battles.

"It's better than looking at you with a big lump on your face," Darryl said.

The intro music of *Call of Duty* started playing. "True. It's just that he thinks he's all that," I retorted.

There was a rap on the door before it opened. Carionis was standing outside, my mother next to him. "Here you are. You boys have fun," Mom said and patted him on the arm.

"Thank you, Mrs. Morrison," Carionis answered.

As soon as the door closed, we all burst into laughter. When Carionis joined in, it helped to alleviate my earlier irritation somehow.

"Carionis, what the hell happened after you took Kevin to the principal's office?" I asked, scooting over to give him some space to sit.

"Just call me Car, okay? Carionis is for Aarmark biz only." I nodded.

"I told the principal what happened."

Darryl had lost interest in the game. "But I heard that you threw the first punch!"

"That's true, but it was in self-defense. He would've clobbered me if I hadn't acted first." Car laughed. "He deserved it. But since I'm a nice guy, I suggested to the principal that Kevin didn't deserve a suspension. He already got what was coming to him. So he put us both on warning."

"Unbelievable," Mark said, shaking his head. "You talked the old fart into giving Kevin a warning?"

Car laughed again. I was slowly learning that this was his way of saying yes. He was one weird guy, and I would know.

"It takes one to know one," Car said.

"I hate when you do that," I said, flustered.

"I'm special." He laughed again. "Do you guys have an extra controller?"

Just like that, the Three Stooges became the Super Friends.

Corpse Flower

We got to the end of the week without any further school drama, or embarrassing tic attacks. To say it was a relief would have been an understatement. It was difficult to impress a girl when I had to spend so much time worrying about my next phonic attack, although I had to admit, Shannon had been a trooper. She rarely jumped when I blurted my F-bombs. Regardless, I still hated not being able to know when the big one would come.

After my morning run, I jumped in the shower for my 'date' with Shannon and the corpse flower. I chose a freshly laundered plaid shirt that didn't have any ink stains on the pocket and fixed my hair to the best of my ability. When I inspected the finished product in the mirror, I didn't look half bad.

"Looking good, Morrison." I did my favorite Captain Underpants pose and chuckled. Then I gathered up my keys and a tube of sunblock and hurried out the door. Sure enough, the sun was beating down, and the temperature was pushing into the high eighties.

Over the course of the last two days in school, Carionis had been quite visible, but he'd stayed out of our way. He would say hello in passing, but otherwise, he kept to himself. If Shannon had qualms about his presence, she didn't say anything, although I'd seen her glance Car's way a few times. So far, he'd kept his distance, which suited me just fine.

I parked my car in front of Shannon's house and texted her to come out. There was a large moving truck in front of their garage. This reminded me that Detherina had mentioned her plan to purchase our neighbors' house. I wondered if the sale had been finalized.

Shannon came bursting out of the front door, lugging her camera, a tote bag, and a wide-brimmed straw hat. She was wearing one of those ruffled sleeveless blouses over very short shorts. I tried not to stare, but who could ignore such a vision?

"Hi, Brian!" she said the moment she got in the car.

"Hey." I tried to sound cool, but my voice squeaked. A total fail.

Shannon didn't seem to notice. "Are you excited to get your picture taken?" She eyed my plaid shirt before her gaze slid down to my khaki shorts. Her face colored, and she looked away.

Did Shannon McKesson just blush because of me?

"Ecstatic," I said in a dry voice.

She laughed at my effort to sound sullen. Once we got on the freeway, I decided it was a good time to ask about the truck.

"Is someone moving?" I tried to sound nonchalant.

"Oh, that. I forgot to mention it to you, but Mother thinks the house will remind us too much of my dad, so she decided to move to a smaller place."

"Oh, yeah?"

"Yes. She found a house in the Los Feliz area." Shannon sound excited and my heart did a couple of happy flips. "In fact, we did a walk through last night, and guess what?"

"What?" I answered too quickly, but I bet she didn't even notice.

"You and I are going to be next door neighbors! Isn't that amazing?"

She sounded happy, and my heart did a quick celebratory moonwalk. Shannon and I would be living next to each other. It was the coolest thing to happen since the Lakers won the NBA championship.

I pumped my fist and hooted. "That's awesome! We can ride together to school every day. When's the big move?"

"We're moving some of our stuff already. I guess the sellers were in a bit of a hurry to leave. We should be all moved in by next weekend."

Then an idea struck me. Did her presence last night in my neighborhood have anything to do with the appearance of the Ergans? That would explain Car's presence, too. As much as I wanted to think that he was watching over me, he had mentioned that his main responsibility, first and foremost, was Shannon. I was fuming, but I tried to keep a straight face for Shannon's sake. Good thing she seemed caught up in her own happy bubble.

We found a parking spot right away and followed the pebbled path on foot to the admission booth. The crowds were already building, despite the heat. After we paid for our tickets, we walked around a bit, looking at plants, flowers, and some of the other oddities the botanical garden housed. We covered most of the displays, including the corpse flower, which was the foulest smelling thing I'd ever encountered. The stench was like being in an enclosed space surrounded by a thousand rotting cheeses. Yeah, it was bad.

After our experience with the flower, we stopped under the shade of a tree. I held Shannon's camera bag while she used her camera's viewfinder to search for an ideal spot to begin my torture.

She pointed her camera in every direction imaginable. When she let out an excited squeal, I realized she'd found her perfect picture location.

"I brought a blanket," Shannon announced, slinging the camera strap around her neck. She spread it down in a grassy area next to a trellis with funky-looking vines everywhere. It was perfect all right, considering a small tree there provided shade from the sun's harsh rays.

"I brought sun block, just in case you forgot," I pulled out the tube from my pocket with a flourish like I was performing a magic trick.

"Good call. I forgot all about that," Shannon said, settling next to me. "Do you mind putting some on the back of my shoulders?" She lifted her shoulder length hair and whipped it up into a ponytail.

Good Lord! I stared at the expanse of her back. It was the most beautiful thing I'd seen in my life. "Um . . . of course." Again, I tried to play it cool. I squirted some lotion in my hands.

I ran my palms along her shoulders and at the base of her neck, covering the entire exposed area. When the lotion sank into her skin, I noticed a weird reddened area and leaned closer to study it. It wasn't a rash, but a mark of some sort. The longer I studied it, the clearer it became. It was circular shape and had an eye in the middle and four spokes radiating from the center.

Crap! Was this something I should mention to her? As I wrestled with the question, involuntary garbage slipped out of my mouth. "Fuck," I blurted before I could stop myself.

Shannon laughed and looked over her shoulder at me. "Are you okay? Do I make you nervous?" Her pale cheeks showed a nice pink glow from the sun.

I stifled a jerk rolling on my shoulder, and I stiffened. "Yes and no." I continued applying sunscreen on her skin until I'd covered everything well. The marking was much more pronounced by now. "There . . . you're now ready to take on the sun." I felt like I should say something about the mark, but I bit my tongue. Maybe Matro would be kind enough to enlighten me about what it meant.

"Thanks." She released her hair, and I caught a whiff of her glorious scent.

Pretending to busy myself with recapping the tube, I moved away a bit. I didn't want her see how much she affected me.

"Here's what I want you to do." She lifted the camera to her face. "Lie down, use my tote bag as a pillow, and pretend that you're reading a book. Cross your legs at the knee and relax."

Did she say *relax*? I was wound up so tight that I could hardly breathe, but I did as I was told, arranging the bag and spreading myself out on the blanket. It took me several tries to cross my legs before it felt natural and comfortable.

I opened the book in the middle and breathed deep. Shannon didn't say anything while she moved around on her knees, circling me. Before long, she was snapping picture after picture from different angles. Since I didn't have to look straight at the camera, I began to relax, and my shoulders loosened up.

"Brian?" Shannon asked after a few minutes.

I looked up from the book. "Yeah?"

I heard a swift *click, click, click* and realized she had stolen a few head-on shots. Although I covered my face with my arms and tried to block the lens, she continued her assault with the camera.

"You think you're sneaky, huh?" I said once the clicking had stopped.

"I have an unwilling model, so I had to get creative." She laughed. "Why don't you sit up cross-legged this time?"

"You're not done yet? You must have enough to fill a whole yearbook."

"Not quite. I want a lot of pictures to work with." She aimed the camera at me again without waiting for me to rearrange myself.

"I have a better idea." I tried to take the camera from her, but I'd forgotten that the camera's strap was around her neck. Shannon fell forward, our bodies pressed together for a brief moment. Despite an urge to kiss her, I recalled my promise not to kiss her until she asked me. I pushed her back instead.

"Sorry, I didn't mean to pull so hard." I let go of the strap.

"What is your brilliant idea?" she asked, her voice sounding a bit shaky.

My heart was stuck in my throat, but I managed to say, "Let's take a picture together."

"How do you intend to do that?" she asked, although she handed me the camera without hesitation. "Do you want me to ask someone?"

"No, I can do it. You just have to move closer."

Shannon hesitated but then scooted closer until our shoulders touched. "Like this?" she asked.

I tried to gauge the angle. "A little closer. I don't want to cut your face off."

She scooted closer. "Better?"

"I think so." I took a picture and then turned the camera to see how it came out. The top of my head was cut off, and only half of her face made it in. When I showed her the photo, she wrinkled her nose. "Okay, let's do this one more time." With one arm, I circled her neck, keeping my other arm extended forward to steady the camera. "Ready?"

Before she could answer, I pressed the button and kept pressing it. With my finger on the button, I blew in her ear, and she began jerking away, giggling. When I reviewed the pictures, I saw that they had turned out just the way I intended, candid and relaxed. We were laughing, our faces toward each other—it looked so natural.

"Take a look," I said, handing back her camera.

Shannon checked out the pictures one by one. Each brought a bigger grin until she was laughing out loud. "You're crazy!" she said after she had seen them all.

Yeah, because of you, I thought, but I had to settle for saying, "Well, if you can't beat them, join 'em!"

Laughing, I tickled her until she fell back on the blanket, giggling. Although she tried to fight back and climb on top of me, she was smaller and lighter, so I was able to wrestle her back onto the blanket, pinning her hands and legs.

"You give up?" I asked, looking down at her pretty face.

She laughed and nodded. "I give up!"

After releasing her, I collapsed next to her and sighed. God, I couldn't remember being this happy . . . ever. There hadn't been a time when I hadn't felt self-conscious, but being with Shannon was liberating.

"What are you thinking?"

131

When I gave her a sideways glance, I found her staring up at the sky.

I hesitated, but decided to tell her the truth. "I haven't had this much fun ever," I replied in a low voice, closing my eyes.

She remained quiet, and then I heard a little sigh. "I feel the same way. With you, I can be myself. You don't seem to expect anything."

"Expect anything from you? Heck, I'm still shocked that someone as popular as you would want to hang out with me."

Shannon snorted and turned sideways, resting her head against her palm. "Do you want to know what I see?"

"Do I?" I turned to face her.

She ignored my question. "I see someone who is smart, funny, and cute. You speak your mind, and you're loyal."

She thinks I'm cute? What does that mean? Cute-handsome, or dog-cute? "Wow, you make me sound like a school mascot."

"Not like that, you dope." She poked me in the ribs. "I used to think you were condescending because you were smarter than everyone else. And of course you have a smart mouth, too."

"Gossip's going to get you nowhere, young lady." Feeling bold, I reached for her hand and held it. I gazed into her eyes. "Do you want to know why I act the way I do sometimes?"

She nodded and threaded her fingers with mine. Her hair fell in her face, so I lifted the strands and pulled them away.

"Since I was little, kids have made fun of my tics. Even some parents wouldn't let their kids play with me because they thought I was contagious. So I figured it was better to just stay away."

"I hate people like that. My parents always told me that I'm as good as the next person. Not better, but not less, either."

I looked at her, and a fuzzy warmth washed over me. If

Shannon could accept me, then the rest of the world could shove their snooty noses up their asses. After all the years of being mocked, it came as a surprise that someone found me interesting instead of pitiful.

We fell asleep there together in the shade. The next thing we knew, two hours had passed, and a security guard was nudging us awake.

"Kids, this is not a hotel. Pack up your things and move." The man narrowed his eyes at us.

Shannon and I jumped at the same time and grabbed our stuff.

"Here." I offered my hand, and she took it. The park was not packed anymore, thanks to the hot weather. We ran through it without stopping until we reached the deserted "jungle" garden.

Canopies of trees, climbing vines, tall shrubs, and large leaves surrounded us, and there was the sound of waterfall in the distance. It was a perfect spot to take more pictures.

Laughing, we rested against a tree until we could catch our breath. Shannon pulled a water bottle from her bag and handed it to me. "Drink, you look thirsty."

I twisted the cap and gave her a questioning look. "How does someone look thirsty?"

"You're sweating like crazy, and you smell different."

Note to self—don't use so much cologne in the morning. "Aw, c'mon. It's a special aroma that compels people to hug me. You can't resist it."

She bought the joke and laughed, pulling me into a quick hug. I closed my eyes to savor the moment, but when I opened them, an Ergan was closing in on us, its mouth gaping open while its ear-splitting howl surrounded us. Another growl came from the behind me, too.

It had to be the adrenaline pumping through my veins that enabled me to move at lightning speed. I took the bottle of Mertest from my pocket and splashed some on the Ergan behind Shannon, then I spun her around and threw what was left at the other one. There was a loud thud when they both fell to the ground, but the one closest to me managed to stick out its paw and graze my arm with its claw-like nails on the way down.

"What's going on?" Shannon asked, turning to look.

"Nothing. There was a hawk diving down. I thought it was going for us."

When she noticed the blood on my arm, she screamed. I pulled her close to me and cupped my palm over her mouth. "Ssh, don't worry. I'm fine."

She pulled my hand away and pointed at my arm. "You're bleeding." There were three scratch marks that were oozing with blood.

"Oh, don't worry about it." Good thing blood didn't faze me at all.

Shannon yanked my arm toward her for closer inspection. "Let me take care of it."

"Really, it's okay. It doesn't even sting." On the contrary, the damn thing burned like crazy.

Shannon didn't listen to me and started rummaging inside her tote bag. She took out a small bottle and popped the cap. "Here, it's what my mother uses for me all the time."

Sure enough, as soon as the clear liquid made contact with my skin, the stinging was gone. I looked up at her. "Thanks. That stuff is amazing."

"I'm glad you're okay. A hawk can do that? Are you sure that's what it was? I thought I heard shrieking." Now I had a new dilemma. *To lie or not to lie.* What should I tell her?

There was no time to concoct a convincing story, so I decided to redirect the conversation.

"Hawks are predators. The bird must have seen prey close to us."

Shannon didn't look convinced, judging by the way she shook her head at me. "You're not making sense. I know I heard something. What just happened?"

Her lips thinned, prompting me to squeeze her hand to reassure her. "Look, just don't ask, because I can't explain. You have to trust that this will go away soon." Christ, this was getting trickier by the minute, and I was on the verge of giving away the secret.

"That scratch didn't look like nothing to me."

We both looked at my arm. Lo and behold, the gash was fading like a distant memory.

"What the hell?" I whispered.

"This is freaking me out." Shannon covered her mouth with both hands.

Desperate to give her some sort of answer, I blurted the first thing that came to mind. "I'm going to find a way to explain later, but for now, let's just get out of here."

She nodded and offered her hand to me even before I asked for it. Together, we ran toward the parking lot, and I was dead sure both of us would be seeking answers to our questions.

Version of the Truth

"Baby-boy, wake up!"

Mom's voice jarred me out of my sleep, and I groaned. I hated it when she woke me up on weekends, especially when all I wanted to do was vegetate. After the day Shannon and I'd had yesterday, some peaceful downtime was what I needed, and maybe a chat with Matro later on.

"What?" I pulled a pillow over to cover my face.

"You're not going to believe who's moving next door!"

I had no idea what had gotten her so excited. "Um . . . "

"Your *friend*, Shannon."

I rolled my eyes at the emphasis she put on the word.

"I spoke with her mother. What a pleasant lady! A bit on the weird side, but she's very gracious."

I heard Mom move to the window, no doubt trying to check the activities next door, and light poured into my room when she drew the blinds.

"Mom, don't you have better things to do than snoop on our new neighbors?" I peeked out from under my pillow.

"I'm just happy to have a neighbor to talk to. The Joneses were a bit eccentric." Everyone was weird, in my mother's opinion. "And you get to hang out with Shannon a bit more." She was starting to sound like a matchmaker.

"Mom, we have classes together. We hang out on a regular basis."

For Christ's sake, it was only seven in the morning. Weren't people allowed to sleep in these days? I threw the pillow on the foot of the bed, sat up, and rubbed my face, but then I smiled.

My mom turned around in time to see me grinning like an idiot. "What's so funny?" She moved to my bed and started fluffing my pillow.

As if I was going to tell her how ecstatic I was to know this day had finally arrived. It was almost as exciting as the time I discovered I had some actual facial hair. "Um, nothing. What's for breakfast?" I asked, changing the subject.

"I made ham and cheese omelets." She pulled off the bedspread. I hated when she did that. "Hop in the shower, then have a quick breakfast. I think the McKessons would love for you to help."

Eager to see Shannon, I got out of bed and marched to the bathroom. After I turned on the shower, I inspected my face in the mirror while waiting for the water to warm up. Not bad. A bit of stubble, but my skin was clear. I grinned at my reflection.

Once I'd washed, dressed, and had my fill of Mom's omelets, I armed myself with my phone and ear buds and strode next door. I gave a cursory knock before letting myself in, and several movers glanced my way. Then I spotted Shannon in the backyard talking to Gilbert.

"You're going to love it here, Miss Shannon." I heard him say while I was crossing the kitchen to the patio.

"I know . . . I'm just going to miss our house, seeing Dad's things . . . you know . . . " She seemed so sad.

"Brian's next door. He'd be great company for you." Gilbert turned and waved when he spotted me. "Oh, here he is now."

Shannon looked over and grinned. "Brian, I'm glad you're here. Did our noise wake you up?"

"It was my mom, actually. She's raving about your mother."

Glancing around, a strange vibe hit me, but I kept my face even. Good thing Shannon didn't notice. Gilbert did, though. He excused himself and pretended to make his rounds, while inspecting the surrounding for any sign of a threat.

"It'll be scary if they start hanging out, huh?"

I shuddered at the picture. "Terrifying."

Her laugh was electric. "I think it'll be fun." She patted my arm in mock sympathy.

"Can I help you with anything? Like lifting a piano or a bed, maybe?" I pulled up my shirtsleeve and flexed my puny muscles.

Shannon's laughter was worth my pathetic attempt at being funny. The twinkle in her eyes was back.

"Let's put those big muscles to work. Can you bring those to my room?" She pointed at a cactus plant and a violin case.

"Are you underestimating my supernatural powers?"

"I wouldn't dream of it." She giggled.

"I didn't know you played the violin."

A wistful expression crossed her face for a fleeting moment. "Dad and I used to play together until he got too tied up with work. He was my teacher. We used to play for charities and family gatherings. It was something we enjoyed doing together.

When his travels took up most of his time, he enrolled me in a class, just to keep me playing. I loved it. I was taking lessons up until a month ago. I figured with school starting, it would be hard to juggle my schedule. But I plan on starting up again sometime soon."

Somehow, I understood her reluctance to pick up the instrument following her father's death. "Would you play for me sometime?" I asked.

"Maybe . . . one of these days."

I picked up the plant and the violin case and followed her up the stairs. Once we reached the landing, we heard a loud crash in one of the bedrooms. We ran, but Gilbert got there before we did. There was no one in the room, but a box was ripped open.

Gilbert and I looked at each other.

"What's going on here?" Shannon asked, moving toward the broken glass near the box. She picked up one of the pieces and recoiled.

I was by her side in a second. I took her hand and inspected the cut on her index finger. It wasn't too deep, but there was a lot of blood oozing out.

"There's a first aid kit inside one of the drawers in the kitchen. Would you be kind enough to attend to Miss Shannon's cut?"

"Of course," I answered. "C'mon, let's get this cleaned up." I pivoted Shannon toward the door, glancing at Gilbert and mouthing, *what's going on?*

Gilbert shook his head and began picking up the shattered pieces.

Shannon protested, but her voice was faint. "It's nothing."

"Are you scared of blood?" I asked, knowing already what the answer was. She looked pale by the time we reached the kitchen, so I searched around for a chair, but everything was still covered with plastic bubble wrap. "Sit here." I lifted her on the counter.

I opened the drawer closest to me, then another, and then the next one until I found the first aid kit. I flicked the spigot and felt the water until it was warm enough. "Let's wash it off before I apply the bandage."

Shannon turned her head away, hissing when I placed her finger under the running water. After I dabbed it dry, I put on the bandage. "See, ouchie's gone," I said, just like my mom used to when I was little.

After I gave her finger a kiss to make it better, she offered me a grateful smile. Without warning, I was hit another overwhelming urge to kiss her, but instead I let go of her hand and returned the kit to its drawer. If Shannon noticed the sudden shift in my mood, she didn't say anything.

"Thank you," she murmured and jumped down from the counter.

When I followed her upstairs, the muted sound of conversation came from the guestroom.

"Do you need help unpacking your boxes?" I asked, trying to distract Shannon. I had the feeling that whoever was inside the guestroom wasn't talking about the weather.

"I'm feeling a little lazy right now. Why don't we just hang out and listen to some music?"

Her bedroom was spacious compared to the matchbox I called my room. Her large bed occupied a huge amount of space, dwarfing the room. We lay side by side on the bare mattress, letting our legs dangle over the edge of the bed, and I handed her an ear bud.

"I'm digging a little dub step right now. Do you mind

listening to Lindsey Stirling?"

"Oh, my god. You like her, too?" Shannon's face broke into a big smile.

"Hell, yeah. You play the violin. I bet you can do what she does."

Shannon shook her head but grinned. "Maybe . . . "

I watched her mouth quirk into a cute, sheepish smile before I pressed play.

It was around lunchtime when Gilbert stuck his head through the door. "Pizza's here!" he announced.

We jumped off the bed at the same time.

"Race you!" Shannon said and got a head start.

I would have beaten her if she hadn't bumped me along the way, throwing me off balance. "You're a cheater!"

Several hours later, I wobbled back to my house, feeling like an overstuffed pig. Not only had I eaten almost an entire large pizza, I'd even gobbled up a half dozen chicken wings.

Of course, being the gracious guest that I was, I also pitched in with unpacking and furniture moving. I would've stayed longer if Shannon hadn't needed to get ready for Brittney's party. At least half of the cool kids were invited.

Then there was me. Spending Saturday night alone. Again.

I rolled my eyes the moment I walked in the house. It was movie night for my parents.

"Hey guys, I'm home!" I hollered from the door before I took the stairs.

"Back so soon?" Mom asked, and Dad grunted a greeting. That told me they were too engrossed in the movie to notice if I responded.

I walked into my room, only to stumble backward in surprise. "What the hell?" Matro was there, laughing while I hurried to close the door.

"That is not a polite greeting, you know." He was lounging on my bed, looking like he was ready to take up residence there.

"Then quit trying to give me a heart attack." I dropped my cell phone on the desk and removed my shirt. "What brings you to this side of town?"

"Well, I said I'd be back, didn't I?"

Matro crossed his legs at the ankles and rested his hands behind his head, the picture of relaxation. At least he had the decency to remove his shoes.

He raised an eyebrow.

"Good. I have questions for you." I sat on my desk and turned the television on. "Just keep your voice down, will you?" To remind him my parents were in the house, I gestured toward the floor.

"The only voice your parents will hear is yours. I would worry more what they'll think when they hear you talking to yourself." He chuckled.

I rolled my eyes. "So no one can see or hear you, but me?"

"Just you, my boy. And Larry and Moe, that is, if I want them to see me."

"Why is that?"

"Because you're the one person I'm allowing to witness my presence at all times."

"What the hell does that mean?" I asked. "Can we skip the cryptic answers? Just give it to me in plain English."

"The little guy has a temper." It was obvious that Matro found this whole thing amusing. He sat up and planted his feet on the floor, but he didn't get up. "Aarmarks are divine creatures. We're like, um . . . deities?"

I narrowed my eyes, not at all pleased by his reply.

He raised his hands in mock apology. "Okay, okay. Where we came from, good and evil are relative. We're a peace loving realm, and we care for our land, work with diligence, and care for one another."

"So you are all just boring farmers?"

Matro turned somber. "Just like most beings, we are independent and peaceful, but we still have enemies. The Ergans and their employers from Pratrim."

"Now we're talking. Tell me more." I leaned back in my chair, making myself comfortable. Then I remembered a more pressing matter. "Wait, we were attacked by those mofos yesterday in broad daylight."

Matro didn't appear worried. "You used the Mertest, right?"

I raised an eyebrow. "Of course I did. I need more."

"Check your drawer and your glove compartment. You're well stocked."

"Dang, you're fast."

"I'm always watching you."

That sounded strange. Why would he let me fend for myself if he was around, risking Shannon's life in the process? "How come you didn't help out?"

"It was a test. I needed to gauge your capacity to protect. Besides, I was nearby even if you couldn't see me."

"Did you see the part where one pawed me and drew blood?"

He nodded. "Shannon took care of it, right?"

"Did she know what it was?" When Matro hesitated, I waggled a finger at him. "Out with it."

"Elizabeth has been using it on all her scrapes since she was a child. To Shannon, it is like carrying a homemade merthiolate."

"A what?"

143

"It's an over-the-counter antiseptic."

"How come it worked on me?" This conversation was getting weirder by the second.

"Because it's a divine product. Our spiritualist made it for us."

"Kinda like the Mertest?"

"Sure."

Whatever. Still the idea that he was nearby and didn't help out didn't sit well with me, and I spoke the thought aloud. "Next time, step in if you think I can't handle the situation."

"As you wish."

"Fine. Now tell me about the Ergans."

He smiled. "Ergans are creatures of the dark. They've been our foes from the beginning of time. Classic good versus evil. We have been in constant battle for as long as I can remember." He stood up and walked over to the window before turning back to face me. "Be careful with those Ergans. They grew desperate after we defeated them and destroyed their territory. Right now, they're scattered, but they are rebuilding. They are cunning and manipulative, and they will employ whatever means available to strike back."

His statement jogged my memory, making me remember what the Ergans had told me some nights ago. "They called Detherina a whore. What was that all about?"

Matro's eyes twitched. "Those bastards will poison your mind. They'll tell you anything to win you over."

"Which means?" I cocked my head. This wasn't making any sense.

"Detherina asked the Prodians for help. Prodians are guardians of the fair—the truth as you call it. Our people are not accustomed to fighting, and we asked for their protection. This made Detherina a *whore* for seeking outside help. The Ergans accused her of escalating the campaign by involving other deities —"

"You called me Shannon's Prodian. But I'm not a deity. I'm just human. Am I supposed to be some guardian of the truth?"

"You are her version of the truth." Matro walked over to my bookcase and began thumbing through the titles.

I scratched my head, getting frustrated. "I already asked you to dumb it down. What does 'her version of the truth' mean?"

"There are things that I'm not at liberty to discuss with you. But I assure you, nothing those Ergans said was true." He pulled out a book on the Civil War and walked back to the bed.

"How do I know you're not just using me like a pawn?"

"You're a smart one. You'll know if you're being played."

That was the thing, though. I couldn't tell. I hoped that the relationship developing between Shannon and me, whether friendship or something more, wasn't going to be built on lies and deception.

"But what do I have that is so special?" This conversation was getting more frustrating with each passing minute. My shoulder jerked once and then again, a bit stronger. I breathed in and out, trying to suppress the next one.

Matro looked up from the book. "Are you okay?"

I hated the intrusion of my ever-present curse. "Why did I make the cut to be her protector? Look at me—I can't even get through the day without humiliating myself. I'm not the hero type."

"Detherina already told you about the vision of our sage. It is predestined. We have no power to change anything. You've been chosen to deal with this. It does not matter if we agree with it or not."

"What's in it for me?" As much as I wanted to be the one to save the day, the question remained. It sounded selfish, but I wanted to know what was waiting for me after all this was said and done.

Matro nodded as though he'd been waiting for that particular question. He closed the book, marking his place with a finger stuck between the pages.

"You're making good friends. More than what you'd expected."

It was a bizarre answer, but true. I watched Matro while he focused his attention back on the book. His pale eyes moved rapidly across the page. Right then, he looked normal to me, like a regular human.

"What sets humans apart from your kind?" I asked.

"Well . . . " He thought for a moment and then looked me straight in the eye. "Nothing, really. We just belong to a different universe. We can travel though time and sense the general emotions and thoughts of lesser species."

I knew it. He could read minds. I should have realized this the moment he started answering my unspoken questions. "That is a big difference in my opinion. Travel through time? Talk about big gas savings." *Wait, did he just call me a lesser species?*

He laughed, amused by my rambling. "What else do you want to know? You're entitled to as much information as I am permitted to give you."

"Why are we keeping Shannon in the dark? I mean, look. This is her life we're talking about. Don't you think she's entitled to know what's going on?" I meant it as an observation, but it came out sounding like a challenge.

"That is the Totren's call. Daughter of our leader or not, we are all subjected to secrecy until one is considered a matured

Aarmark. Even Shannon." He paused. "I know you feel it's not fair on her. She knows enough to get by, but until the Totren—or in this case, her mother—is ready to give her all the details, then it will remain a secret from her."

"I believe in full disclosure. My life and my choice." I felt a tremendous amount of sympathy for Shannon. What would happen after they told her? They would whisk her away to an unknown place instead of letting her make the decision for herself? Gone to a place where I wouldn't see her anymore?

The idea unhinged me. How would I live after that? The past weeks had been the best I'd ever had. It didn't matter what I had to do, as long as I was able to see Shannon every day.

"Human values are well-intentioned, but they don't apply to our way of life."

"But Shannon is being raised as human. You can't turn her point of view on and off like a freakin' light switch, you know." How could they manipulate Shannon's life without giving her room to choose for herself?

"We can argue all night long, but our rules are different from yours. There's nothing I can do. We all have our own burdens to carry. This is Shannon's."

"Totally unfair!" I shouted like a pouting child before I remembered that my parents might hear me.

Matro flew at me—literally flew—to cover my mouth with his hand. Then we heard footsteps outside my door.

"Son, is everything okay?" My dad knocked on the door.

"Answer him," Matro whispered, removing his hand from my mouth.

"Yeah, Dad. I'm on the phone," I answered, trying to infuse a good amount of irritation into my voice.

Dad lingered outside for a moment before the sound of his

footsteps faded away. I breathed a sigh of relief.

"I told you to keep your voice down," Matro said.

"Whatever. I still believe Shannon has the right to know what's going on. She's not a child, and I hate to be added to the list of people lying to her."

He started putting on his shoes. "It's not your call, buddy. I'm sorry if you don't agree with how things are going. This is for her protection."

"That doesn't mean I have to go along with it," I answered.

Matro narrowed his eyes at me. "Don't do anything rash, my boy. Once things are done, it is difficult to take them back." He lifted the book and waved at me. "I'm going to borrow this. Until we see each other again."

"Wait!"

"What?" He sounded annoyed.

"How do I get in touch with you if I need to talk?"

"Go get yourself a shrink!"

"Ha ha. You're so funny," I shot back.

"Here's my calling card."

He threw something on my bed and vanished. Just like that, I was all alone in my room. I picked up the flat, dark thing and was surprised it wasn't as light as I'd expected. The surface was coarse. It felt like its weight was similar to that of a little rock. I inspected the swirling inscriptions in yellow ink, but there was no way of knowing what they said. There was no number or other useful information. It was just a rock! I threw it in the wastebasket.

The wastebasket began to glow. Dumbstruck, I stared at it for a moment before realizing I'd better keep the darn thing, just in case it could be a real ticket to salvation. I retrieved the rock and placed it on my desk.

After a quick shower, I was getting comfortable in bed when my phone rang. I picked up after glancing at the caller ID.

"Mark, what's up, bro?"

"Someone nominated you as homecoming king," Mark said on the other line, sounding annoyed.

"Must be a joke," I replied.

"Has to be. Who would do such a thing?" he asked.

It wasn't rocket science. "Kevin Masters."

"That SOB. If he wasn't a teammate, I swear I would've kicked his butt a long time ago." Mark was angry.

If he weren't going for a college football scholarship, I was certain Mark wouldn't hesitate to introduce his fist to Kevin's face. I sighed, feeling like a total loser. Being nominated as a homecoming king was supposed to be an honor, but this was meant to humiliate me, especially if I was going up against Kevin.

"Bro, are you still there?" Mark asked after a minute of silence.

"Yeah. Don't worry about it. I'm sure Kevin did this so he could show everyone how great he is." *And what a big loser I am.*

"One day, you'll get even with that asshole."

"Who knows, I might win," I teased, trying to lighten the mood. *Yeah sure, Morrison. Dream on.*

After we hung up, I lay in bed, staring at the ceiling in the dark until sleep found me. It was past midnight when I woke up from another terrible dream. This time, Shannon was being herded into a corner by the Ergans, but I was nowhere in sight. I could hear her crying out for me. Terribly upset, I sat up in bed and glanced out the window. I couldn't shake the panic the dream had stirred in me, so I got up, put on a shirt, and without making a noise, ventured out of the house.

I just wanted to check on Shannon. To make sure she'd gotten home in one piece. After all, being her Prodian, it was my duty to protect her. With just the porch light to guide me, I made my way across our lawn to theirs. The grass was still wet, so I stopped and folded the hem of my PJ bottoms. When I straightened up, I almost screamed when I found Shannon standing in front of me, grinning.

"What the hell are you doing out here?" I asked, lowering my voice when I realized I'd shouted.

"I should ask you the same thing." She placed her hands on her hips.

"I can't sleep," I muttered.

"I have the same excuse," she said.

Reumdag

We stood there in the darkness, the wet grass soaking our feet, and stared at each other. This was not an ideal place for Shannon to be, so vulnerable to the creatures of the darkness.

"You should go back inside." I held her shoulders and turned her around to face their house.

She resisted and wiggled out of my grasp. "I'm not sleepy. Why can't we just hang out for a bit?"

I considered her proposition, and then asked, "Your house or mine?"

Shannon was thoughtful for a moment. "Yours."

She took my hand and led me to my doorstep, not giving me a chance to voice a protest. I turned the knob ever so gently, praying that the door wouldn't squeak. When I pushed it open a little, there was no sound. I stuck my head in first, making sure it was safe to proceed before I opened the door wider, holding my breath. With a sigh of relief when the door didn't make its usual squeaky noise, I let Shannon in.

Even the hardwood floor gave me a break. Our steps didn't create the creaking noise I expected. We tiptoed into my room, and I locked the door. I went straight to the bathroom and changed into dry shorts, pulling a towel from the rack on my way out.

Back in my room, I turned on my desk lamp and handed the towel to Shannon. "Dry your feet. We don't want you catching cold."

"Thanks," she said and started to dry off.

When her face broke into a smile, I wanted very much to be privy to her private thoughts, but I knew better than to pry. My gaze slid down to the creamy skin peeking out above her pajama bottoms, but then I inhaled deep and turned around. Any more skin showing would wake a sleeping dragon. I busied myself with the remote control, feeling my hand tremble when I pressed the On button.

"What would you like to watch?" I asked, not sparing a glance in her direction.

She didn't answer right away, so I figured she was deliberating. I dared not look at her again to check, so I kept facing the television.

"Do you have *Hangover*?"

When I heard her stand up and realized she was heading to the bathroom, I let out a long sigh of relief. "Who doesn't own *Hangover*?" I asked in mocked horror.

I heard her laugh in response. Hoping Darryl or Mark hadn't borrowed the movie, I rummaged for the DVD on the shelf. I found it and was popping the disc into the player when Shannon emerged, looking too damn cute with her hair tied in a ponytail.

There was that mark again, which I'd forgotten to ask Matro about. My hands shook a little. This was destined to be a night of torture, shut in my room alone with her. Why did she have to be so pretty?

To distract myself and keep her from noticing how nervous I was, I asked, "So, how was the party tonight?"

She sat on the edge of the bed. "It was all right."

"Just *all right*? All the popular kids were there. How could it be just all right?" I pressed further.

"Well, Kevin showed up with his friends. You know, the boys who think they're all that." Shannon rolled her eyes.

My blood boiled upon hearing Kevin's name. The bastard had better have stayed away from her. "Did he give you a hard time?"

She nodded and wrinkled her nose at the memory. "He was drunk. He had that glazed look in his eyes, and his breath smelled like beer."

"What did he do?" I asked, trying not to get all worked up and pressing the play button.

"He was getting all handsy again, so I pushed him, and he fell on his butt." She admitted with a smile.

"You did? Nice job!" I raised my hand for a high-five, and she slapped her palm against mine.

"Yep. Mark and the other guys on the football team held him back. I left early, and Veronica drove me home."

I hated that once again, Shannon had been subjected to Kevin's asshole behavior. Nonetheless, I was relieved that she'd come out unscathed. I rubbed my jaw, feeling frustrated.

"You need a bodyguard," I muttered.

"Are you volunteering?" She laughed and picked up the remote.

That caught me off guard. "I guess I am." No matter what, Shannon going anywhere by herself was going to be dangerous. It was either Kevin hounding her or the Ergans coming for her.

"Then you're going to go to the homecoming dance with me?" Her smile got wider, and I stared at her, dumbfounded.

Homecoming? Was someone playing a cruel joke on me? The dance would be the last place I wanted to be if I were smart.

"You're asking me to the dance?" I asked, feeling dumb. What if she was just joking? The uncertainty was pure agony. I hadn't been to any dance, let alone with the prettiest girl in school.

Shannon smiled. "I guess I am. So . . . are you going to take me?"

The thought of the potential ridicule I'd face made me cringe. But how could I pass up a once in a lifetime chance to go on a date with Shannon? I should be thanking my lucky stars for this opportunity. I nodded my head, still unsure if this might blow up on my face.

Shannon squealed in delight, which confused me. I mean, she was a kind person and all, but was I just a charity case?

"Fantastic!" She clapped her hands. "We'll make plans later, okay?"

Then I remembered Mark's call earlier. "Did you know that someone nominated me for homecoming king?"

Shannon shook her head. "That is even better. We get to wear our crowns together," she giggled.

I had a sinking feeling that she was making fun of me, so I started the movie and focused on it, trying my best not to look worried.

After a few minutes, I decided to enlighten her. "You know, that nomination part is a prank someone's playing. I'm going against Kevin, so don't even hold your breath." I jammed my fingers through my hair, trying to keep my voice even. "It's going to be humiliating, but I'm not going to pass up the chance to take a beautiful girl to a dance."

"Win or lose, we're going to have fun." She tugged at my arm. "Stop pouting."

"I'm not pouting," I countered, and she laughed out loud, making me jump.

"Shh . . . we don't want my parents to wake up and fuss over your being here," I whispered.

"Then let's watch the movie." Shannon scooted to the end of the bed and leaned against the headboard, then patted the space next to her.

I reluctantly followed her but left a wide space between us. For the first half of the movie, we had to try hard to control the volume of our laughter, reminding each other several times to keep our voices down.

Eventually, we both dozed off. The next thing I knew, I was waking up from another vivid nightmare, gasping and disoriented. Then I realized that I wasn't alone. I turned to find Shannon's head resting on my arm. She was sound asleep. Once I'd pulled my arm free, I raised my head to see the time. I jumped when the clock showed it was almost six in the morning.

Shannon stirred and opened her eyes. "What's going on? What's wrong?" she asked sleepily.

"Shannon, you gotta go. My parents will be waking up soon, and we're going to have a lot of explaining to do if they see you."

"What?" She sat up in a panic. Looking at the time, she gasped. "I have to go." Then she jumped off the bed and started looking for her tennis shoes. After she found them, she looked at me. "Brian, what's wrong? You look shaken."

"Nothing, just a bad dream." I dismissed her question with a wave of my hand. "Let's get you out of here." Careful not to make a sound, I opened my door and peeked outside. The house was quiet. My parents hadn't gotten up yet, which was a good thing. "Let's go." I pulled her along behind me.

Once again, we tiptoed along the hallway and down the stairs. The front door creaked when I opened it, but it didn't matter anymore. We skittered across our lawn to hers. When we got to her door, Shannon turned around.

"Thanks for being a good friend," she whispered.

Then she did something I didn't expect. She wrapped her arms around my waist and gave me a hug. A hug that I awkwardly returned.

"I'll see you later," I whispered back.

She turned the knob and waved before closing the door. I stood there, still stunned beyond words, and lifted my hand for a belated wave.

Then I heard a chuckle behind me. I pivoted on my heel in surprise.

"Wow, if I had words to describe that dreamy look on your face, I'd be selling romance books like crazy," Matro said, appearing before me.

"What the hell? Don't you guys ever sleep?" I asked, walking back toward my house.

"Remember, boy, that's my niece in there. One wrong move, and I'm all over you in a heartbeat." Matro followed me.

I turned around and glowered at him. "Hey, I'm not a pig, you know. I'm saving myself for the real deal."

Matro laughed, and I couldn't help but join in. "I think you're doing just fine, baby-boy," he teased.

I reached the front door. "I'm going back to bed. Do you mind not watching me?"

"I'm going to be as invisible as I can be." He laughed again and turned to leave.

"Hey, what's with the rock you left me?" I asked, remembering his 'calling card'.

"Rub it, and I'll come running." He disappeared before I had the chance to respond.

Like a stinking genie in a bottle?

Back in the comfort of my room, I began to wrack my brain for details of the dream I'd had earlier. This time, the victim was someone I knew. This was somewhat disturbing. It was Mr. Peters, my photography teacher. He was in a store, a smaller one. It didn't look like a big grocery store like Ralph's or Vons. From what I could remember, it was more of a convenience store, or maybe even one of those little liquor stores in a strip mall.

While he was paying for his purchase, two armed men came into sight. They were holding up the store. Mr. Peters cowered to the floor, afraid for his life, and moved away from the line of fire.

I saw the shaking cashier empty the cash register and hand the loot to one of the masked robbers. Then they laughed at something, but I couldn't make out what was being said. Before the two men left, they shot the cashier and pointed the gun at Mr. Peters.

That was all I could remember. Then I'd woken up, drenched in sweat.

I glanced at the clock. It was close to seven in the morning. As much as I hated to wake up Mark, I needed to unload to someone who might be able to help. I scooted over the bed and reached for my cell phone on top of the nightstand. I pressed his speed dial.

It took four rings before he answered.

"This better be good," he mumbled.

"I had another bad dream," I said and launched into my story. After I'd recounted every single detail I could remember, I was met with a whole lot of silence.

"You're freaking me out, Brian." Mark's tone was serious.

"Why do you think I'm calling you? I'm scared! I want to tell Mr. Peters, but I don't know where he lives. And even if I did, would he believe me?"

"Let me see what I can do. I'll call you right back." Mark hung up.

Staring at the ceiling, I tried to make sense of my vision. If something happened to Mr. P, I wouldn't be able to forgive myself. But if I jumped the gun and nothing happened, then I'd be a laughing stock. *What else is new?* I'd gotten used to having a freak status anyway. It wouldn't bother me one bit. All I wanted was to be certain that Mr. P would be all right. I happen to like the man, even if he was a bit odd. I laughed. It'd take one weirdo to recognize another.

I powered up my laptop and waited. Although it felt like Mark was taking too damn long, I knew only ten minutes had elapsed. In an attempt to distract myself, I logged on to Facebook. It was a rare occasion that I went there to post anything. My friends had forced me to create an account, saying that social media was a great tool to make friends. So far, I had very few. Most were students from the yearbook committee and some cousins from Minnesota.

So I'd become a lurker, content to browse through the newsfeed and leave an occasional 'like' on friends' posts. I preferred to be invisible, but it was a pleasant surprise to find that the rarely used friend request icon was active today. It was a friend request from Shannon. Eager and happy, I accepted and went on to check out her profile. Then my phone rang.

"Bro, I got his address." Mark sounded quite pleased with himself. "Want me to come with you?"

"I think that's a good idea."

"I'll be over in half an hour."

Forty-five minutes later, Mr. P was looking at us as if we had lost our minds. He shook his head. "Are you kids playing a prank on me?"

"No, Mr. Peters. This is real. I've been having these dreams, and they've come true. I'm here to warn you," I said.

He narrowed his eyes at me. "I'm on my way to purchase a lotto ticket, and you think that something unpleasant will happen to me?"

I nodded. That was all I could offer. The vision had cut off, so there was no way of knowing what happened to him.

"I'm going to pretend that you kids did not show up on my doorstep today trying to fool me. I'll see you both in school tomorrow." He waved his hand to dismiss us.

"Please, Mr. P. You have to listen to me," I pleaded.

"Enjoy the rest of your weekend," he said and closed the door.

I fought the urge to pound on his door and beg him to listen. Then I looked at Mark, and he shook his head.

"We tried."

I sighed. "We did."

It had to be the Ergans' doing. I was certain they had somehow messed with my vision. After all, Matro had warned me.

Mark and I drove home in silence. There was nothing we

could do but wait.

For the rest of the day, I was tethered between restlessness and dread. I tried to push my vision to the back of my mind, immersing myself in my homework. Although it kept my mind occupied, the panic came back after I finished the last of my weekend assignments.

I left the house in search of something to do. Without a destination in mind, I backed my car out of the driveway and cruised around the neighborhood without purpose, until I ended up on the street that led to the Observatory. After parking my car by the sidewalk, I sat and stared at the city lights. It was getting dark, and the multicolored lights that defined LA twinkled before me.

How in the hell had I gotten myself into this situation? Was it my destiny to be Shannon's Prodian? If Matro had been telling the truth, did I have what it would take to protect her?

A wisp of air swirled around me, alerting me that I had company, then Matro appeared, holding several weapons. "I think someone needs a friend."

Eyeing the gadgets in his hand, I reached for one. Surprisingly, he let me take it. "Are we having lessons today?"

"It's as good a time as any." He took a step back. "First lesson, hold it with the sharp tip pointing down."

"What is it, anyway?" I closed my fingers around the middle of the weapon.

"It's called the Reumdag."

"Wicked." I inspected the unique weapon.

The Reumdag, as Matro called it, was about three feet long and an inch wide, tapering in the middle. The glass-like blades were filled with crimson liquid. One tip was sharper than the other and had the appearance of metal. I tightened my hand on the narrow handle and was surprised at how it molded to my grip right away.

When I looked up, Matro was smiling. "You like it?"

"What can it do?" I asked.

Matro lowered the rest of his stash onto the grass except one weapon similar to mine. He swung it with one hand, his wrist flicking in a circular motion, until all I could see were twirling flashes of the liquid inside. "This is the primary weapon of Tranak. It was developed after we realized that we could never go back to our peaceful past. Unlike the Mertest, which incapacitates our enemies first before disintegrating, Reumdag's sharp tip will melt them on contact."

I looked down at the lethal weapon in my hand and swallowed hard. "Can it kill humans?"

"Nah. It would be nothing but a splash of colored liquid to you guys. The appearance is meant to confuse humans so carriers can walk around with them." Matro laid down his Reumdag and walked behind me. "Ready for your first lesson?"

"As ready as I'll ever be."

Matro placed his hand on top of mine and closed his grip, then he began to move the weapon, twirling it like a baton. He repeated the step until I could perform it on my own, moving aside to give me room.

"Remember, sharp tip down until you have to strike. If you intend to stun your opponent, use the blunt tip."

It took hours until I built up enough confidence when handling the weapon, and then Matro went on to show me the footwork. "There is a little recoil whenever you strike with the sharp end, so spread your legs apart. They must be shoulder-wide." He did a short demo, which I watched with admiration. His movements were fluid as he twisted, spun, and rotated. Then he thrust forward as if going for the kill. "You got it?"

"I think so."

"Now you do it."

Remembering everything I saw, I started moving sideways while twisting the weapon. It was clumsy at first because my coordination sucked, but Matro was a patient man, repeating the steps and having me practice until I was moving with more ease and grace.

The next lesson was the defensive stance, to show me how to use the weapon to deflect any blows or weapons coming my way. This process was more tedious since Matro had to use himself as a target.

With utmost concentration, my movements were slow, mindful of which tip was pointed at him and bracing myself for his blows. The sound the weapons produced was like the clinking of two glasses. It created a melody while the lights danced before our eyes.

Matro didn't announce that our training session was over until close to midnight. With reluctance, I got into my car, feeling exhilarated.

He stuck his head in the driver's side window. "You did a great job," he said with a smile.

I pushed the ignition button. "Will I be able to keep one for myself?"

"In time."

He bowed and was gone in a blink of an eye.

Fighting Back

It wasn't a surprise that I woke up with a pounding headache. After coming home around midnight being unable to sleep, it was difficult to get an early start. Mr. Peters' refusal to listen lay heavy on my mind, despite the excitement of my first lesson in fighting. When I reached the school, I continued to struggle with the remnants of my headache but still noticed the somber atmosphere on campus. There was no doubt something was wrong.

By the time I got to the classroom, Shannon was already sitting in her usual spot with her head bent low.

"What's going on? What's with the long face?" I whispered, dropping my backpack on the floor.

When she looked up, I recognized that she'd been crying.

"Haven't you heard?" she asked.

"Heard what?"

Most of the girls in class were crying, and even the guys appeared grief-stricken.

"Mr. P was shot last night at a gas station." Shannon's voice quivered.

"Where is he?" Maybe I could pay him a visit at the hospital or his home and give him lecture for not listening to my warning.

"Brian, he's dead."

My whole body went cold. *No! No! This isn't happening.*

Guilt wracked me, and I buried my face in my trembling hands. I should've forced him to listen to me. He shouldn't be dead.

"Are you okay?" Shannon touched my arm.

I shook my head. How could I tell her that I'd seen this and failed to stop it from happening?

Shannon scooted closer. "What is it?" she whispered. "You're scaring me, Brian."

Before I had the chance to respond, heavy footsteps stopped in front of us.

"Isn't this a lovely picture? My ex-girlfriend is getting all cozy with the weirdo," Kevin said in his usual mocking voice.

Despite my grief, anger coursed through my veins when I felt Shannon stiffen. I looked up to find Kevin scowling at her.

"Will you shut up? You just said the magic word, Kevin. *Ex-*girlfriend! In case you forgot what it means, it's over. O-V-E-R!" Shannon yelled.

Kevin's expression darkened while he glared at her. In one stride, he seized Shannon's arm, yanking her to him. "You used to be all over me, but now that you're hanging out with this loser, you have the nerve to talk shit?" He skimmed his mouth along her cheek.

Shannon recoiled. "Stop it." She tried to push him away.

At this particular moment, with guilt and grief short-circuiting my better judgment, I jumped from my seat and gripped Kevin's shoulder, snatching him away from her.

"You heard what she said. Get your hands off her," I said, pushing him back.

He dragged Shannon back with him, but I caught her waist. Although I'd expected a tug-of-war, he released her arm at once to focus his wrath on me.

"You think you can tell me what to do, freak boy?" Kevin threw his fist at me.

Reacting fast, I sidestepped to avoid the hit and then punched him in the stomach. He staggered backward and the room erupted in applause.

Then out of nowhere, Kevin barreled into me like a battering ram, his head hitting my ribs. The sound of a crack came just before we hit the floor, and pain radiated across my body. My anger kept me going, fighting him with every ounce of energy I had. We struggled with each other until we heard the principal's voice above the clamor around us.

"Stop it, right this minute!" Mr. Delson ordered.

Several kids separated us, dodging Kevin's attempt to get in another kick.

My eyes burned with unshed tears of rage. The sharp ache in my chest made breathing hard, so I tried to keep my breaths shallow.

"Both of you in my office! Now!" Mr. Delson shouted and turned around, leading the way.

Despite the excruciating pain, I was able to follow, my head held high and my hand clutching my side. I'd broken something for sure. When I glanced back to check on Shannon, I found Kevin right behind me, literally breathing down my neck.

I wasn't scared at all.

While we waited outside the principal's office, I fought

against the unbearable pain, refusing to give any sign of discomfort. My pride wouldn't allow me to wimp out, and nothing was allowed take away from the thrill of standing up to Kevin.

After half an hour, my mother came running down the hallway.

"Brian, what's going on?" She rushed to my side.

"Nothing," I straightened my body and tried to mask my discomfort, but the stress was bringing on my tics again. My shoulder tightened while I fought the pressure to shake.

"Fuck!" I blurted out before I could clamp my mouth shut. I leaned against my seat, unable to suppress the violent movements I knew were coming.

Kevin snickered, and my mother swung her head in his direction to glare at him. Her comforting hand rubbed my back while I struggled with the barrage of jerks and shudders.

Soon after, a man with graying hair and beard entered the office. With his swagger and the striking resemblance to Kevin, there was no doubt that he was Kevin's father.

"Kevin, what have you done now?" he shouted.

The door to the Mr. Delson's office opened. It struck me as funny how I had avoided trips like this to his office over the past. Since meeting Shannon a few weeks ago, I had been racking up the points as if I were making up for lost time.

"Mr. Delson's waiting for you," the secretary informed us.

I dragged myself up and tried to ignore the stinging burn, piling into the principal's office with the others.

Mom looked at me with concern. "Where does it hurt?" she whispered.

Not wanting to call unnecessary attention to myself, I tried to walk straighter. "I'm fine," I said, although I was unable to hide my grimace.

166

We sat on chairs lined up in front of the desk. Mom sat on my right, while Kevin took the one next to me. I looked straight ahead, avoiding the principal's condemning eyes.

Mr. Delson cleared his throat. "As you already know, your children got into another fight. We have zero tolerance for violence in this school. I've spoken with a few eyewitnesses, and I believe I have my facts straight. This is the second time this has happened, so I'm not going to be lenient." He stood up, moved around the desk, and stopped between Kevin and me.

"I will suspend you both for a week. After that, you'll be on probation. If something like this happens again, expulsion will be next." Mr. Delson's head swung from Kevin to me, as though expecting a response.

My mother gasped in obvious disbelief, but I had been expecting this.

"Is there anything else?" Mom asked. At Mr. Delson's shake of the head, she got up, tugging at my hand. I tried to stand, but the pain blazed across my chest. I slumped back in the chair, and another round of freaking tics hit me. It was impossible not to cry out.

Mr. Delson rushed over and knelt on the floor. "What's wrong, Brian?" he asked.

Through gritted teeth, I tried to answer. "I think . . . I broke . . . my rib."

Mr. Delson called his secretary. "Call the nurse," he ordered.

The pain continued to radiate, and I closed my eyes, overcome.

When I opened my eyes again, unfamiliar white walls and the sterile scent I associated with hospitals surrounded me.

"He's awake," I heard Shannon say.

I turned toward her voice, but the slight movement brought back the pain. When I made a noise of protest, she took my hand

and squeezed it. The warmth of her hand was reassuring.

"Oh, thank God." Mom rushed over to my side.

"Where am I?" I asked, feeling weird.

"The emergency room. We rushed you here when you passed out," Mom answered, smoothing my hair.

I moved my head to avoid being petted in front of Shannon. Passing out was embarrassing enough, but having my mother treat me like a two-year-old was downright mortifying.

"What are you doing here? Shouldn't you be in class?" I asked Shannon, making the effort to turn my head in her direction.

"I asked permission to come with you," she said.

"Now that I'm awake, we can go." I moved to sit up, but the next thing I knew, I was flat on my back again.

"Mr. Morrison, you'll have to take it easy for the next few weeks. You've broken a rib. I suggest you stay in bed and let your body heal," a man wearing green scrubs said.

The doctor scribbled something on a piece of paper and handed it to my mother, while Shannon stayed next to me, still holding my hand.

"Take one pill three times a day for pain and then another to help you to sleep. You're going to be sore for the next few days."

I nodded, feeling like a complete idiot. How was I going to protect Shannon if I couldn't even get out of bed?

On our drive home, I watched my mother and Shannon from the back seat, but no one spoke. When we stopped in front of my house, Shannon turned back to me and smiled, although it looked strained. "I'll call you later," she said.

Dad took it easy on me that night. He asked almost nothing about the incident from school, and his reprimand was mild.

After dinner, I walked ever so slowly back to my room. Every movement made me groan. Without trying to get out of my school clothes, I lowered myself back into bed.

The sleeping pill took effect, and I conked out for another five hours until a noise at my window woke me. I gingerly turned my body toward the window, and to my surprise, it slid open and Shannon let herself in.

"What are you doing?" I asked.

"What does it look like? I'm visiting you." She cleared the windowsill.

Whatever possessed her to climb up to my room? I coughed, and a round of tics overcame me. Once the worst was over, I glared at her. "Damn it, Shannon! We have a door. Use it."

"Will you just shut up and sleep?" she retorted, making herself comfortable next to me. "Besides, I can't have your parents know I'm here." She wrapped an arm around my shoulder.

"You're silly," I heard myself say before I succumbed to the warmth of her presence and fell right back to sleep.

Cannus Ride

It had to be a dream. I was one hundred percent sure. Shannon and I wouldn't be spooning in my bed if it were real life. I couldn't kiss Shannon as if she were mine in real life. My real life couldn't hope to compete with this dream.

I snuggled closer, running my nose through her hair and inhaling her scent. My arms tightened around her waist, staking a claim. It felt good, even if it was just make believe. No chance I was letting her go anytime soon.

A strange yet familiar voice pulled me out of my reverie. "Dream on, lover boy."

I opened my eyes. Sunlight poured in from the window, stinging my eyes. Matro was looking down at me, his eyes filled with contempt and his mouth turned up into the annoying smile I'd grown accustomed to. My body still ached like a mother. I sank into the mattress.

"What the hell are you doing here?"

Matro walked to my desk and sat down. "I'm watching Shannon, of course."

He must have been making sure I wasn't going to make a move on Shannon.

Matro smirked and shook his head. "Um . . . no. I wouldn't go there. Someone had to keep an eye on our princess while you were snoring away. She left an hour ago to get ready for school."

I took a deep breath. Although the pain had incapacitated me, I had to find a way to be with Shannon and take care of her.

I rose, favoring my injured chest. "I'll just shower and head to school," I muttered to myself.

"Sit back down," Matro ordered. "You may be her Prodian, but you're still human. You're not going to do her any good right now."

I shook my head. My responsibility was to watch her, to protect her.

"I can't leave her on her own," I protested, even though the pain in my chest intensified with every movement.

"From what Car told me, you got hit hard, but you fought back. That is impressive. Besides, you're suspended, boy. I don't think your principal would appreciate seeing you in school right now."

Matro rose to his feet and walked over to my bookshelf. He checked the titles before pulling out a book.

"But she can't be alone," I said, moving in the direction of my bathroom.

"Don't worry. Car is there and he's got Mark and Darryl watching her."

Somehow, the idea should've comforted me, but instead I felt sick to my stomach.

"Jealousy is not healthy, my boy." Matro glanced my way. "Go shower if it'll make you feel better. I'm going to wait here. There's something I want to show you afterward."

I took my time in the shower. I ached all over, and the warm water helped. Afterwards, I felt a bit better. Being suspended may not have been an ideal way to close out my high school record, but finally having the balls to stand up to Kevin made it worth the trouble. If it had happened pre-Shannon, I'd have had many things to occupy my time, like reading, taking pictures, or playing video games all day. Now, I couldn't think of anything better to do but ogle Shannon.

Once I'd toweled dry and changed into shorts and a cotton T-shirt, I combed my hair with my fingers and hurried out. Matro was sitting on my bed, looking all comfortable and holding another one of my favorite books.

"This looks interesting."

"It has its moments." I'd read the book so many times. The spine was showing wear.

Matro got up and slipped the book in the waistband of his pants.

"Where are we going?" I asked, taking the pill bottle from my nightstand.

"I'm going to show you what happened while you were sleeping."

"Hold up. Let me pop a pain pill, and I'll meet you outside." I turned to the door.

"Your parents left, so there's no need for me to hide."

Matro followed me down the stairs to the kitchen. The house was quiet except for the humming of the refrigerator. The coffee maker buzzed and shut off.

172

"Coffee?" I asked.

Matro shook his head. "Thanks anyway," he said, walking to the back door. He ran his fingers along the vertical blinds, making them sway like tree branches on a windy day. I opened the fridge and grabbed the orange juice, popped the pill in my mouth, and drank straight from the carton.

"Your mother wouldn't like that," he commented.

"Yeah, and you're not my mother." I recapped the lid and shoved the carton back inside the fridge.

Matro chuckled. "Fair enough. No breakfast for the champion?" he asked.

"I'm ready." I started for the front door. When I didn't hear Matro's footsteps behind me, I looked over my shoulder and found him still standing in the middle of the kitchen with his eyes closed.

I walked back, feeling like I was interrupting something important. Then I noticed the swirling air at his feet, like a mini-tornado. His eyes opened then, and they were glazed over. The color was like a kaleidoscope, dark but mesmerizing.

"What the hell?" I stumbled backward.

"Hop in. I can take you with me." Even Matro's voice had changed from its normal booming bass to something more like a wisp of air.

Reluctantly, I stepped forward, feeling the cool air brush my legs. He held onto my shoulders and pulled me closer, and the column of air rose, faster, swirling until I could no longer see anything beyond it. We were surrounded by walls of twisting air, fierce and deafening.

My heart pounded against my chest, but surprisingly, my ribs didn't hurt. In the darkness, I felt us lifting, like we were taking off. As unmanly as it seemed, I grabbed Matro's waist and held on to him like a pansy. This was freaking me out.

After a long minute of nothing but shades of black, white, and gray flashing around us, the dizzy swirling stopped and the sounds faded away. Then I was struck by the feeling of flying and tightened my grip around Matro's waist even more.

He laughed, a pure and gleeful sound that made me realize how stupid I must look to him. Still, I couldn't let go for fear of falling. He tried to pry my fingers away, but I gripped tighter.

"Boy, it's okay. You can let go now. I promise you won't fall."

I shook my head. "What the hell are you doing? Are you planning on killing me?"

"Tempting, but no." Matro gave me a brief smile and pried me off him.

I wanted to scream, but a little yelp was all that came out.

"Stop resisting," he said.

"I'm going to fall." I started pumping my legs to try to keep aloft.

"Stop and stay still. Trust me." Matro shook me by the shoulders, urging me to listen.

Despite his assurances, I kept trying to push myself up, but after several minutes, my legs began to tire. That was when I noticed that Matro wasn't moving at all, just watching me and grinning. Filled with trepidation, I stopped flailing my legs. Nothing happened. I didn't drop. I was just there, suspended in space.

"How is this possible?" I asked, still feeling anxious.

"You're inside a Cannus."

"A what?"

"It's a vacuum we use for transport. In here, humans can see what we see, but no one else can see us while we're inside."

It felt like we were traveling at high speed, but looking out, everything seemed to be moving at a normal pace. We covered a good distance before he pointed at something. A figure was moving underneath a dark cloak, running. It had a ferocious expression and a face that was closer to animal than human.

"That's an Ergan. That's what they look like to us." Matro pointed to another one. It was galloping like a horse.

"You said they can't see us?" I asked again, concerned.

"No, but they can track our scent. They know we're in the vicinity."

"Scent? What are we supposed to smell like?"

"I have no idea, but they seem to know when we're around."

"They're the ones who stink," I said, recalling my last encounter with them. The sound of their gnashing teeth made me want to cover my ears. How could Matro stand it?

He answered my unspoken question. "It's not easy, but years of practice tuning them out helps."

We were approaching my school, I realized. "What are we doing here?"

"You see that mark on the wall by the front door?" He pointed to a symbol painted on the edifice, but I couldn't quite make out what it was. It looked like three circles linked together, with a three-pronged spear running through them. Despite the graffiti's large size, nobody seemed to notice it.

"That's the symbol of the Pratrim, our oldest adversary. No one but Aarmarks can see it." Matro's face darkened.

"Then how come I can?"

"Because you're in the Cannus with me. Like I told you. In here, you will see what I see."

I nodded. "I thought they'd been here all along, watching Shannon."

"The Ergans are the soldiers. They're just smalltime combatants, the front-liners employed to do reconnaissance. It's typical for the symbol to appear only when one of the Pratrim leaders is present. This could mean that they're coming together and gathering strength." Matro glanced around, his brows furrowed.

"What does that mean?" I felt an unfamiliar dread spreading through me.

"Can you sense any danger right now?" Matro asked instead of answering my question.

"What do you mean?"

"Close your eyes and feel. Do you sense anything around you? Don't pay attention to the Ergans. They're always around, so you're most likely immune to their presence by now."

I did what I was told, closing my eyes and allowing my hearing to capture the slightest sound.

"I hear faint murmuring in another language, and someone's laughing. That's all." I opened my eyes and glanced around.

Matro nodded. "We'll head back to your place now." Just as he spoke, the school bell rang.

"What were those voices? Do they mean anything?" I asked, watching through our invisible vacuum while students burst out the front door like liberated soldiers returning from a war.

"Nothing yet," he said and motioned with his hand.

"What do you mean, 'nothing yet'?" I insisted. All this gibberish was beginning to irritate me.

"That's need-to-know. I can't tell you any more right now."

I was too busy pondering his cryptic explanation to notice that we had landed back in my kitchen.

"Has Shannon asked you about anything lately?" he asked, the funnel of air slowly dissipating around us.

"Aside from the Ergans, no. Can't we tell her anything?"

"She's a precious child, and if we can preserve her that way, the better for all of us."

"I want to remind you that hiding things will blow up in your face someday."

The funnel disappeared at that moment, and my pain came rushing back.

Matro pointed at the door. "She's here," he said and disappeared.

I walked to the door in slow, easy steps, giving myself time to compose myself. The short ride with Matro had freaked me out, but the knowledge that a greater threat was in our midst was more disconcerting.

When I opened the door, there was Shannon, all smiles.

"Hey, how are you feeling today?" she asked, stepping inside.

Before I closed the door, I took a quick glance outside, and Mark and Darryl waved from the car before speeding away. There was nothing else but the same faint voices I'd heard earlier. A whole lot of goose bumps hit me, and I slammed the door, which made Shannon jump.

"I'm sorry. I'm a little edgy today."

"You don't look too well. Do you want me to go?"

"No, I want you to stay here." I took her hand, and we climbed the stairs together in slow, grandpa steps.

"Okay." She laughed and squeezed my hand. "I have your homework with me. We can do it together."

"Sure."

I led her to the desk before I sat down on the edge of the bed, as close to her as possible. She emptied her backpack of its contents and spread them across my messy desktop. Her hair was pulled back in braids, and I had this damn urge to undo them.

She looked up and caught me staring at her. Her blue eyes sparkled when she smiled. "Are you okay? You looked dazed."

"Yeah." I looked away, feeling foolish for being caught staring at her.

"Do you want to work on Sweeney's first?" She handed me a piece of paper with some scribbled notes on it.

"Might as well." I tried to retrieve my backpack from the floor, but Shannon beat me to it. She handed the bag to me and I took out the book and sat down on the floor.

For the next two hours, we discussed the next scene of *The Glass Menagerie*. As we'd agreed before, it was Shannon's turn to write the analysis. I watched her while she got busy writing our combined work.

She often smiled as she wrote, her hand moving in beautiful arching motions. A few times, her mouth turned into a pout while she thought. She was fascinating. I could watch her all day long.

"Are you just going to keep staring at me?" Shannon asked, a hint of a smile twitching at the corner of her lips.

"I-err, yeah . . . I-I can't um . . . take my eyes off you," I stammered.

"You're such a funny guy, Curly." She slid off her chair and sat next to me on the floor.

I made a sweeping gesture with my hand. "Always at your service, ma'am. My one and only goal is to put a smile on your face." *Jesus! What did I just say?* She must think I was the lamest guy ever to walk the earth.

"You're sweet, too." She took my hand. "Curly, don't you ever wonder why we got thrown together this way?"

Tough question. What should I tell her? "All I know is we have to stick together because of Elizabeth's prediction."

Shannon didn't answer right away. "Are you okay having me around all the time? I mean, your friends must hate having me around, too."

"Hell, no. We like to hang out with pretty girls, and you, my dear Shannon, are the fairest of them all." *Geek alert. Geek alert.*

From Shannon's smile, she didn't seem to think it was geeky at all.

Once again, we fell into silence. Shannon finished her homework, but mine took longer. It was difficult to concentrate when all I wanted to do was stare at her. After several attempts to focus, I managed to wrap it up. While I walked Shannon home, I had to lie several times when she asked if I was in pain.

Mom insisted that I at least have some soup. After I ate, I felt a bit better. I'd made up my mind that I wouldn't jeopardize Shannon's safety by taking the pain pill. It would dull my senses and make me sleep longer.

Dad came by my room just before bedtime. "Son, how're you feeling?"

"I'm okay."

My dad didn't do a lot of talking. He was a quiet man. His visit must be about something important.

"What's going on?"

"I have another job offer in New York City, and I'm considering it. How do you feel about moving there?" He sat on the edge of my bed.

I shot up and instant pain radiated from my chest, but I didn't let it distract me. This was more important. "No way. I'm happy here."

"You're happy?" Dad asked, narrowing his eyes. "That Masters kid is bullying you. You're getting into fights—"

"I'm fine. It's all growing pains. Besides, I'm graduating. It's better if we stay here until then. C'mon, Dad, please."

He closed his eyes, his expression pained, as if he were blocking out an unpleasant thought. "I just want what's best for you. I'm scared of what might happen."

I inched closer, more careful of my injury. "What are you talking about?"

Dad's eyes snapped open. "Nothing. I'm going to bed. We'll talk about this another time." He hurried out of my room, leaving me confused and worried.

The Battle

My throbbing ribs woke me up before my alarm clock went off. It had been a rough night without the pain medication. There had been moments throughout the night when I thought I was going to lose it. Even the simple act of breathing was difficult.

I lay in bed and stared at the ceiling. It was too early to call Shannon or even to send her a text message. I wondered why she hadn't shown up like she had the other night, though it wouldn't have surprised me if she'd been grounded for sneaking out. The mental picture of her climbing the trellis made me smile.

I turned toward the window with great difficulty. Not taking the pain pill had been a dumb idea, but I couldn't take any chances.

Dad's comment the night before still bothered me. What had he meant about bad things happening?

Another hour passed before I decided it would be okay to

text Shannon. When I picked up my cell phone, I noticed I had several missed calls. None of the numbers were familiar, but one. I ignored the unknown callers and dialed Jude, our yearbook editor.

As it turned out, the homecoming game was coming up, and he needed two people to cover the pictures. Shannon had signed up for one spot, so I agreed to take the other. It would be nice to work with her. After Jude and I hung up, I sent her a text.

I'll drive you to school. I'll honk at 7:30.

Her response came back real fast. **You rest. Mark and Darryl will pick me up. I'll be okay. Don't worry.**

The hell I wasn't going to worry. Finding out that the Ergans were loitering like dirt on the road was enough reason to get me all fired up. As much as I trusted my buddies, my chest constricted at the idea that they were with Shannon instead of me.

I'll take you. I'm feeling better.

Yeah, right. Lying didn't feel so bad when it was supported by good intentions.

I walked into the shower with difficulty.

Soaping my body was an excruciating task. It felt like I was being skewered. I might have been acting like a baby, but it really hurt.

I bit my lip while I finished dressing. Moving with care, I retrieved my keys and the bottle of Mertest from my desk. Combing my hair would cause unnecessary discomfort so I pulled on a baseball cap, slung on my backpack, and headed downstairs.

"Baby-boy, I made your favorite Mickey waffles," Mom hollered from the kitchen.

Mickey-shaped waffles. I'd gotten sick of them like ten years ago, but Mom always made sure that I had them whenever I came down with the flu or something.

"Coming!" I answered and tried my best to hide my discomfort when I walked in the kitchen.

My father looked up from his usual spot at the table, setting aside the newspaper. "How are you feeling?" he asked, forking a piece of waffle.

I took my seat and held my breath, bracing for the pain that followed each movement. Dad watched me, his eyes narrowing.

"I'm good," I said, hoping he'd buy it.

He looked doubtful. "Are you taking your medication?"

"Yeah, but I'm going to switch to the over-the-counter ones. I don't like feeling nauseous." Good thing I'd read the side effects on the label.

"Breaking a bone is no picnic." He gave me another long once-over before picking up the newspaper.

"Here's your Mickey waffle, baby-boy." Mom handed me a plate with three large waffles on it and hovered over me.

I wasn't too hungry, but she'd be disappointed if I didn't gobble it up, so I picked up the maple syrup.

"Thanks, Mom," I said after the first bite.

She smiled, satisfied.

I swallowed down one waffle, and then I was ready to bail. "Sorry, I can't finish it. I'll save it for later." I carried my plate to the microwave and put it inside. As a child, it had been something I'd always done, just to keep my mother from forcing me to finish.

"What are you up to today?" Mom asked before I could make it out of the kitchen.

My injured rib protested when I spun around a little too quickly. "I-I'm going to the library. I'll see you guys later."

183

I braced my hand on the wall the moment I stepped out of the front door and let out a groan, taking shallow breaths until the pain subsided. Then I walked slowly to my car and managed to back it out of the driveway without screaming. I honked once, and Shannon appeared at her front door in less than a minute.

She bounded down the walkway. This time, her hair was free from braid or ponytail, and I watched in awe while it flapped behind her. Her skinny jeans hugged her body like a second skin, and her loose-fitting USC sweatshirt did nothing to hide her blossoming figure.

Shannon smacked my arm once she got in the car.

"Aww! What was that for?" I rubbed my arm and glared at her.

"For staring at me like I'm a piece of meat." She fastened her seatbelt and turned to face me. "Have anything planned for the rest of the day?"

I shook my head and maneuvered the car out onto our street. As I waited to make a left turn on the main road, I felt her eyes on me.

"Did you sleep well last night?"

"Yeah, good enough, although, there was someone missing." I grinned at her.

Shannon blushed. "Well, I wanted you to have a good night's sleep, so I stayed away. Besides, you're already cramped in that bed to begin with. I was trying to be nice." She laughed a little, but I noticed the nervousness in her voice.

With a surge of confidence, I took her hand and kissed it. "Well, I slept well," I lied, "but I've gotten used to your snoring. I missed it last night."

She yanked her hand back, but I didn't let go. Instead, I rested our twined hands on my lap while I drove with one hand on the steering wheel.

The moment we turned onto the school's street, a remarkable screeching noise began buzzing in my ears. I looked left to right, trying to see if I could track down the Ergans. There were two loping by, and more about five hundred feet down the street.

"Hey, what's wrong? Why are you so quiet?" Shannon asked, looking in the same direction I was.

"Nothing. I thought I heard something." I parked the car in front of the school entrance where Mark and Darryl stood, waiting for her. Their faces lit up when they saw me, and they jogged over. I turned to Shannon, still holding her hand. "I'll be waiting out here by the time school's out. Make sure either Mark, Darryl, or my cousin walks you out."

"You're such a worry-wart. Kevin won't be around. I'll be fine." She smiled and gathered up her backpack. Then she looked at our hands pointedly. "I'm going to be late."

"Oh, yeah!" I laughed and let go of her hand.

I watched her climb the steps, Darryl walking alongside her. Mark stayed behind, and after the two made it in, he leaned into the passenger side window. When I glanced in the rearview mirror again, another Ergan streaked by.

"Bro, you look like shit," Mark commented.

"Thanks. I feel like it, too." I let my body relax a little and slumped against my seat.

"We got it covered, man. I'll text or call if anything's up. Car is like a dog. He follows her everywhere she goes."

My chest hurt, and I knew why. This was a different type of distress. I nodded and looked away. It wasn't the time to be jealous, but I couldn't help it. I wanted so much to be with Shannon myself.

"I'm going to pick her up after the last period. Please make sure you're with her."

"No worries, man. See you in six hours?" Mark reached in and held his palm to me.

I slapped mine with his. "Cool," I said and added, "Thanks, bro."

Mark snorted. "Anything for you, buddy."

After the first bell rang, I sat inside my car, deliberating what to do next. I glanced at my rearview mirror and noticed Kevin walking toward the front entrance. What was he doing here? I ducked my head, pretending like I was pulling something out of the glove compartment. I watched him after he passed by, and I noticed that he was mumbling something to himself.

I continued to observe him while he stopped by the front entrance, looking intent on something. When the last bell rang, he turned around and bowed his head. For some bizarre reason, I felt the hair on my arms rise. Sensing an unseen threat, I fished for the bottle of Mertest in my pocket and waited. Matro appeared next to my car, as well as Carionis, looking ready to rumble.

Although the movements were blurry, I could see what was happening. Kevin was talking to a hooded figure, and the Ergans were bounding toward us. I opened the glove compartment and took out two more bottles of Mertest before I got out of the car. Pain lanced across my chest when I tried to stand, making me slump to the ground.

Matro touched my arm, and an electric current coursed through me, erasing the throb of my broken rib.

"Car, go for it," Matro said and pulled me to my feet. "Here." He handed me a Reumdag.

One Ergan swept by, and Matro struck it with his weapon. The sucker melted on contact, fizzling into thin air. I braced myself to face the incoming herd while Carionis ran across the street, using throwing stars of some sort and striking anything that crossed his path.

I looked at Kevin, who was already slumped to the ground, moaning. The hooded figure looked up and met my gaze before disappearing.

"Behind you!" Matro yelled while he assaulted another Ergan.

I spun around, and the thing let out an ear-piercing screech. It got up on its hind legs, its front claws almost grazing my face. I jumped back, and it moved forward. Remembering what Matro had said, I braced my legs, rotated my weapon, and stunned it with the blunt tip. The Ergan stumbled backward, so I ran toward it and thrust the sharp point of my Reumdag as hard as I could into its chest.

It shrieked before melting right before my eyes. Panting, I looked around to see that we had cleaned house. However, several shocked bystanders were beginning to run away.

Eyewitnesses. Me in the middle of a weird battle in front of school. No doubt this would make the news, and not in a good way.

"What do we do with them?" I turned to Matro.

"I'm on it. All they need is a little spell to block out this particular information from their memories," he said before he disappeared.

Carionis returned just as I was about to collapse inside my car. "Dude, the stress too much for you?"

Leaning my head against the steering wheel, I tried to catch my breath when the pain came back tenfold. "Shut . . . up . . . "

He reached for the weapon on the passenger seat, and the moment he touched it, the thing vanished into thin air. "Just making sure you don't hurt yourself."

If I hadn't been in agony, he would have been my next target. Then my tics decided to take over. A massive spasm vibrated from my shoulder, radiating down to my chest, my vision blurred, and then there was nothing.

When I opened my eyes again, I was still slumped against the steering wheel, and Matro was sitting next to me.

"What happened?"

"You took a nap." He chuckled.

I glanced at the dashboard clock and was surprised to see that an hour had passed.

"Tell me I just dreamed we had a battle in front of my school," I groaned.

Matro shook his head. "Bystander memories are all handled. Nothing to worry about. Now that you're awake, I'm going to go take care of some business."

Before I could respond, he was gone. I was baffled by the turn of events, but I realized I shouldn't be seen in the vicinity of the school while I was under suspension. With a jab at the ignition button, I started the car and drove away.

Still in a fog, I drove around the general area of the school, looking for clues, although I had no idea what to look for. After a few minutes of circling the neighborhood, I decided to head to a nearby coffee shop to kill time.

With an iced coffee in hand, I settled at a corner table and turned on my laptop. For the next four hours, I typed every word and detail I knew related to the creatures I'd had the pleasure of meeting in the hopes of discovering more information about them. I came up with nothing. Their names were non-existent, even in comic books.

I pursed my lips in frustration. Matro had given me some

useful information, but I knew he was holding back. Why me? Should I just believe their explanation? Was I being naïve?

I slapped my face. It stung, so I knew for sure that I wasn't dreaming. Believing everything Detherina and her friends told me might be a risk, but the glory of having Shannon in my life made me want to throw caution to the wind.

When it was time to pick her up again, I gathered my things together and purchased another drink for her. Back at school, I parked my car in the same spot where I'd dropped her off and noticed that the marking on the wall by the front entrance was visible. Up until now, I'd only been able to see it through Matro's funnel. Something had changed since this morning.

How on earth had I ended up chin-deep in this mess? I took my backpack from the front seat, pulled out paper and a pen, and copied the symbol as closely as I could.

When Shannon came out of the school, flanked by Mark and Darryl, I saw Car emerge behind them and head to his motorcycle parked by the curb. He glanced in my direction, and when our eyes locked, he flashed a thumb's up and inclined his head, then drove away.

Stunned at the unexpected approval, I managed to compose myself by the time Shannon slid in next to me. Mark and Darryl saluted before heading to the basketball court.

On impulse, I blurted out, "Why don't we watch a movie?"

Shannon smiled, her eyes twinkling. "Let me call my mother to ask if she can do without me for a couple of hours."

I'd forgotten that Wednesday and Fridays were her days to help at Elizabeth's tarot shop.

Shannon called her mother while I pulled out of the parking space, glancing at the students on the street.

"I'm good to go," she said once she'd ended the call,

seeming excited. "I don't even have to work at all tonight. That'll give me a little time to go shopping for a dress for the homecoming dance."

I smacked my forehead with my palm. "I'd forgotten about that."

"How could you?" Shannon pouted.

"I'm going to run to the tux shop tomorrow, I promise."

When we got to the theater, it didn't take long for us to agree on a movie. Nothing could have been more perfect than another scary movie.

Concentrating on the movie was difficult. All I could think of was the way Shannon leaned against me when the scenes got tense. I lay my arm around the back of her seat, trying to make it appear innocent. When another horrific scene came on, it was natural for me to pull her close and hold her.

We stayed that way for the remainder of the movie. The throbbing ache in my injured rib, though present, was ignored.

After the movie, we wandered through the shopping boutiques, and I waited while Shannon tried on several dresses. I gave her my biased input whenever she asked for my opinion. I wasn't much help. As far as I was concerned, Shannon could wear a burlap sack and she'd still be the most beautiful girl in my eyes.

Finally, she found the perfect gown. I was astounded when she came out in a lacy black outfit, the front falling to just above the knee, with gold ribbon running around the waistline. The back had a small train that made her look like a princess. It was a fitting outfit for the daughter of an alien leader. It reminded me of what Detherina had been wearing when I first met her, except Shannon's outfit hugged her body well.

After she paid for the outfit, Shannon pulled me aside.

"You're very patient. Most guys would have run away at the thought of being dragged from one store to another."

"I'm no ordinary guy," I replied, wagging my eyebrows.

Shannon laughed. "You can say that again. Since you're in such a great shopping mood, I'm going to take advantage of it. It's time to accessorize!" she said and then pulled me into a shoe store.

Sleepover

The rest of the week passed at a snail's pace. The healing process went even slower. I'd gotten better at hiding the pain, and I stuck to my resolve to avoid anything that could alter my state of mind. My schedule for dropping off and picking up Shannon from school continued. At night, she'd climb up to my window, and we would spend the night chatting until we fell asleep.

Over the weekend, I spent all my waking hours inside the house. Dad thought it would be a good idea to rest my injury. It wasn't all bad since Darryl and Mark dropped by to play video games.

Shannon had the entire weekend open and spent time with me, too. So far, I had restrained my teenage desires and kept everything chaste. Although I would have loved to explore a deeper relationship between us, there was one glaring issue. I wasn't sure where I stood with her, and I was too afraid to ask.

Sunday night, a light tap on my window alerted me to my nightly guest. I got up, still feeling the sting in my chest with every movement. I pulled the blinds aside to give Shannon enough room to get in.

"Just in time," I said, reaching out to help her down from the ledge.

Shannon laughed, the same sweet, jingling sound I never tired of hearing. She straightened and smoothed her shirt. "I'm always on time."

"I'll give you that."

She went straight to my bed, which told me that she felt very comfortable with me. I sat next to her, leaning against the headboard.

"So, what do you want to watch tonight?"

"We can skip watching tonight. I want to talk instead." Shannon made herself comfortable and hugged a pillow to her chest.

"What do you want to talk about?" I asked.

"Are you excited to go back to school?"

"A little, I guess." I shrugged. School might be hell, but since Shannon came into my life, I was more than happy to be there.

"It wasn't the same without you," she said.

"Why do you say that?" I peered at her, hoping she'd give me some clue of how she felt about me.

"Well, I missed sitting next to you in class. I've gotten used to your tics, and it gets quiet sometimes. You know what's scary? I can hear myself think." She laughed.

Okay, that was unexpected. At least she had accepted my presence in her life, tics and all.

"Don't I make you nervous with my jerks and F-bombs?" I joked.

She didn't laugh. "I'm never nervous around you."

I raised my eyebrow, inviting her to explain further.

Shannon rolled her eyes. "Okay, fine . . . it was awkward at first. I had no idea if you were just being obnoxious. I heard other students call you names, but I thought it was a joke since I'd never paid close attention. You're the first person I've known with Tourette's."

"My favorite is 'freak boy'." It was a disgusting name, but I had to admit, Kevin was rather inventive.

"Kevin is an idiot, self-serving, and so full of himself. I can't believe I let myself get involved with him."

I'd often wondered what she was doing with a prick like Kevin. As far as appearances went, they were perfect for each other. Mr. Cool and Ms. Popular. But it ended there. Shannon was a compassionate person, caring and easy to get along with, while Kevin was the spawn of the devil.

"I wondered the same thing."

She frowned. "Kevin's been around school for the last three days. I have no idea why."

"I saw him once. He seemed distracted."

"He's acting weird." Shannon made a face and shuddered.

"Did he try to approach you? Like to talk?"

She shook her head. "Mark wasn't going to let that happen. And that cousin of yours. He's always around, watching. He's a little creepy. He doesn't talk to anyone except Mark or Darryl. He doesn't even listen in class. He's always looking out the window or staring at me."

I thought of Car. He was another puzzle to me. I recalled Detherina explaining that he was a Binarian. By definition, from what I understood, they had no powers except the ability to recognize danger and help an Aarmark go through their transition. Car seemed a bit more useful than that. The night he tangled with the Ergans was a prime example. He saw them, knew them almost as if he'd encountered them many times before.

Shannon nudged me. "What are you thinking that's making you frown?" she asked.

"Nothing," I shook my head, hoping she'd move to another topic.

No such luck. "C'mon, we don't keep secrets anymore." She even batted her eyelashes.

Like a fool, I was mesmerized. But I wasn't stupid. "I'm just thinking . . . why are we friends? People are wondering why Miss Popular is hanging out with Freak Boy."

She shrugged and made a tsk, tsk sound. "Shame on you for listening to other people who should be minding their own business."

"You didn't answer my question."

Shannon thought for a moment. "I like being around you. You seem to be content with who you are. I'm sure you're wondering if I'm here because of what the tarot reading said. I always think about that. I don't want to use you. You're genuine. You don't take advantage of our friendship. That's what makes me feel safe."

I tried to find the right words in reply. Instead, I focused on a lock of stray hair that had escaped from the twist on her neck. I reached out and wound it back in place.

"Brian?" She tugged at my arm. "How do you feel about this whole thing? About me?"

The uncertainty in her voice made me want to kiss her. I

stifled the urge and concentrated on an honest answer. "I find myself drawn to you more each day," I admitted, expecting her to laugh at me. When she didn't, I continued. "You're not what I expected you to be."

"What did you expect?" she asked, leaning closer.

"I don't know . . . you're popular and pretty. I thought you'd be snooty, a bit self-absorbed. You know. Someone who wouldn't pay attention to a guy like me."

She shook her head in amazement. "You don't think that way anymore?"

"Not since day one. I'm the self-proclaimed president of Shannon McKesson's fan club."

This made her laugh, but we soon cupped our hands over our mouths and held our breath when we heard scraping footsteps approach my door.

"Brian, are you talking to yourself again?" Dad asked, his voice muffled.

"I'm watching TV, Dad!" I replied, fumbling to turn the television on.

"You better catch some sleep. It's your first day back to school tomorrow." There was some reproach in his tone.

"Yes, Dad."

After we heard the sound of his retreating footsteps, Shannon giggled. "Whew, that was close."

I got settled and patted the pillow. "Time to sleep, gorgeous."

She smiled, turned off the lamp, and nestled right next to me. I wrapped my arm around her and after a few minutes, her breathing evened out. The soft sound had become my nightly lullaby, soothing me to sleep.

I was watching the homecoming game, except it was between the Ergans and Mark, Kevin, and the rest of the

Barrister football team. The official counter ticked down to the end of the game.

Ergans = 3, Barristers = 0.

The field erupted in cheers when Kevin launched a Hail Mary pass to Mark.

Then a hush fell over the crowd while everyone followed the ball's trajectory toward the twenty-yard line. It was close to the end zone when there was a sudden snap and the lights went out. Total darkness blanketed the field.

I scrambled to my feet, calling Shannon's name. I heard a muffled sound, a faint crying, then a curse. I ran, trampling over people's feet in my haste to pursue the fading sound.

Groping in the dark amidst the cries of protest of students and spectators alike, I made it down the bleachers, moving as fast as I could. Then as if nothing had happened, the lights came back on.

Looking around, I noticed black rose petals everywhere I could see. I shuddered, fearful of one thing.

"Shannon!" I shouted.

Then I woke up.

It was just after one o'clock in the morning. Disoriented, I jerked into a sitting position. I reached for Shannon, relieved to find her sleeping like a baby.

Damn it. I thought the dreams were over. Too disturbed to go back to sleep, I got the bottle of ibuprofen and tiptoed to the kitchen to get a glass of water. I downed three caplets and stood there in the dark.

It was such a confusing dream. I'd seen every event unfold as if I were standing in the middle of it, but there were some patches that seemed to have been blotted out of the scene.

I walked back to my room, still worrying over my latest

vision. Unable to decode it, I gave up and climbed back into bed, and wrapped my arms around Shannon protectively. She leaned into me.

Waking up to my alarm hours later, I ran my hand over the space next to me. I wasn't expecting Shannon to be there, but a little part of me hoped to find her there. As fast as I could manage, I went through the motions of getting ready for school. After I endured Mom's perky chatter, I ran out of my house just as Shannon stepped out of her front door.

"Good morning," she greeted, much too chipper for me, especially after the dreadful nightmare I'd had the night before.

Then a distinct scent permeated the air. It was the sort of salty aroma I might associate with food, but this smelled more like sweating bodies. Ergans!

"Shannon, get over here, fast!" I shouted.

Mr. Ax

Shannon's eyes widened, and she assumed a fighting stance as if by instinct.

"Brian, what do you see?"

"Just run here, now!"

She blinked like she was waking up from a bad dream and streaked across the lawn, her momentum carrying her to me. I tucked her into my arms, protective in the face of the threat from our unseen enemy.

"What's going on?" Shannon asked after she caught her breath.

I surveyed the half-empty street. There was a man walking his dog and watching us, maybe wondering what the hell these two teenagers were up to. Then I scanned our front yard and the neighbors'. When the surroundings checked out okay, I let her go.

"Sorry. It's just my paranoia kicking into high gear. I thought I heard something." It was a lie. There was a lingering scent burning my nostrils, even though I couldn't see anything.

Shannon seemed unconvinced. "That didn't look like nothing. You're scared." She tugged at my hand. "Look at me, Curly."

The panic in her eyes made me wish I could erase her fears and the threat to her safety.

"Let's go. I don't want to be late to school on my first day back." I winked at her, hoping she wouldn't see right through me, and led her to my car. I opened the door for her while glancing around.

Again, I heard faint murmurs, which grew louder by the second, echoing in my ears. There were unfamiliar voices, foreign sounds, screeching and bellowing. My neck started getting stiff and my shoulders jerked involuntarily while I walked around my car and slid behind the driver's seat. I gripped the steering wheel when a few tics erupted.

Shannon placed a comforting hand on my thigh while I went through the embarrassing round of spasms I hated so much.

"I'm good." I lifted Shannon's hand and placed it back on her lap without looking at her.

Her expression said it all. She was showing compassion, and I was blowing her off like it meant nothing to me.

Shannon didn't say anything while I maneuvered the car onto the street. We drove in silence. She was undoubtedly a bit pissed at me for not taking her offer of comfort with grace, and I was worrying over the new developments.

The minute the car stopped, Shannon opened the door without waiting for me as she had for the past week. She walked toward the school entrance without even glancing back.

As much as my body hadn't completely healed, I forced myself to ignore the pain and ran after her. When I caught up to her, I took her hand.

"Hey, what's going on? Why'd you just walk away?"

She pulled back her hand and continued walking. "Nothing."

Time with Shannon had taught me a few things about girls in general. My brush-off had struck the wrong nerve.

"Shannon, please. Can we talk?"

She stopped.

"Hey, look at me. I can be an asshole. You know that already, right?" I tipped her chin so she was looking straight into my eyes, and she nodded. "I can't change overnight, but I'm trying. I just hate being reminded that I'm so different from everyone else."

Wow. Shannon had changed me. Never in a million years would I have expected to be talking about my condition so openly with someone.

"I understand. It's just annoying when you push me away," she said, looking as lovely pouting as she did smiling.

"Can you forgive me?" I brushed a finger along her cheek. She didn't seem to mind my touch one bit. From the corner of my eye, I saw Mark and Darryl by the steps, snickering at me.

"There's nothing to forgive. Just promise you won't do it again."

I placed a palm over my heart. "You got it." Emboldened, I twined our fingers together. "Happy?"

Shannon flashed her million-dollar smile. "Shall we?"

We climbed the steps and headed to our respective classes. I had been gone for only a week, but it felt like it had been a month.

The hallways were plastered with campaign signs, most of

them with my name on them. I was surprised to see that groups I wouldn't have expected to know I existed had endorsed me.

Mark nudged me. "I think the joke is turning around, bro. You might have a chance," he said, sounding proud.

"This is freaky," I muttered and nodded at some students who pumped their fists in the air when we walked past them.

"I have my money on you, Curly." Shannon winked at me.

Kevin was standing just outside the classroom with his group. He glanced our way, and his eyes narrowed. Shannon nudged me to keep going, and we took our seats right away.

The day wouldn't be the same now that Mr. P wouldn't be around anymore. From the gossip circulating, a new teacher would take over and replace the substitute who had covered the class. The students piled in, scurrying into their seats, followed by a rather young looking man wearing dark sunglasses. He closed the door behind him and strode to the desk, placing his backpack on the table.

He took his time taking papers out of his bag before he addressed the class.

Then he sat on the edge of the desk and cleared his throat. "I'm Mr. Bon Ax, and I'll be taking over Mr. Peter's class for the rest of the year."

The class started murmuring, and the new teacher waited until everyone quieted down before he continued. "I apologize for not removing my glasses, but the glare is not good for my eyesight."

More whisper rippled across the room while the class reacted to this.

One boy in the back raised his hand. "Sir, it's school policy for everyone to remove their sunglasses while in class."

Mr. Ax's shoulder tensed a bit, but after a moment, he

smiled. "I've got a prescription for mine, and Mr. Delson has approved it. Now, let's proceed with class." He handed out papers to the front row to be passed back to the rest of the class.

While sheets of paper were passed around, he glanced at his copy. "I'm revising the remaining subject curriculum for the rest of the year. I'm going to schedule photo tours with smaller groups of students. We'll focus on landscape photography, as well as the use of filters."

Mr. Ax continued talking, but I started tuning him out. I turned my attention to where Car usually sat during class. The seat was empty, which made me wonder where he was.

"Who here are members of the yearbook committee?" I heard Mr. Ax ask.

Shannon and I raised our hands, and he looked over the rim of his glasses at me. The moment our eyes met, the hair at the back of my neck rose. His irises were acid yellow with a little black dot in the middle.

"Did you see that?" I whispered to Shannon.

She looked at me questioningly. "See what?"

"His eyes." I looked again, but his sunglasses were back on.

Shannon snuck a glance and shook her head. "I didn't see anything."

"You in the blue shirt. Would you like to share with the class what you are discussing back there that can't wait until class is over?" Mr. Ax stood up and moved closer.

I straightened in my chair. "It was nothing, sir."

Kevin snickered together with some of his friends, and Mr. Ax turned to him. "Is there anything you want to say, Mister . . . "

"Kevin Masters. I'm sorry, sir."

Mr. Ax paced, stroking his chin before addressing the whole

class. "This goes for all of you. If you want to talk, raise your hand so I can call on you to share with everybody. If not, I expect you to hold your tongues until this class is over. Are we clear?"

Feeling suddenly out of sorts, I tried my best to concentrate and listen for the remainder of the class. My skin was prickling, and my gut was screaming that something wasn't right with our new teacher.

A hard tug on my shoulder announced incoming twitches, and by the time class ended, I was tired from holding them back. The pain in my rib wasn't helping either.

Thank God the rest of the day went by faster than I'd anticipated. By the end of sixth period, I was overwhelmed and in a great deal of discomfort. After dropping off Shannon at her house, I went straight to bed and fell into a deep, but troubled, sleep.

The next thing I knew, Matro was shaking me awake.

"You wanted to see me."

Stifling a yawn, I glanced at the clock and wondered if anyone was home already. "I didn't rub the rock," I muttered, irritated by interruption of my nap.

Matro grinned. "You don't have to. I sensed your need. What can I do for you?" He walked over to the window and glanced outside.

"I have this feeling that something is going to go wrong. And there's a new scent that's been bugging me." I propped myself up into a sitting position. The aroma of mom's fettuccine and shrimp permeated the air, making my stomach growl.

Matro looked over his shoulder at me with a questioning look. "You can actually smell them?"

I nodded.

"Describe the scent to me."

Pushing my gnawing hunger aside, I thought about the best way to explain it. "It smelled like salt, but more like sweat. It felt like something or someone was close by, even though I couldn't see anything."

He sat on the foot of the bed. "You're right about that . . . " His voice trailed off, and he studied me intently.

I waited for him to say something more, but he didn't. "Is there anything you know that you're not telling me?"

Matro shook his head.

"I'm going to freak out any time now," I warned him, sliding out of bed.

My words snapped him out of his momentary stupor. "No. You're doing fine. Those bastards just know how to scare humans."

He walked over to the door and pressed his ear against it before disappearing without a word. Just in time. There was a knock, and Mom opened the door.

"Dinner's ready, baby-boy," she said.

"I'll be right down." Leaning against the headboard, I plastered a neutral expression on my face.

She walked in and glanced around. "I thought I heard you talking to someone."

I raised an eyebrow. "I'm all alone here, Mom. Who would I be talking to?"

"Hmm . . . okay." She didn't sound convinced. "Are you keeping something from your mother?"

"Mom, c'mon, gimme a break. Why would I keep something from you?"

She still looked doubtful, but thank God she turned on her heel and started for the door. Then she pivoted and added,

"Come down now."

"I'll be there in just a minute." I escaped to the bathroom and closed the door. That had been a close call.

Matro reappeared, leaning against the wall. "Your mom is sneaky. She suspects something, so it's better for us to limit our talks."

"Okay," I agreed. "Now if you'll excuse me, I need some alone time, unless you want to stick around when the bomb drops?"

He grimaced and was gone in a flash.

Once alone, I thought about the new teacher, Mr. Ax. I couldn't tell if my mind was playing tricks on me. After all, I had been under a lot of stress with the whole Prodian thing.

Matro returned just as I was about to leave my room. "I know there is something else on your mind."

There was no escaping a mind-reading creature. "We have a new teacher who started today. He's…" I tried to think of the best way to explain it. "I'm not sure if it was just my imagination, but I saw his eyes. They didn't look human. Tell me I'm not going insane here."

Matro paled. For a good long time, an uncomfortable silence loomed between us, and when he answered, his voice was hard. "You're not losing your mind. What's his name? Describe him to me."

"It's Bon Ax. He's about your height. What are you, six-foot-three?" Matro nodded. "His hair is almost white, like platinum, silver, whatever, but his eyes were the clincher. They were yellow with a black dot in the middle."

Matro bristled. "Go on. Did he leave a scent?"

"No, not really. Why?"

Another long stretch of silence passed.

"What are you thinking?"

Matro shook his head as if dispelling an unpleasant thought, then he gripped my arm. "Listen to me. Have the Mertest handy at all times, and call on me right away if you need anything. Most of all, be safe. Don't trust anyone with Shannon's life or yours, except us and your friends."

If his statement was meant to scare me, it had worked. "You're freakin' me out."

His expression softened. "The portal between Pratrim and Earth is open. Our enemies are in our midst, yet I don't see all of them. I'll be damned if I let anything happen to you guys. We're going to need more sentries to help out."

With that, he disappeared again, leaving me and my emotions in upheaval.

Dinner was low-key. Mom and Dad seemed preoccupied with something, but that was good for me since Matro's warning was still causing havoc in my mind.

After dinner, Shannon made her usual appearance, armed with her backpack. I was surprised to see her wearing her pajamas.

I eyed her warily. "Why are you wearing PJ's?" I asked, inching away.

"I figured, after we're done with our homework, I'd already be dressed for bed."

Hmm, this is going to be a long night. I suppressed a groan. "Okay . . . shall we start?"

Shannon sat next to me on the floor. I scooted further away when she leaned closer to check on my work, my raging hormones taunting me. I swore to walk her home the minute we finished our work.

It was past eleven when the last of our assignments were

finished. At my wits' end, I tried to stand up, but my healing rib protested. I shrank back down and clutched at my chest.

"You better get to bed," Shannon said, worried.

That was my cue. Despite the pain, I sucked in a breath, straightened my shoulders, and started gathering her books. "Let me walk you home, and then I'll get to bed."

She looked at me with a puzzled expression. "Are you trying to get rid of me?"

I shook my head. "Of course not. I need to take my pain pill, and that will knock me out, that's all." Without another word, I opened the door and stuck my head out, getting a feel for my parent's whereabouts.

There were faint sounds of the television and conversation coming from their bedroom. It was our chance to get out unnoticed. "C'mon." I tugged at her hand and led her to the hallway and down the stairs.

Once we got to her door, I handed her the books. "Same time tomorrow?"

Shannon didn't say anything. I felt bad, but I had to do this. I would end up attacking her if I didn't put some space between us.

"Don't forget to bring your camera, and try to have a good night's sleep."

"Okay," she said and closed the door.

Weary and worried, I climbed onto my bed, hoping Shannon wouldn't hold this against me. It was for her own good, and my sanity.

The next day, I honked twice and waited for Shannon to come out of her house. The moment she walked out the door, her face lit up with a smile. Thank God there were no hard feelings from the night before. Giving her a goofy grin, I waved to her.

"Are you ready for your first job as a school photographer?"

"You bet."

We chatted about our assignment all the way to school, and everything was right in my world again.

The pep rally was scheduled for lunchtime. After the end of third period, I waited outside Shannon's classroom. The hallway was bustling with kids eager to attend the rally or just to have extra time for themselves. The entire school was buzzing with excitement about the homecoming football game on Friday. The good news was our team actually had a chance of beating our cross-town rival this year. Having a decent defense made the difference.

Shannon walked out a moment later and waved at me.

"Ready?" I took her backpack and slung it over my shoulder.

"I'm excited. This is my first gig, and I can't wait." Shannon glanced at a few of the whispering girls behind her and glared at them for a brief moment. "Let's go, baby."

That threw me off for a second or two, but I regained my composure right away.

"That was sweet of you."

Shannon acted innocent. "What are you talking about?"

"You know exactly what I'm talking about." I left it at that and took her hand instead.

With the busy foot traffic and impossibly noisy exodus to the rally, further conversation between us was impossible. We walked in comfortable silence until we spotted our yearbook team converged not too far from the football field.

Laying our backpacks on the ground, we busied ourselves right away with getting our cameras ready. Ron, our team leader, ambled toward us. "Brian, your assignment is to take pictures during the pep rally. I'm counting on your quality shots."

"Sure thing." I hung the camera strap around my neck and gave him a thumb's up.

Then he turned to Shannon, who was switching to her favorite short lens. "I need you to cover the team picture, as well as their individual shots. Can you handle it?"

Shannon grinned. "You bet I can," she said, obviously pleased with her assignment.

"Better get a head start now." Ron continued to talk to the rest of the group.

Shannon beamed, and it was damn near impossible not to be happy for her. "See you in a bit?"

"I'll be waiting here."

There were too many things going on at the same time with the music, electric atmosphere, and rambunctious kids. I lost track of time as soon as the rally started. The marching band performed well, surprising everyone with music from the eighties. Next were the cheerleaders with their colorful pompoms and swinging short skirts, leading the students in colorful and funny chants against our rival, Belmont High. Next, a student dressed up as Kermit the Frog in our midnight blue football uniform did a short skit with someone else as Gonzo, who wore a tattered uniform from our rival school. Ms. Piggy rocked the scene with her own version of cheers, leaving everyone in high spirits.

Finally, the football team was called in. This was my cue to cover every angle, from the group running to the middle of the field holding their helmets, to the crowd rising to their feet. As captain, Mark took the microphone and invited everyone to join in singing our school song. In his proud but slightly off-key tone, he led the students through the anthem. Snapping picture after picture, it took some time for me to note that Kevin was missing from the group.

I scanned the multitude of faces to look for Shannon, and abandoned my post when I couldn't locate her. Starting a frenzied search, my first stop was the bleachers. She wasn't there, so I ran to where we left our things, hoping she might've finished her assignment early.

My heart rammed against my chest as sweat trickled down my forehead when I found our things still lying where we'd left them.

Breaking out in a run, I sprinted across the field, looking for anything that would give me a clue. There were a whole lot of kids, but not Shannon. I found Veronica with the other cheerleaders and decided I didn't care if I was crossing the popular students' boundary.

"Veronica, have you seen Shannon?" I asked, my voice coming out in a croak.

Some of the girls giggled, but I was beyond caring. The only thing on my mind was finding Shannon. Veronica tossed her honey blonde hair before answering. "No, I thought she was with you." Then she added, sounding like it was meant for the rest to hear. "I don't know why she's hanging out with a loser."

"Thanks for helping out," I said, pointedly, and took my leave.

Then out of nowhere, the stench I had associated with the Ergans drifted around me. "Oh no, not your nasty asses again." I checked my surroundings, but not one of those suckers was in sight. This wasn't good.

A strident sound came from the direction of the locker room, and I sprinted toward it.

The distant hooting from the ongoing festivities couldn't compete with the loud thudding of my heartbeat when I headed to a deserted area of campus. Then I heard Shannon's pleas reverberating above the din, coming from the locker room.

Inside, she was struggling against Kevin, who had her cornered against the wall.

"Get your hands off me," Shannon shouted.

"What does that geek-face have that I don't?" Kevin asked while pressing his filthy body closer.

That was when I saw red. No one was going to disrespect Shannon this way—over my dead body. Fueled by a burst of adrenaline and red-hot fury, I plowed toward them with speed that even surprised me. Without considering the consequences of my actions, I pummeled into Kevin with force, almost hitting Shannon. Caught off guard, he fell to the ground. As an athlete, he was fast and was back on his feet before I had the chance catch my breath. My ribs protested, but I was not going to give in.

"Just who do you think you are, barging in here? This area is off limits to weirdos."

"Oh yeah? Then what are you doing here, you piece of crap?"

At my words, Kevin barreled in my direction. Luck made my feet catch a piece of equipment on the floor, and I stumbled backward, avoiding what would've been a hard blow.

Kevin managed to brace his fall by landing on top of me, and that was when all hell broke loose. We grappled together on the ground, rolling, kicking, and exchanging punches.

"For the last time, keep your hands off her!" I socked him in the face real good, and blood squirted from his nose.

"Stop it, Stop it!" Shannon's voice echoed in my ears, but there was no stopping me. I was nowhere even close to easing up. Rage and adrenaline kept me going, landing punches and kicks without pause. I'd had enough of Kevin trying to take advantage of her.

"You son of a bitch!" Kevin howled and swung at me, catching me across the jaw.

All of a sudden, a familiar stink drifted around us and we were yanked to our feet.

"What's going on here?" Mr. Ax grunted under the force of my resistance.

"You broke my nose, you dipshit." Kevin spat out some blood.

An excruciating pain radiated from my chest, but pride kept me from crying out while I tried to catch my breath. "I'm not done yet, you bastard," I said through gritted teeth.

"You're going to get expelled, you piece of scum," Kevin roared. His face was a mask of rage as he took a step in my direction.

Mr. Ax yanked him back, and then tossed him to the ground. "He's not going to get expelled. You are."

Sputtering with anger, Kevin jumped to his feet. "But . . . you told me to—"

"Enough!" Mr. Ax cut him off. "You're in big enough trouble as it is." Then he turned to me. Behind those dark glasses, I sensed the dagger glare he threw my way. "I'm watching you, Morrison."

Shannon rushed over and wrapped her arms around me. "Mr. Ax, thank God you came. It was Kevin's fault. He was going to attack me. Brian came in time to help me."

"If that is the case, then you should come with us to the Principal's office." Mr. Ax turned on his heel and found Kevin smirking at me. "You're not going to like what's going to happen next. If I were you, I'd cut my losses now and shut up."

Once more, we found ourselves being hustled to the principal's office.

After several hours of intense interrogation, I walked out of Mr. Delson's office with a final warning. Engage in another fight, whether it was my fault or not, and I'd get booted out. Shannon testified against Kevin, and Mr. Ax confirmed her statement. The whole process gave me some time to study the new teacher, and more than ever, I believed there was more to the man than met the eye. And I would make sure I found my answers soon.

The whole event left me baffled. It left so many questions that needed answers. What was Kevin trying to say before Mr. Ax cut him off? And what was the photography teacher doing near the locker room?

In the end, I was just relieved that Shannon had escaped without a scratch.

Grounded

Shannon and I left the principal's office in a hurry, trying to avoid crossing paths with Kevin again. Now that he'd been expelled, the situation was bound to get worse. We hurried to my car, and once we got inside, Shannon started fussing at me.

"Brian, you can't keep fighting like this." She touched my jaw, and I fought hard not to react under her watchful eye. *I won't kiss her. I won't kiss her,* I chanted in my head.

"In case you hadn't noticed, I was trying to protect your virtue." I pulled away, afraid I wouldn't be able to control my physical reaction to her proximity.

"I can defend myself. Besides, you're going to be expelled if you get in another fight."

Shannon glanced ahead, and we saw Kevin walking out when we passed the school. His expression said it all. He wanted payback.

For the first few minutes, nothing much was said as we headed home. I had so many things running through my mind, but focusing on them would only provoke my tics. There was no point in worrying about anything other than Shannon's safety.

"Did you smell that stink back there? Or was it only me?" she asked.

At least it wasn't just me. "It came with Mr. Ax, I swear."

"What's up with him? He scares me." She shuddered.

I reached for her hand and held it. "Don't worry. I'm going to be watching him from now on."

Shannon shot me a glare. "Of course I'll worry. He looks really pissed at you." She shook her head. "What I'm trying to figure out is what Kevin was trying to say. You heard it, right?"

I nodded, knowing full well we had another puzzle to solve. "From now on, avoid Ax at all times. If he comes near you, run away."

Shannon laughed. "He's our teacher. I can't avoid him."

"I'm trying to look after you," I whispered.

"Why? Is there something I should know?"

It wasn't something I could discuss with her, but before I could stop myself, I blurted out a different sort of secret. "I . . . think I'm falling for you . . . "

I let go of her hand and looked away, expecting a rebuff. Shannon didn't say anything, and an uncomfortable silence followed. When I couldn't take it anymore, I shot a furtive glance at her.

Her expression confused me. I'd expected her to laugh or tell me that I'd overstepped a boundary. Instead, she was smiling.

"That wasn't so hard, was it?" Shannon tugged at my arm. "And don't let go of my hand."

She wasn't upset. I had been stressing for no reason at all.

"I'll call later." I kissed her hand as soon as we'd parked in my driveway.

Shannon smiled. "Sure. I'll be waiting."

After I got her safely inside, I got back inside my car and headed down the road. I needed to go somewhere I could summon to Matro without witnesses so I could talk to him and not be seen talking to myself again. Mark's place would be the safest bet, I figured.

My phone buzzed with a text from Shannon as I was pulling up to Mark's house. I parked and read her message.

Hope ur doing ok. Running errands with mom. Don't worry. Gilbert is with us. See u 2night. Same bat-time, same bat-channel.

Despite myself, I grinned at her attempt to make me laugh and responded, "KK."

No sooner had I hit send than Matro appeared in the passenger seat, startling me.

I glared at him. "Don't you have a warning bell or something?"

"Testy. You'll just have to get used to it, my boy." He stretched his long legs as best he could in the cramped space. "You got in a fight again."

"Well, duh!" I replied. "Aren't you supposed to be watching out for us?"

The expression on his face stopped me from continuing, however. Matro rubbed his chin and sighed.

"I can't see you when you're in school. It's weird. And Car's out of pocket. I've been calling him, but there's no answer."

Matro's clear distress showed he wasn't lying. If we didn't have backup at school, it posed a greater problem for me. Kevin had no grasp of when to stop, even more than usual. Although I didn't know Kevin well on a personal level, it was clear that he hadn't been himself. He seemed almost dazed most of the time.

"How is that possible? You see everything." It was meant as a question but sounded more like an accusation.

"It's that teacher, right? I'm guessing he must be one of the leaders. He's blocking my vision. I can't explain it, but it's like my radar shuts down. There's this big *bleep* in the middle." Matro opened the car door with a rough push.

"So does this mean I'm on my own there?"

Matro looked remorseful. "Forgive me. It will never happen again. You'll never be on your own."

"Hey, I know what I have to do. No worries, man."

"Regardless, I'm to blame for that. From now on, I'm sticking to you guys like glue. I need some time to find out what's causing the glitch." We walked together to Mark's house, and Matro patted my shoulder. "For now, just sit tight. There's nothing much they can do while you're near Shannon."

When I rang the doorbell, Mark answered right away. He gave me a cursory glance, then looked at Matro, then back to me. "You look like shit."

"Gee, thanks. I have a habit of rearranging my face every now and then."

We made our way to his room. Once there, Mark and I settled down to play video games, but Matro stayed by the window, staring into space.

Nothing more was said until we paused to rest.

"I heard what happened," Mark said, his face scrunched in disgust. "What is wrong with Kevin?"

"At least I didn't get expelled with him." The scene played out in my mind again. Nothing made sense. What did Kevin want with Shannon? Couldn't he take no for an answer?

"Well, Mr. Ax sure came through for you." Mark shook his head and turned to watch the screen. "What's up with that guy, anyway?"

"Mr. Ax?"

"Yeah. What went down? When did he show up?"

I tried to remember. Where had Ax come from? Once I'd spotted Shannon and Kevin, everything else had been a blur.

"He just appeared from out of nowhere. It was like he'd been watching the whole time."

Mark scratched his head, obviously as bewildered as I was.

After an hour or so, Matro and I drove back to my house so I could get ready for dinner. He excused himself after receiving an urgent summons from Detherina. Although my curfew wasn't enforced most of the time, I thought it would be wise to be around when my parents got home. I had a sinking feeling that this latest incident might not sit well with them, especially my dad. Even though they'd let the two prior brawls go without much drama, I suspected that they wouldn't react the same way this time.

When I came down to dinner and my parents saw my busted lips and the bluish discoloration around my cheek, Dad dropped his utensils and glared at me, his nostrils flaring. A sign he was harnessing his temper. Mom was utterly still. To mask my nervousness, I busied myself with scooping a glob of mashed potatoes onto my plate.

"You got into another fight in school?" Dad asked.

"Yeah," I answered and began cutting through my steak with more force than necessary.

"Care to tell us what happened?"

I stopped slicing the meat and looked at my father. Mom still hadn't moved. "I was at the pep rally this afternoon covering the pictures. I noticed Shannon was missing so I went to look for her. Kevin trapped her in the locker room and was trying to do something to her."

Dad pounded his fist on the table. "You know I don't condone fighting. I let those two earlier incidents slide, but I'll be damned if I'm going to ignore this one. Starting tonight, you're grounded. Home and school, that's it!"

My mother gasped and stood up, turning her back on us. "Excuse me." She ran out of the room.

I stared at my father in disbelief. "What? I'm not the one who instigated it."

"Better watch your tone, young man," Dad said. "Ever since you started hanging out with Shannon, you keep getting into trouble."

I twitched in response. A spasm rolled from my shoulders, radiating through my neck and arms, and for the next few seconds, I shook like crazy.

"Dad, why?" I kept my tone low, even if I wanted to scream. This had to be the worst thing he could do to me, but I didn't want to take the chance of making it worse still.

He observed me, and for a moment, I thought he'd relent. "It's for your own good. One week. After school, you're expected to head straight home."

I pushed my chair back and rose. "If you'll excuse me, I've lost my appetite."

Stomping my feet, I headed upstairs, hurried to my room, and flung open the bedroom door. "I can't wait to get out of this shitty place. A few more months, and I'm gone," I muttered.

"That's not a nice thing to say," Shannon said, startling me.

I glanced at the clock, not having expected her back so soon. "You're early. Is something wrong?"

Shannon stood and wrapped her arms around my neck. "Thanks again for coming to my rescue earlier."

"You're welcome," I answered, feeling my skin flush with embarrassment.

For a little while, I savored our proximity, but then I noticed her puffy eyes. "Hey, what's going on?"

Shannon glanced away. "You're always getting in trouble because of me."

"It's okay. I'm a big boy. I can handle myself."

I led her to the edge of the bed and we sat down. "Can you tell me what happened?"

"I asked Kevin for a picture, and he told me to follow him to the locker room. He sounded calm and friendly, so I did. Then once we went inside, he started talking gibberish. He smelled funny, too."

I rubbed her back, trying to comfort her. "That bastard is head over heels in love with you, and I can understand why. What I don't understand is why he keeps insisting on pushing himself on you."

"I don't know." Shannon shook her head. "I'm scared that he might take it out on you, now that he's been expelled."

"Don't worry about me. I'll be fine." With a light touch, I tilted her head up to see her face. "Are you okay?"

She nodded. "So what are we going to do now?"

"Since Dad grounded me for fighting—"

"You're *grounded*? What about the game? The homecoming dance?"

"I'll figure something out." It was easier said than done, of course. Then a brilliant idea hit me. "Let's go out and celebrate my grounding. Bring your backpack."

"But . . . "

I picked up my own bag from the floor and headed to the window. "After you, my dear."

Shannon giggled and started to work her way down the trellis, and I followed close behind.

"So where are we going?"

"Doesn't matter."

We drove around until we found a donut shop. After we got some hot cocoa, a sprinkled donut for Shannon, and a bear claw for me, we settled into a booth at the end of the room.

"If you're ready to work on TGM, then we can start," I said.

"TGM?" She looked puzzled.

"Oh, sorry. *The Glass Menagerie*. I shortened it." I took a big bite of my bear claw.

That made her smile. For the next hour, we worked on our analysis, pausing to read lines or bounce ideas off each other. After that, I moved on to my math homework while Shannon listened to music on her phone. In the silence that had fallen while I was in deep concentration, I glanced up to find that she'd fallen asleep, her head resting against the wall. Although I felt like a stalker, I decided to let her sleep for a bit while I watched over her.

Why do things have to be so complicated? I nudged Shannon, but she didn't stir. The place was empty, but this was hardly a spot we should be hanging around until the wee hours of the morning. Too bad. Shannon looked tired. A rush of tender protectiveness coursed through my veins while I watched her. Studying her features and feeling a bit lightheaded, I stifled the urge to brush my mouth against her parted lips.

It felt like it would be a crime to wake her. However, we had to get home. Gathering our things, I nudged her once more. "Hey, wake up."

Shannon's lids fluttered, and then she opened her eyes and jumped. "Oh, my God. Was I sleeping?"

I chuckled. "Like a baby. Let's go home."

During the short drive, I reflected that things were getting deeper between us, even if Shannon hadn't said anything about her feelings toward me.

I parked in the driveway and walked her to the door. "Good night."

She reached over and touched my cheek, caressing. "You're amazing, Brian."

When I climbed the trellis back to my room, I found Matro leaning against the wall and grinning. "Restraint is a good thing. You've done well, Brian. I'm so proud of you."

I groaned and flopped on the bed. It was close to midnight, and I doubted sleep would come soon. "I'm going to go nuts. Thanks for the vote of confidence. Do you mind? I need some sleep here."

"Sleep well." Matro chuckled then dematerialized.

The remainder of the week was hell, but as any teenager would do, I figured out a way around the grounding. Mark and Darryl came home with me after we dropped Shannon off and would leave a few minutes before my parents got home. Also, Matro was more visible than ever. He even had henchmen with him.

Two dilemmas remained—the football game that night, and the homecoming dance the next. I could forgo the game, but there was no way I was going to miss taking the prettiest girl in school to the dance.

My biggest concern was leaving Shannon defenseless against the Ergans during the football game. I couldn't possibly hang around the house while she was out there and vulnerable.

Concocting an excuse was going to be difficult since Dad had been vigilant the past few days. He went to great lengths, checking in on me regularly and sending text messages that nearly drove me insane. Mom remained subdued, which puzzled me. I brought it up once, but she shrugged it off, so I left her alone.

Good things come to those who wait, it turned out. By the time six o'clock rolled around, I heard my parents getting ready to go out. A glimmer of hope burned in my chest while I waited to find out where they were going.

The much-awaited tap sounded, and Dad pushed open the door and stuck in his head. "We're going to a fundraiser tonight. Your mom left you a casserole in the fridge for dinner. Don't wait up. We're going to be late." He glanced around, as if he'd expected to find someone in there with me.

I nodded, trying to appear indifferent. Dad bought my act, and his features softened. "I'm glad you're taking your grounding well. A few more days, and you'll be off the hook. I hope you realize this is for your own good."

I resisted the inclination to comment, and he headed back downstairs.

The moment I heard the car drive away, I dialed Shannon's number. It rang several times and then went to voicemail. With a curse, I threw on jeans and a jacket, packed up my camera, and left the house. A quick rub on the rock to summon Matro, and he showed up right away.

"Have you seen Shannon?" I asked, stepping on the gas.

"She drove to the school with Veronica and Brittney." Matro stared straight ahead, looking a little preoccupied.

We sped through the busy streets, weaving in and out of small openings between cars.

I glanced in his direction again. "What's wrong?"

"I just have a bad feeling about tonight."

An unpleasant sensation washed over me. "I haven't even told you about the dream I had last night."

"What dream?" he asked, turning his full attention to me.

"A major calamity. Rocks, water, a long bridge, ground shaking, and fire everywhere. People will die. And I can't even tell when or where it'll happen."

"There's nothing to give the location or the time frame?"

"No."

Matro fell quiet and I was left to my own thoughts once more.

Parking was the pits. It took me several turns to find a spot. Once I'd shut off the car, I noticed Matro had a weird expression on his face. "What's wrong?" I asked as we began the long walk toward football field.

"You have the Mertest with you?"

I nodded.

"Be careful out there. I'll be watching you." He looked tense.

"Why?"

"I can't see a thing again. Something's not right." Matro stopped walking and gestured for me to keep walking.

I shrugged and continued on my way.

Then he said, "Know your surroundings, and trust no one."

That was exactly what I planned to do.

Homecoming Game

The marching band had already taken the field by the time I made it through the long line of students to the spot where our group would meet. I spotted Shannon with Darryl, and I breathed a sigh of relief until I also saw Mr. Ax standing next to her.

I paused midstride and searched for Matro. Sure enough, he wasn't too far behind.

What could they be talking about? Then I remembered—photography teacher. Duh! I jogged toward them, and Mr. Ax met my eyes, sans sunglasses. My whole being shuddered at the darkness I saw in his.

Suppressing the terror that gripped me, I approached with caution. Shannon waved once she saw me. Mr. Ax put his arm around her shoulder, as if he were trying to taunt me. Then he whispered something in her ear, and I swore Shannon's body quivered ever so slightly.

"Hello, Brian," Mr. Ax greeted.

I searched Shannon's face, looking for evidence of discomfort, anything that would give me an idea of what he'd said to her. Her expression gave no indication at all.

"Mr. Ax," my response was curt before turning to Shannon again. "What's your assignment tonight?"

"I'm going to spend time with her tonight going over panning and flash usage," Mr. Ax answered.

"Why don't I work with you and let Shannon do the stills?"

Mr. Ax's face darkened. "Are you telling me how to do my job?"

Actually I am. I bit my tongue. My alarm bells were clanging, and I knew vigilance was the key.

Instead of responding to him, I turned to Darryl. "Hey, bro."

"'Sup?" Darryl shifted on his feet, looking uncomfortable.

"If you want to learn those techniques, you could follow them around," I told him pointedly, hoping he'd get my drift.

"Oh, yeah—can I join you, sir?" Darryl asked. He sounded intimidated.

Mr. Ax studied Darryl for a moment. "You're going to have fun, young man."

By this time, the marching band had exited the field amid the loud clapping and foot stomping, and the crowd was chanting, "Barristers! Barristers!"

Shortly after, the team piled onto the football field, and a deafening roar erupted. While the noise rose to a crescendo, I planned how to juggle taking pictures while keeping tabs on Shannon, too. With all the chaos going on around us, it would be impossible to keep an eye on her every move.

"Hey, can I have a word with you?" I pulled Shannon by the arm, and we walked a few feet out of earshot.

"Is everything okay?" Shannon asked.

"Yeah." I raked my fingers through my wild hair, not sure how to tell her how I felt. Terror was making me edgy. "I want you to have your cell phone in your pocket. Call me if Ax starts acting suspicious."

"You're scaring me." She clutched my arm with a clammy hand.

"Tell me what he said to you." I glanced at Mr. Ax. He was surveying the crowd, and Darryl stood next to him, looking quite on edge, too.

"He said he'd give me what I needed. That's all."

"What kind of a lesson is that? No . . . no . . . I don't want you with him."

"What are you talking about? He's a teacher. Are you crazy?"

"Maybe I am."

"Brian, I may like you, but don't try to start telling me what to do," she said, looking annoyed.

Getting Shannon angry was a complication I didn't need. Shit. "Look, I'm sorry. That came out wrong. I'm worried about you, but it's your call. Either way, don't let your guard down, okay?" I pulled her hood up over her head and then tightened the strings. "It's going to rain."

"Tell me what you're thinking."

"That's the thing. I don't know. I feel like something's wrong, but I can't pinpoint what it is." I rubbed her back. "Call me, okay?"

"Yeah."

It was time for us to take our positions. I stayed on our team's end zone, while Shannon, Mr. Ax, and Darryl stood near the fifty-yard line. Marshall won the coin toss, and the game began. The crowd jumped to its feet the moment the whistle blew.

Watching the game was fun. Mark in particular kicked some serious ass. I snapped shot after shot to edit later, taking more of Mark than was necessary. In a way, it was my apology for the times I'd ditched his games. I chronicled every hit, every fall, and every celebratory chest bump and huddle. It was exhilarating, even from the sidelines.

During halftime, while I was reviewing my pictures, a familiar and annoying voice spoke from behind.

"Miss me?"

I swung around to find Car, looking ill at ease with his hands in his jeans pockets.

"Son of a—what the hell happened to you?"

"I had a family emergency." He offered his fist, and we bumped knuckles. "How much have I missed?"

"A hell of a lot," I retorted.

He laughed. "I spoke with Matro just a few minutes ago. He said he's unable to see anything here."

I nodded. "I can't explain it. It's like I know there's something here, but my wires are all scrambled. I get bits and pieces, but I have no idea what they are."

A rumble of thunder roared, and the first drops of rain trickled down. I grabbed the protective cover for my camera and covered my gear. Car remained standing next to me, surveying the crowd.

"What are you feeling right now?" he asked, glancing over at the fifty-yard line where Shannon was deep in conversation with Mr. Ax.

"I see green clouds drifting in and out of the field. It's very subtle. And there's the sweaty stench again. It's freakin' weird."

229

"I'm getting that, too." He sniffed hard, then continued scanning the crowd. I watched him for a moment before returning my eyes to Shannon.

"What the hell are you?" I blurted after a minute.

"I think Detherina told you already." Car shot me a glare.

"Bullshit," I coughed. "You're not a Binarian. If you think I'm buying that crap, you're wrong."

"We can discuss that another time." He motioned to the field. The band had finished their segment, and the team was running to take the field again.

"Whatever." I changed the subject. "He's creeping me out," I said, pointing to Mr. Ax.

"Who?" Car followed with his eyes.

"Him. There's something evil seeping from that guy. I can feel it but I can't explain it."

"Darryl?" Car asked with a puzzled grimace.

"Bro, I'm not talking about Darryl." I pointed again. "Him. The teacher standing next to Shannon."

"What the hell are you talking about? There's only Shannon and Darryl." Car said, sounding exasperated.

Mr. Ax was standing next to Shannon in plain sight. As if on cue, our eyes met, and he saluted in my direction.

"Him. Mr. Ax!" The noise around us started to get louder, making conversation difficult.

Car's eyes widened and shouted back, "Ax? Fucking Axhatas?"

"What did you say?" I asked.

"Axhatas!" He pulled an unusual looking weapon from his jacket. "He's one of the Pratrim leaders. No wonder Matro's all freaked out and I can't see him. We have hard time seeing him or the others away from our realm. It's an advantage he has over us."

"You can't see him right now?"

Carionis shook his head and moved forward, pushing several students out of his way.

"Where are you going?" I held him back. "What the hell is that in your hand? Is that a throwing star?"

It was made of transparent metal or some type of glass. The shape resembled our version of hira shuriken—palm-sized wheel blades with six spikes—except Car's weapon had black liquid inside. With its multiple sharp points, it looked lethal.

"It's called kordag and is our best bet for incapacitating him." Car responded, shaking off my grip.

"How in the world are you going to aim at someone you can't see?" I asked. I was starting to panic.

"I won't, but you will."

"What? We can't fight here. There are hundreds of witnesses."

"We don't have much of a choice."

"This is insane," I shouted above the clamor of the crowd.

Car stopped and turned, his face menacing. "You think your presence alone can save Shannon? Bro, you better get your head straight. These beings . . . they're going to kill."

That decided it. I realized I was willing to murder these creatures I hadn't even known existed a mere month ago to keep Shannon safe. "Fine, tell me what to do."

"You've watched cartoons. Just do what they did." He pressed the weapon onto my palm and pushed me forward.

We jogged toward the sidelines. "I'll aim wherever you throw for backup, even if I can't see him. Matro's already on alert."

My camera hung limp around my neck, and the crowds

hooted and hollered around us. After another rumble of thunder, the sky opened, and rain came pouring down. Most of the spectators went for cover, creating instant pandemonium.

We got close, but before I could launch the kordag, Mr. Ax seized Shannon by the neck and blew something in her mouth. Green smoke puffed around them while she struggled against his hold.

"Watch out!" I yelled, causing several students to whip around. They stopped in their tracks, which made it impossible to get through without pushing them out of the way. Darryl sprang into action. He pulled Mr. Ax back, but Ax struck him in the chest with his fist, sending him flying across the grass. Then five Ergans appeared out of nowhere, running over the students who blocked their way.

"Ergans!" I dug my feet harder into the ground. Car was already slinging one kordag after another, and Matro and his group engaged the monstrous creatures. Screams of terror broke out from witnesses, and they scrambled around, making it difficult for us to fight. "He blew something into Shannon's mouth," I yelled to Matro.

"Oh, hell!" Matro cursed, veering in another direction to fight off an Ergan that was running toward me.

Mr. Ax sneered when we locked eyes. I couldn't hear what he said, but I understood the movement of his lips.

She's not pure anymore!

Furious, I threw the kordag in his direction and was surprised at the speed of the weapon. My throw wasn't bad either, although it only grazed Ax's shoulder. Then just like that, he disappeared, and Shannon slumped to the ground.

Am I too late? I had failed to do my job. Terror shot through me like a runaway train.

"Shannon!" When I reached her, she was writhing on the ground. I dropped to my knees and pressed my ear to her chest. Good, strong heartbeat. I cradled her in my arms. "Shannon, please. Please say something."

Darryl moaned a few feet away.

"Car, can you check on Darryl?"

"Got him." Car rushed over to him. Meanwhile, Matro and the others finished off the remaining beasts.

The chaos continued, screams competing with the furious storm. The downpour soaked the students who lay scattered across the field. Frantic instructions from Mr. Delson came over the loudspeakers. "Stay off the field. Everyone get off the field."

Shannon groaned, her rapid heartbeat slowing down.

"Hey, baby, say something."

She shivered in her damp clothes and peered through the haze of lingering green smoke around us.

"Are you okay?" I asked, swiping the damp hair off her face.

She nodded weakly. "I'm lightheaded."

I glanced at Car, who picked up Darryl like he weighed nothing and slung him over his shoulder. "We need to go."

"Let's take them to my place. It's less than a mile away," Car said.

"Where's Matro?"

Matro appeared by my side within seconds. He checked on Shannon first, then closed his eyes for a brief moment. When he opened them, he turned to the rest of his men. "Wipe out everyone's memory. Make sure you cover every witness." He led them away in grim silence.

Mark came running to us with his helmet in his hand. "What the hell just happened?" he asked.

"We'll explain in the car." Car began walking fast, his boots making sloshing sounds on the rain-soaked ground.

I followed, with Shannon in my arms. "What is going on?" she asked.

"You'll be fine." I brushed my lips against her hair.

"I'll drive." Mark offered. When we reached my car, I helped Shannon stand up. She leaned against the car door while I tossed the keys to Mark. Then we got into the back with Darryl, while Car took the front passenger seat.

Car and I recounted the series of events for Mark. Once we had finished explaining, he shook his head in utter disbelief. "Are you trying to tell me that Mr. Ax isn't human either? How come we can see him and Car can't?"

"That bastard is using mind tricks against us, making it difficult for us to track him outside Pratrim and Tranak." Car heaved a sigh. "This is just shitty."

I agreed. Until we had Shannon somewhere safe, I wasn't going to be able to process everything that had happened. Then I had an idea. "Matro!" I exclaimed, rubbing the rock-card in my pocket.

Almost at once, a whirlwind surrounded the car, lifting us off the ground.

"What the hell?" Mark shouted.

"Relax. Matro's taking us on a shortcut," Car answered.

In just a blink of an eye, we arrived at Car's house.

"House" was an understatement. The place was a fortress, set deep in the higher hills of Griffith Park. Secluded as it was, there was no way we could have found our way on our own. The moment the car hit the ground, we all spilled out of the car in a hurry.

The walls and fences surrounding Car's domain were made of gleaming metal. It looked like a movie set rather than someone's home.

"This is the only way we can stay hidden," Matro explained, reading my thoughts. "Ergans and their leaders can't penetrate metal. They won't be able to catch our scent or hear our conversation."

I raised an eyebrow at this piece of information.

"It's a long story. We'll talk about it another time."

Shannon looked up to me, ignoring the conversation going on around her. "I can walk."

It was obvious that she was way too weak to make it on her own. "No. Let me carry you."

I didn't wait for her protest and gathered her in my arms. We headed into a long, dark hallway that led to a metal door, which was etched with a familiar symbol.

"What does it mean?" Mark asked while we walked through it.

"That's the crest of Tranak. I'm sure you've seen it before." Car flicked his fingers and the darkened room we'd entered was suddenly bathed in light.

It dawned on me where I'd seen the symbol before. It was identical to the marking on Shannon's neck.

The house was remarkably cold—the metal must have had something to do with the abrupt drop in temperature. When we approached the last bedroom in the hallway, Car pressed a button on the wall. The door swung open, revealing a spacious room with a rather large bed in the middle that was covered with a black canopy.

"Help her onto the bed."

"Is she going to be okay?" I asked, lowering Shannon down with extreme care.

Rather than answer, Matro gave her a quick inspection once

she'd been tucked in. Then he shook his head, his eyes flickering with rage.

"She's going to be fine, but I'm sure Detherina won't be happy," he said in a low voice.

Car signaled for us to follow him out of the room.

I patted Shannon's arm. "I'm going to find something warm for you to drink. Just rest here."

"What happened?" Her hold on my hand tightened.

"I'm trying to find out, okay? Get some rest. I'll be back."

I followed Matro to another room, where we found Mark and Car sitting on a sofa by the fireplace.

"Let me go check on Darryl," Matro said, and left the room.

I took a seat between Car and Mark. "Is Darryl going to be okay?"

"Yes. Axhatas only pounded him with low-grade voltage. If he'd gone for more, Darryl would look like a fried chicken," Car said.

Matro returned. "Darryl's fine. I gave him something for the shock."

I released a relieved breath at the news. "I want to know what the hell Mr. Ax meant when he said—"

A swish of air blew around us, cutting me off and scattering embers from the hearth. In the blink of an eye, Detherina was in our midst. Mark shrank back, caught off guard by her abrupt arrival.

"He got to my daughter!" Detherina's eyes burned with rage.

Dagger

A fearful hush swept across the room like frigid air.
Detherina's gentle demeanor had been replaced by a ferocity that
sent chills up my spine. I glanced at the rest of the men in the
room, and noticed that even Matro appeared unnerved.

Car managed to offer an almost inaudible response. "I
couldn't see Axhatas, your grace."

"Silence!" Detherina floated across the room toward him as
if her feet weren't touching the ground.

Mark's gasp was as loud as my pounding heartbeat. I pressed
against the wall, out of the line of fire. "Keep quiet," I murmured
to him.

"I gave you one simple task—to watch my daughter and
keep her away from that creature. Now she is tainted." If fury
had a face, this would be it.

Matro stepped forward, his head bowed, and spoke.

"Detherina, you know Axhatas plays a dirty game. He's using our inability to track him against us."

Detherina pivoted in his direction. I could see that she didn't appreciate the interruption. "Did you train the boy?" She pointed at me.

I tried to shrink inside my skin. I had to say something before she turned her wrath on me.

"I—"

In a heartbeat, Matro had moved to me and placed a hand on my shoulder to keep me from talking. "He's had a little training. It's my fault. I just felt that he needed more answers first."

The man spoke in riddles. I turned my head to look at him. "What are you talking about? I clipped Ax on the shoulder."

Detherina's glare moved over to me. "Axhatas. You got him?"

"Yeah. My kordag hit him on the shoulder before he disappeared. I'm not sure how much damage I did, though."

This seemed to appease Detherina. "That is good enough for me."

"Is there more stuff I need to know?"

"There are many things you will soon learn." The sting in her voice was gone, but her tone was still hard and forceful. "There are secrets that were kept from you, but I'm afraid the time has come for you to learn who you really are." She turned to Matro. "You're going to stick to them like glue. You will not leave his doorstep. You will not conceal yourself from them anymore. And I want you to arrange for all necessary back-up."

The rest of her instructions were spoken in a language I'd heard just once before. I stared at them, wishing someone would answer the questions that were swirling inside my head.

"Yes, your grace." Matro's gaze rested on me before he

bowed his head to her in reverence.

"Tell Elizabeth to stay home from now on. No more posing as a clairvoyant. Also, find a way to get this boy ready to leave. Where is Shannon?"

Ready to leave?

"She's resting in the bedroom." Matro straightened up and led Detherina into the hallway, leaving the rest of us behind.

Carionis looked like a wet puppy, pitiful and embarrassed. It was a solid minute before any of us uttered a word.

Mark broke the silence. "What the hell is going on here?"

My shoulder twitched once, and before I could brace myself, a barrage of spasms rocked my body and my mouth let loose. "Fuck! Fuck!" I bit down on my lip hard to keep the profanity from escaping. No one laughed. Car gave me one of those compassionate looks that I hated, but Mark knew better.

As if Car knew what I was thinking, he cleared his throat and strode to a window that overlooked a whole lot of nothing besides the walls that protected his property.

"There is much to do now that Axhatas has marked Shannon." I got the impression that he was as pissed as I was.

"What did he do to her?"

"You remember the green smoke?"

I nodded.

"Every single Aarmark becomes a target as we close in on our prime. When our enemy manages to spit that green smoke, it's like a homing beacon. They will know her location anywhere she goes. So it's going to be hairy from this point on."

"What can we do about it?" Axhatas *spat* on her? What in the hell did he mean? A few more jerks rocked my body, and I braced my hand against the wall.

Car threw me a quick glance before returning his attention

outside the window. "It can be reversed, but her days here are numbered anyway."

"Numbered? What the hell are you talking about?" I felt a surge of anger and fisted Car's jacket collar, pinning him against the window.

His eyes flashed, but he didn't fight back. "She has to leave after she turns eighteen. I know Matro already explained the maturation process to you."

The thought of Shannon leaving made me want to cry. "What's next?" I released Car and rubbed my temples.

"You will graduate and finish your business here while Matro gives you a crash course on everything you need to know." Car turned and looked at me. "There are things you will learn about yourself that will change everything you believe about your life."

I smacked my palm against my forehead in frustration. "What are you talking about? You know I'm getting sick of all these vague hints."

"I'm not at a liberty to say. Detherina has ordered Matro to fill you in." The earlier rage I'd seen in his eyes made way to gloom. "Just brace yourself. It will change you."

With a sigh, I turned on my heel and sat down next to Mark. "I guess all I can do is wait for the 'right' time." I muttered with as much sarcasm as I could muster.

"I wish I could offer you answers, but I would only confuse you more," Car said.

Mark was fidgeting in his seat, something he hadn't done before. 'Mr. Cool' was acting like he was ready to bolt.

"If you can't offer answers about me, why don't you tell me what you really are."

Car turned to us, a shadow crossing his face. "I'm not a

Binarian. I come from a long line of protectors to the throne. When Detherina was threatened, I came here to help out. I wish I could do more, considering Shannon is . . . "

I moved to the edge of the sofa. "Shannon is what?"

He took a deep breath and closed his eyes. From my vantage point, I could see his pained expression.

"I have been watching Shannon all her life. I didn't expect it would come to this."

"Are you in love with her?" That was the million-dollar question, even though I didn't want to hear his answer. I didn't think I could handle it.

"What I feel is not important." He sighed, as if in resignation. "You're her Prodian. That is your destiny."

A twitch rocked my shoulders again, and I bobbed my head back and forth in an attempt to keep tics at bay. I felt like a bomb ready to explode.

"Her protector?" I stood up and paced, my hands in my pockets to hide the tremors. "I can't even control my Tourette's."

"It will leave you in time."

Bingo! His words were the answer to my years of prayers. The end was in sight. But at what price?

"I can't answer the when and the why. That is for you to discover." Car reached inside his pocket and produced a pack of gum, popping a stick in his mouth. "Want some?"

I shook my head. However, Mark raised his hand, acting more like his old self. Car tossed him a stick, and Mark caught it. Silence followed while Car rocked on his heels.

"I'm going to bounce. Coming?" I asked Mark. He nodded and rose to his feet. Then I turned to Car. "Can I see Shannon before I go?"

Car shrugged. "Darryl should be clear to go with you. I'll

241

check on him in the morning and see you guys in school."

"How are we getting home?" Mark asked once we stepped into the hallway.

"Matro will take you guys home," Car replied before the door closed once more.

I retraced my way back to the room where we'd left Shannon, and Mark set off to get Darryl. When I entered the bedroom, I found Detherina staring at her daughter's resting form. Debating whether to stay or go, I hovered by the door.

Why in the hell was this happening to us? Why me? Why Shannon? It was one thing to be her designated protector, but another to be surrounded by unanswered questions.

"You're right. There are things you will need to know soon, but I'm afraid the information you want is held by another person." Detherina didn't look away from Shannon while she spoke.

"Another person?" I inched forward and stood next to her.

Detherina nodded. When she turned to me, exhaustion was clear in the drooping of her mouth, the bags underneath her eyes, and the sag of her shoulders. "Yes. I am not the one who may reveal these details."

"Would I know who to ask? Or is that person going to come to me with the truth?" It looked like I was back at square one.

"There is no denying that the time has come for you to discover the truth."

With a wave of her hand, she produced a small dagger. The blade was wavy and double-edged, and it broadened toward the hilt. The sheath and handle were made of wood. It reminded me of ancient weapons I'd seen online.

"This is for you."

"For me?" I took the diminutive weapon and studied it. The

blade was rusty, but nothing a good scrubbing couldn't fix. There were carved markings on the wooden handle. A strange sensation flowed through me while I held it. There was a sense of familiarity I couldn't explain. "Why are you giving this to me?" I asked.

Detherina smiled and looked at Shannon once again. "I will answer that question as soon as you receive your revelation. For now, just know that it is very special."

There we went with the riddles again. If it didn't stop soon, I was going to go crazy. "Anything else I *don't* need to know?"

Detherina pinned me a glare. "You seem so impatient, and yet I sense hesitation in you. Once you learn the truth, I assure you that you will come to appreciate the cocoon of your ignorance."

Rather than reply, I asked a different question. "Will Shannon be okay?"

Detherina closed her eyes for a brief moment. When she turned to face me again, her eyes were like a television. Events and characters flashed before me like they were on a screen. I stumbled backward, and a round of tremors rocked my body. She caught my arm to steady me.

"Is that Shannon and me?" I asked, unable to cope with what I'd seen. We were saying our goodbyes.

"Yes, it will be happening soon."

"What did Axhatas mean by Shannon not being pure anymore?"

Detherina's face darkened, and her eyes turned cloudy. "She's putrefied. He did it to weaken my position. For every Aarmark family, there is one particular member whose fate also affects the head of the unit. In our case, that person is Shannon, since she's my offspring. Our position was already compromised by her father's death. I'm afraid that the progression of the putrefaction would force me to surrender my position and allow our enemies to wage an all-out war with us again."

"What is putrefaction?" I asked, not liking the sound of the word at all.

"It's a terrible decomposition of the corporeal being. It is fortunate that this happened here. The effects won't be as intense as they would have been if she were in Tranak, and we will soon be able to reverse the process."

It took me a few moments to digest the information. Shannon stirred on the bed, and I shot a quick glance at her.

"If that's the case, why would you move her there?"

"The reversal must be performed in Tranak. The circumstances are complicated, but I can assure you that she'll be fine. I will not allow it to progress. Shannon will be her old self in a matter of hours. She won't remember much of today's events until her birthday. The day after, she will be taken to our home, and the process of removal can commence. The method is tiresome, but it's her chance to expel Axhatas' hold on her."

"So after her birthday, she goes?" The prospect was enough to trigger another set of tics. While I shuddered and tried to control the spasms, Detherina touched my arm, and a vibration flowed through my system, effectively halting any further shaking.

"What about . . . her and me?"

"The future is always full of surprises. Don't give up just yet. Now, you should go home." Detherina pulled me into a brisk hug.

Once she released me from her fierce embrace, I walked to the door to give her the chance to be alone with Shannon.

"And, Brian, don't worry about calamities you can't prevent.

They are going to happen whether you know ahead of time or not. The Ergans are toying with you, making you question your sanity so you will want to step away."

A few minutes later, I walked out of the house and to my car trailed by Mark and Darryl, who still appeared dazed. I had one lingering thought. How could I *not* worry about my dreams when innocent people were the ones being targeted?

Aarmark Maturity

Luck was still with me. Thanks to Matro, we all made it home in plenty of time. When my parents came back from the fundraiser around midnight, I was already showered and in bed.

There was a knock on my door, and I pretended to have been asleep. "Hi," I said in a groggy voice.

Dad poked his head in the door. "I'm just checking on you."

"How was the fundraiser?" I asked, wiping the pretend sleep from my eyes. At the rate I was going, an acting career might be in my future.

"It went well. Your mother won something at the silent auction. She is now the proud owner of an autographed book by Dr. Phil."

"Are you kidding me?"

Dad shook his head and laughed, and I joined in. Then he opened the door wider and stepped into my room. I sat upright, not knowing what to expect.

"I was thinking things over tonight," he began, making himself comfortable next to me.

All ears, I leaned against the headboard and waited for him to continue.

"I don't want you to miss your first-ever dance, and I hate the thought of you being grounded on your birthday, too."

Dad was right. This would be my first time attending a dance, or any social function for that matter. But the real reason this one was special was because I was taking Shannon. With all the excitement and commotion, I'd forgotten that it would be my birthday as well. Eighteen wasn't a big deal to me, except that I would be able to emancipate myself from my parents, if necessary.

"Thanks, Dad," I said, grinning like an idiot.

"There is one thing I want to ask of you." He waited for me to settle down. "Pick your battles. Life is difficult enough as it is, so think things through before you act. Always remember that a handful of patience is worth more than a bushel of brains." He pulled me into a tight hug. "I love you, son."

"I love you, too, Dad," I answered, feeling a sense of déjà vu.

He released me and left my bedroom, and I thought about what he'd said. Before my run-ins with Kevin, I'd led a pretty quiet life, content to stay in the background. I did wonder about the reasons behind his change of heart, but I wasn't going to complain.

I was about to turn off the light when another light tap sounded on my door.

Dad came back into my room. "I want you to have this." He held out a pendant of a rose in the center of a circle that was attached to a tri-color rope. It was about the size of a half dollar and quite heavy.

"It was your grandma's. I want you to have it. Just a reminder of how much you mean to me. You can give it to someone special one day."

"Thanks Dad." I wasn't sentimental by nature, but couldn't stop the tears that pooled in my eyes. "It's beautiful."

When he left, I swore I could see tears in his eyes. A bit too emotional to think about anything else, I turned off the lamp and stared into the darkness, fantasizing about the perfect dance with the perfect girl.

Sleep, which had once been my escape from reality, had turned into torture, the visions coming at me in waves. It became a constant struggle to accept that I couldn't save everyone. That night was no different. I woke up drenched in sweat after yet another dreadful nightmare.

Countless catastrophes and senseless deaths flashed before my eyes, haunting me while I padded along the dark, quiet hallway and down to the first floor. I turned on the kitchen light and pulled out a carton of milk from the fridge, wracking my brain for a clue as to what needed to be done.

At such an ungodly hour, I doubted that Mark or Darryl would appreciate a wakeup call, so I returned to my bedroom, feeling drained. This time, I sank into a restless sleep, tossing and turning and waking up every hour. At around six in the morning, I gave up and turned on the television. There was nothing on but infomercials, so I went ahead and popped a DVD into the player to pass the time.

It was about nine when I jerked awake to discover the sun was peeking through the blinds. I got my phone to reach Mark, but the call went straight to his voicemail. "Hey Marko, call me as soon as you get this," I said and hung up.

A few minutes later, a grouchy Mark returned my call. "This had better be good," he said.

"Bro, I had another dream." I recounted all the details while Mark listened. Once I'd chronicled each frightening aspect, I asked, "What should I do?"

When Mark spoke this time, he sounded awake. "You mentioned Detherina said something to you about your dreams last night."

"Yeah. She wants me to keep quiet about the visions, but I don't understand why I can't try to prevent them."

"Look, if we don't have the when, who, and where, there's not much we can do anyway. You said yourself that you have no idea who'll be hit."

"I guess all I can do is keep an eye on the news to see if I come up with any clues. It still doesn't feel like I'm doing enough, though."

"I'll help as much as I can," Mark said. "Oh, before I forget —happy birthday, dude. We'll have to celebrate tonight."

"Thanks, bro. I'll see you later."

Once we'd hung up, I got up and went to shower. Now that I was allowed to go to the dance, I didn't have to hide any preparations from my parents. My closet was filled with raggedy school clothes, so I had eight hours to find something decent to wear and get a corsage for Shannon.

The house was humming with morning activity by the time I made an appearance, ready to tackle the task at hand. Dad looked up from the newspaper when I walked into the kitchen.

"Good morning," I said with a grin, moving through the kitchen to give my mother a sloppy kiss on the cheek.

She turned around and beamed at me. Dad joined her in

singing "Happy Birthday" to me while she took a cake out of the fridge. When they'd finished, Dad produced a lighter and lit the candle.

"Make a wish," Mom said.

I closed my eyes, wished for Shannon's safety, then blew out the flame.

Mom put the cake on the table. "We'll have some after breakfast."

"Okay," I smiled, totally on board with the plan. It was carrot cake, after all—my favorite.

Then she took an envelope from her apron pocket. "This is for you."

"Thanks, guys."

"They watched me attack the envelope, in which I found a hundred-dollar gift card from a local game store. This was a big change from all birthday presents I had gotten in the past. Grateful for their thoughtfulness, I pulled both of them into a hug. "You guys are so cool! This calls for a shopping trip."

"You seem . . . happy," Mom observed.

I nodded to my dad. "Dad gave me the go-ahead for the homecoming dance."

Mom's mouth hung open for a beat before she broke into a big smile. "Oh, that's great! Your first dance!"

"Actually, I'm headed out after breakfast to find something decent to wear."

"Gerald, why don't you take him to your tailor? I bet he can put together something 'cool' for him." She winked at me before turning her attention back to the bacon sizzling in the skillet.

The way she emphasized 'cool' made me want to squirm. "Um, I can go to the mall and find something," I muttered.

"Nonsense. Omar will have you looking spiffy in no time."

Dad rose from his seat and folded the paper.

Spiffy? "Really, I don't want to take up your time, Dad." Somehow, I managed to avoid sounding unappreciative.

"Finish your breakfast, and we can leave in an hour. Let me call Omar so he can meet us at the shop."

I ate, torn between happiness and misery. Hideous Elvis outfits, stiff-looking suits, and candy-colored blazers flashed before my eyes. Resigned to the inevitable, I met Dad in the garage.

With the roadster's top down, conversation was next to impossible, so we drove in relaxed silence. Watching the buildup of early Saturday traffic, I began to daydream about Shannon. I also worried some about the dagger Detherina had given me. Carrying weapons to school-sanctioned events was forbidden, but I wondered if it would be smart to carry the dagger anyway.

We stopped in front of a shop that wasn't even open yet, but the moment we stepped out of the car, the glass doors swung wide and a smiling, short man came out to greet us.

"Gerry, it's a pleasure to see you." The gentleman shook dad's hand and ushered us inside. Apparently, the shop didn't open until noon and this was a VIP service he was offering to one of his most treasured clients.

"Omar, thanks for coming on short notice. I owe you one." Dad made himself comfortable on one of the plush leather sofas.

I looked around, and my earlier qualms disappeared. Rows of mannequins, decked out in cool suits, lined the display window.

Omar regarded me with interest, running his gaze up and down until I wanted to squirm. "So you're about six-one, around one hundred seventy pounds. Am I correct?"

Close enough. I nodded and stashed my hands in my pockets

to keep the tics from rolling. Being inspected like that made me nervous.

"Follow me. I'll show you the suits we have."

We walked through several rooms until we came to an area with clothing that looked appropriate for people my age. I'd heard Dad talk about Omar being a celebrity favorite, but I hadn't believed him. Now that I'd seen the shop, I swore never to doubt my father again.

Omar stopped by a rack, pulled out a dark grey suit, and held it up. "What do you think of this one?"

My knowledge of fashion was limited to T-shirts and jeans, so this was a good time to defer to an expert. "That looks cool."

He beamed at me and then took me to the dressing room "The slim cut will make you look taller."

I nodded in reply.

He came back and handed me a crisp white shirt and a tie that would match Shannon's outfit. We were done and back in the car in less than two hours.

"Where to now? You need a corsage for Shannon, right?" Dad merged into the swelling weekend traffic.

"I can go by myself if you have stuff to do."

"Oh, c'mon. I'm never too busy for my son." He reached across to pat my back. "But before we go to your mom's florist, let's grab some lunch."

That was another surprise. My dad was a busy man, and I respected his work enough not to make unnecessary demands of him. We had a good relationship because we honored each other's boundaries. Besides, I was pretty much self-sufficient at my age. Even so, I wouldn't turn down an opportunity to spend some time with him. "I'd like that."

"Pick the place," he said.

For the next hour, we chowed down on hotdogs while he reminisced about his high school days. He regaled me with stories about playing football, his friends, and the pretty girls he took to different dances. These were things he hadn't told me before.

It was shortly after two by the time we got done with all our errands, leaving me with some spare time to relax and get a few games in before I had to get dressed.

I sent Shannon a quick text. **Are u ready for 2nite?**

She responded right away. **So excited. How are you going to get past your parents?**

Dad ungrounded me. Will pick you up at 6PM. Be ready.

Awesome. I'll be ready. Can't wait to see you.

To kill time, I played a game of *L.O.L.* then tuned in to the news as Mark and I had discussed. There was nothing out of the ordinary being reported. I watched for thirty minutes before heading for the shower.

For once, my hair cooperated, and the suit did make me look taller, just as Omar had predicted. It fit just right. I felt like the star of a spy movie. After I'd decided against bringing the dagger, I stowed the kordag and Matro's calling card in the inner pocket of my jacket.

"You're so handsome, baby boy." Mom glowed with motherly pride when I made my appearance in the living room.

Uncomfortable under her heavy scrutiny, I mumbled a quick thanks.

Dad didn't help at all. He snapped one picture after another, and all the attention was making me nervous, triggering some unwanted tics. I squared my shoulders and tried my damnedest to look unruffled. Once my parents were satisfied, we trekked across the lawn to our neighbor's house.

Gilbert opened the front door, nodding his approval at my appearance, then dipped his head in greeting. "Hello, Dr. and Mrs. Morrison. I am Gilbert, Elizabeth's cousin from out of town. Shannon and her mother will be right down." He ushered us into the living room to wait. "Have a seat. May I offer you anything to drink?"

"We're fine. Thank you," Dad replied, while Mom merely shook her head.

Gilbert disappeared, and within minutes, the sound of descending footsteps came from the stairwell. Shannon paused at the foot of the landing, looking more stunning than ever.

In awe, I stood up with my mouth open, holding onto the box containing the corsage. Elizabeth followed her, fussing over Shannon's gown. The black dress hugged her curves like it had been designed for her. The gold ribbon twisting across her waistline reminded me of a Greek goddess, and the tiny braid framing her face made her look regal. I stared at her, holding my breath and unable to move, until she took my hand and squeezed it.

"Curly, is there something wrong?" she whispered, her blue eyes searching my face. Up close, she was even more gorgeous. Best of all, there were no signs that she had any permanent damage from the incident the day before.

Dad jumped to the rescue. "I'm betting Brian is thinking you're a vision of loveliness."

This snapped out of my trance, and I smiled awkwardly and cleared my throat. "Y-yes, you're breathtaking."

Shannon blushed at my praise. "Thank you."

Still feeling giddy, I opened the corsage box, which held a white rose surrounded by tiny flowers. "This is for you."

"It's beautiful."

"Just like you are," I whispered in her ear. She reddened again. In a louder voice, I added, "Here, let me put it on you."

I spent long, excruciating seconds trying to figure how to attach the corsage to her gown without making it seem like I was playing 'pin the tail on the donkey'.

Elizabeth took pity on me and stepped in to help. Once it was secure in its place, Shannon pinned a boutonniere on my lapel (without any problem, much to my embarrassment). After another round of picture-taking, this time from both Dad and Gilbert, the parents began chatting among themselves, leaving Shannon and me to our own devices. The reprieve let me relax, and it gave us a few minutes of alone time.

She pulled me onto the patio. "Close your eyes," she said.

"What's going on?"

"Just close them, will you?"

I complied. The sound of her footsteps faded away but soon returned.

"Okay, you can open them."

Shannon was standing in front of me, holding a bunch of balloons in different colors and a wrapped present.

"Happy birthday!" she squealed. "You thought I forgot, huh?"

"To be honest, I'm the one who forgot about it."

"You're something else. Who forgets his own birthday?"

We laughed together. It was a nice feeling, being with her. The night was just beginning, and we were already having a great time.

"Open it." She held out the gift to me.

"Now?"

"Now," she said with a little hint of impatience.

I ripped open the paper. Inside the box was a picture frame

that held the photo of us laughing together at the Huntington Garden. It was the candid shot I had taken of us on that trip.

"Thank you. I don't know what to say." I looked up to find Shannon giving me a wide smile.

"Say you'll put it on your nightstand."

"You bet I will."

Murmuring came from inside the house, and we saw the adults watching us from the opposite side of the glass door. Mom had tears in her eyes, and Dad was whispering in her ear and rubbing her back. Shannon and I glanced back at each other, both blushing dark pink.

A few minutes later, Mark and Darryl arrived with both dates and parents, and the barrage of pictures and posing started up again. Once the photographic assault came to an end, we were able to pile in the limo. I didn't let go of Shannon's hand during the duration of our ride to the hotel.

When we reached the venue, my arm was resting around Shannon's shoulder as if it was the most natural thing in the world. It was nice knowing that, for a change, there was a girl who wasn't embarrassed to be seen with me.

"Ready?" I whispered in her ear.

Shannon gave me a big smile when she looked up. "Ready as I'll ever be."

The Prom

Everything was a first for me that evening, from the limo to attending a party with other kids my age—not to mention having a *date*. I savored every minute of the experience.

Throughout the evening, I showered Shannon with compliments. She had no idea how her blushing reaction boosted my confidence. If I could have this effect on Shannon McKesson, then the whole world had better be ready for me.

Shannon was my main focus all night, so it didn't escape my notice that she tapped her foot with the beat of every song. I tried to distract her with small talk, hoping my engaging personality would make her not mind that we weren't dancing.

It didn't work. As soon as a popular, extra-bouncy song blasted from the speakers, she tugged at my arm. "Would you like to dance?"

Okay. This was going to shatter my perfect night. My

shoulders sagged at the thought of making a fool of myself in the middle of the dance floor with my two left feet.

"I can't dance."

Shannon's face fell.

Darn it. Here goes nothing. "Just kidding!" I said. "You gotta see my moves." I tried to paste on an enthusiastic smile. *What in the world am I thinking?*

Shannon looked worried anyway. "Are you sure you're up for this?"

"Of course." I waved my hand with a flourish and stood, ushering her to the dance floor. Other kids crowded the dance area and were hopping around like grasshoppers. Running through a quick plan in my head, I intended to jump around and pretend I was having a seizure. It might just pass as a cool dance move.

We sandwiched ourselves between Darryl and Mark and their dates. Despite my reluctance, I let go of Shannon's hand and straightened my jacket. Then I plunged into the abyss and began moving with a confidence I didn't possess. Looking like an idiot was unavoidable, but I had to try for Shannon's sake. She was too pretty to be a wallflower.

Shannon's eyes widened, and then she giggled. Caught off guard, I threw a quick glance to check if anyone else was paying attention to me. Darryl howled in laughter before mimicking my moves. My best friend was doing me a favor by risking looking like an idiot. That was what I called loyalty. Thanks to him, I wasn't the only fool on the dance floor.

To my surprise, Shannon and Mary Kate started following our routine. Before I knew it, all the kids were dancing like we were. The sight was too weird, but at least no one was making fun of me. By the time the music ended, my jacket was clinging to my sweat-drenched body, but I felt more at ease. I couldn't believe that I had actually enjoyed myself.

Mr. Delson approached the stage and motioned for everyone to settle down. "Listen up. We are about to announce our homecoming King and Queen."

The jubilant students clapped, adding to the already charged atmosphere

I clasped Shannon's hand while Mr. Delson conferred with the homecoming president. Then he walked back to the microphone. The next thing I knew, my name was being called and everyone was congratulating me.

I had no idea how my shaky legs managed to carry me to the stage amid the backslapping and congratulatory handshakes. The fact that I didn't stumble was a plus. Good thing the nerd gods weren't out to get me tonight. I had to squint when I stood under the bright stage lights.

"Congratulations," Mr. Delson said, shaking my hand and placing the oversized plastic crown on my head.

A short tremor went through me while I struggled to keep the crown from sliding off my head. "Thanks, Mr. Delson."

"You've come a long way, kid. Just keep your nose clean." He clapped me on the back and then returned to the microphone.

"Our homecoming queen won by a landslide—none other than Shannon McKesson!" Mr. Delson beamed.

I jumped up and down on the stage. The constellations had aligned. I was the luckiest boy on the planet.

Shannon had more poise than anyone I'd ever known while she walked to the stage. Her gown made her look like a queen. Our eyes were locked to each other, and my body felt as if it was going to melt. Overwhelmed, I kept my hands inside my pockets to prevent another round of tics.

Once Mr. Delson had lowered the crown on her head and handed her the scepter, he waved me to come forward and introduced us together as king and queen. Another round of applause erupted, and I took Shannon's hand without even thinking about it. It seemed so natural. Mr. Delson raised his hand to silence the crowd. "Hold on, we have Mark Stanton here to make an announcement."

"This should be interesting," I whispered to Shannon, who grinned back at me.

Mark cleared his throat. "Hey guys, how're you doing tonight? Having fun yet?" Everyone in the room screamed in response. Mark knew how to rally a crowd. "I just wanted to take this time to announce that today is also Brian Morrison's birthday. We're lucky to call you a friend, bro. Congratulations!"

Darryl took the microphone from Mark. "C'mon guys, say happy birthday, Brian." All the students repeated after him, and then my two buddies laughed and slapped me on the back. I had no idea what to make of it. People were cheering for the freak-with-a-tic.

"Now, let's welcome the homecoming king, queen, and their court for the customary dance," Mr. Delson announced.

"Here goes nothing," I mumbled to myself while ushering Shannon down to the middle of the dance floor. When the music began playing, I felt a shiver run down my spine, which had everything to do with my overflowing affection for the girl in my arms. Thank God we moved seamlessly together without any disasters until the song ended. It felt so good to be accepted for the way I was, like I wasn't an outsider looking in anymore. But the best part was that Shannon was positively glowing in my arms.

We kept dancing when the next song began, and soon Car

appeared with a jaw-dropping woman on his arm. She looked like she'd just walked out of a fashion magazine, making the girls around her seem like little children in their best party dresses. Her hair was black as night and reached the small of her back, and her dark gown hugged her curves, leaving every boy in the room dry-mouthed.

"Congrats, guys," Car said when they moved closer to us.

Shannon and I murmured our quick thanks.

Car wasn't bad-looking himself. His hair was slicked back, and without his usual garb, he seemed almost normal.

"This is Orida. She's a friend from out of town," he said by way of introduction.

The woman's smile was gracious when she inclined her head. Her violet eyes flicked to Shannon for a brief moment before she turned her attention to me.

"It's nice to meet the stars of the night." Orida's voice sounded like sweet velvet—husky and smooth, and I fought not to gape at her.

The music turned fast again, and this time, I strutted around with confidence. Darryl and his date joined us a few minutes later, and we ruled the dance floor until our feet ached. Shannon didn't seem to mind that my version of dancing was just a lot of twitching, coupled with spastic jerks.

At midnight, exhausted but happy, we piled into the waiting limousine.

"How about a late night birthday dinner?" Mark asked while the driver guided the vehicle away from the hotel.

"Denny's!" Darryl and I said in unison.

Mark lowered the glass divider and spoke with the driver. "Hey, Mike. Can you take us to the Denny's on Vermont, please?"

I was famished. The hotel's chicken had tasted like plastic, and eating had been the last thing on my mind while I was busy dancing with Shannon.

During our drive to the restaurant, I felt my skin prickle several times. I looked out the window and wasn't surprised to find several Ergans running alongside our vehicle. With a subtle nod and raised eyebrows, I managed to send Mark and Darryl a silent message. They looked outside and patted their pockets, understanding my warning.

It was not a surprise to find Car and Orida waiting on the sidewalk at the restaurant. Leaning against Car's motorcycle, they looked like biker models. Then Matro showed himself to me, and I knew that this had something to do with our unwanted escorts. It made me wonder if Orida had any idea that she wasn't hanging out with an ordinary group of kids.

They met us by the entrance, and Car held the door for us. "Don't worry your regal head about anything tonight. We've got you covered," he whispered.

With that promise, I allowed myself to relax. We sat at a long table, Shannon to my right and Orida next to her. The server was taking our drink orders when a news report on the television caught my eye.

In all the excitement, I'd forgotten about the dream that had plagued me. "Excuse me," I exclaimed and moved closer to the television by the counter. "Can you increase the volume, please?" I asked another server. She threw me a disgruntled glance but did as I'd asked.

"The tsunami has left twenty people dead in the small Caribbean nation," the newscaster was saying. "According to initial reports, the phenomenon was caused by an underwater disturbance. Geological and volcanic experts have gathered together and are predicting that further seismic events are likely, and the death toll could be high."

"Hey, guys!" I beckoned Mark and Darryl, trying to ignore the feeling of tics building and rolling into a tight coil inside me. The moment of shock had pushed me close to the edge. How could I have missed it? The threat was massive. Nothing and no one could take an event like this lightly.

The guys rushed to my side, and Car also turned to watch the news unfold.

"Fuckkkkk." I clamped my mouth shut and braced my shoulders while a round of tics shuddered through me.

"What the hell is going on?" Mark asked.

"This is the dream. It's going to happen. So many people are gonna die. What should I do?" Panic was in my voice.

"Calm down, boy, it will be a while before we find out what's going on," a man seated at the counter piped in.

I ignored his remark and shook my head. "We have to tell someone. Warn everyone. Give them time to prepare."

"The trouble is, we don't know where it's headed yet," Darryl said, glancing back at the television.

"He's right. Who do we even call?" Mark asked.

Car came up and pulled us aside, out of earshot. "Those bastards are getting you worked up," he said. "This is something that was going to happen no matter what. They're trying to get you all scrambled and worried so you lose your focus. I'm almost positive that they are working on something as we speak."

Mark, Darryl, and I looked at each other. "I don't know if I can sit around and wait." I was beginning to feel light-headed, so I loosened my tie.

"Well, you have to. Let's wait for the next report. In the

meantime, we'll let Matro know what's going on. He'll figure out what to do. I suggest that you don't lose sight of what's really important. You need to protect Shannon." Car glanced at the women and whispered, "This is how cunning our enemies are. They've got you wrapped around their slimy fingers."

"What should we do, then?" Mark sagged against the wall.

"Sit tight and go about your business. Orida and I will keep an eye on everything."

After a few minutes of deep breathing, I calmed down enough to return to the table. Shannon took my hand, and her warm fingers entwined with my clammy ones. "Brian, what's going on?"

She'd used my real name, a rare occurrence. I knew she could sense that something was wrong. In an attempt to reassure her, I said, "Oh, I just got a little excited over the news. I've been following tsunamis since I was a kid." Okay. That made me sounded geekier than ever.

She narrowed her eyes at me for a long time before she spoke. "I know you're keeping something from me, but I won't press tonight. You can tell me in the morning."

Under normal circumstances, I would have joked about it and maybe even teased her, but I had the sinking feeling that she wasn't going to let it go, so I nodded instead.

I chewed on my country fried steak without tasting it, trying to maintain the celebratory atmosphere for Shannon's sake. It was supposed to be a magical night, and regardless of my fears, I intended to leave her with wonderful memories. I wouldn't let anything ruin the evening for her.

Casualty

The limousine dropped us off in front of Shannon's house. From a distance, I could make out the idling engine of Car's motorcycle. The distinct, fetid scent of sweat wafted in the air, reminding me of our enemy's presence. I guided Shannon up the darkened front steps. The porch lights came on, and Gilbert opened the door.

"I was getting a snack when I heard the limousine pull up," he explained and threw a quick glance outside before stepping aside to let Shannon in.

I assumed a goodnight kiss wasn't happening since we had an audience. Though I was disappointed, Shannon's safety came first. That was the rational part of me speaking. The other part of me was pitching a fit that I had to miss this chance.

"I'll talk to you in the morning?" Shannon asked, flashing a sweet smile that made me want to take her into my arms.

Instead of reacting to my adolescent urges, I slipped my hands into my pockets and kept them there. "I'll call you."

To my utter surprise, Shannon leaned forward and kissed me on the cheek. A flush of heat radiated across my body at the contact, and all I could do was grin back like an idiot. Good things were worth waiting for, and she was a perfect example of something that was worth the wait.

"Thanks for the perfect night, Curly," she whispered before closing the door between us.

Perfect. What more could I have asked for? Whistling, I skipped across their lawn to ours. It felt like I'd conquered the world. Nothing could dampen my high. I let myself into the house and was surprised to spy a light under my parents' bedroom door. With no reason now to tiptoe, I climbed the stairs, all the while basking in the glow of Shannon's lips touching my skin.

I stopped in front of my parents' bedroom door and pressed my ear against the wood.

"Brian, is that you?" Mom asked.

"Yeah." I turned the knob and pushed the door open. I expected to see her reading while my dad sprawled on the bed, snoring. Instead, she was in her housecoat and pacing the floor. Her puffy eyes met mine.

"What's wrong?" I looked at the empty bed. "Where's Dad?"

"I don't know. It's so unlike him not to call if he's running late." She stopped pacing to pull a tissue from the pocket of her robe.

"Maybe his phone battery died?" Yeah. That sounded lame even to me.

"I don't know. I have a bad feeling about this." Mom sniffed.

True. Dad had always been responsible when it came to

calling if he was caught up in surgery or a meeting. Besides, being a cosmetic surgeon, most of his surgeries were scheduled during the day and never on weekends. He always was home right after work, and if there were functions or galas, Mom went with him.

"C'mon, Mom. Maybe Dad went out for drinks with his friends. He'll be home soon." I tried to sound upbeat, hoping it would settle her frayed nerves.

"I'm going to wait up for him. Go to bed. It's late."

Late? It was early morning, but I wasn't going to point that out. "Okay, but you have to get some sleep, too." I kissed her on the forehead.

The door was almost closed when she called out, "How was the dance?"

I poked my head back in the door. "It was fun. I'm homecoming king."

Despite her obvious misery, Mom smiled and beckoned me. "My little boy is all grown up." She wrapped her hands around me. "I'm sure your dad will be so happy to hear about it."

"It's gotta be the suit, Mom."

She tried to smile. "It's all you baby boy."

In my bedroom, I lay awake for some time, worried about my dad. The floorboards made steady creaking noises while Mom continued her nonstop pacing. I rubbed Matro's calling card. Maybe he could help find my father.

He came right way. "You rang?"

"My dad hasn't come home. It's so unlike him not to show or call. Can you just do a drive by his office just in case?"

My own concern was reflected in his eyes. "Sure I can. Try to get some rest."

Sleep came soon. Instead of happy dreams of Shannon, the

same old nightmare plagued me. I was awakened around 5 a.m. by a loud wail from my parent's bedroom.

I stumbled out of bed and ran to their room. "Mom, what's going on?" I found her slumped on the side of the bed, her face buried in her hands.

When she looked up, terror and anguish were written all over her face. She sobbed, then hiccupped, and I dropped to my knees to gather her in my arms.

"A night cleanup crew . . . found your dad . . . " She broke down before she could finish.

"What, Mom? What about Dad?"

"He's dead," she said and dropped her head on my shoulder.

Life as I knew it began to crumble. Dad had been healthy. How could he be dead?

"What do you mean dead? We were together yesterday. He was fine."

Her continued sobs answered me. My heart pounded, and tears started to fall. I couldn't believe it. Dad was still young. "No . . . no . . . no . . . " I kept shaking my head. Maybe if I believed hard enough, it would prove to be nothing but a bad dream.

Mom and I sat on the cold, hard floor, hanging on to each other and crying over our loss. I tried my best to console her, in spite of my own grief. Many minutes passed before she pulled away. She held my face with shaking hands.

"We have to see him now."

Never had I wished for anything as fervently as I wanted him alive. I wanted to hug him and tell him how much I loved him.

The drive over to the hospital took forever. I didn't trust myself to drive, but under the circumstances, I was in better shape than Mom. She didn't say much on the way, not that there was anything either of us could say to make us feel better.

When we reached the front desk, the nurse ushered us to the waiting room, where a man in a disheveled suit flashed his badge at us.

"Mrs. Morrison, I'm Detective John Sander. I was called in when your husband was found."

This brought another bout of tears from my mom. I swallowed the lump in my throat and tried to speak. "I'm Brian, his son. What happened?"

The detective turned his beady eyes on me and nodded. "The coroner does not believe this was a natural death. We did find an empty bottle of prescription sleeping pills he'd just filled yesterday, so it looks like an overdose is a possibility."

"What?" I couldn't believe my ears.

"Overdose? Why would he do such a thing?" Mom asked in a faint voice.

"I'm sorry, but that's all the information we have at the moment. There are no overt signs of foul play, but we've dusted for fingerprints. We'll try to find out more once the autopsy is performed. We will be conducting a full investigation, but without more information, we can't rule anything out yet."

"How long before we can see him?" Mom asked. She swayed, and both Detective Sander and I helped her to the nearest chair.

"He's been transferred to the morgue. If you head over there, they can arrange for you to see him."

Hearing the word "morgue" brought fresh tears to my eyes. It sounded so final.

He was gone. It was real. But why? There was no way I'd believe that he wanted to kill himself.

The next few hours passed in a blur. We were ushered into a

cold, bright white room, where I listened to my mother's lamentations during the painful wait. Seeing his body lying cold and lifeless on a gurney hurt more than I ever thought possible, and a nurse had to help me when Mom collapsed, crushed by the weight of our overwhelming loss. It might be days before we found out what killed my father and could give him a proper burial. Deep in my heart, I knew it was the Ergans' doing, just like I knew they had caused Mr. Peter's death.

During the drive home, my guilt got the best of me. I should've spent more time with him instead of playing video games. I should've tried harder to communicate instead of running out of the house to be with my friends. There were no words that could bring him back, so I stayed silent and held my mother's hand.

When we got home, Mom did not argue when I led her to her bedroom. "You need to get some sleep," I said in a dead voice. My body shook from the tics I'd been holding in all day.

"I should make some phone calls," she said when I lifted the comforter so she could slide in. "We'll have to make arrangements, and—"

I was gentle, but firm. "You can make the calls later."

A sob tore through her when she finally rested her head on the pillow. There was no comfort I could give her, though. She would be lost without him. Things would never be right again for our family.

I turned down the wooden blinds to block out the sunlight. "If you need me, I'll be in my room," I said, leaving the door ajar when I stepped back into the hallway.

Once inside my room, I sagged to the floor, unable to handle the sudden turn of events. One minute I'd been on top of the world and the next, I was in hell. The weight of my grief began to sink in, and the tics were unleashed. I pulled a pillow from the bed and crushed it against my chest while the waves of tremors and twitches ravaged me.

"Fuck! Fuck! FUCK!"

By the time the spasms ebbed, I was drenched in sweat and angry tears streamed down my face. My father should not be dead, and no matter what the investigation found, I was certain he hadn't committed suicide.

"I think you're right," Matro said from the corner of the room.

I whipped my head around and lashed out, "Will you stop trying to give me a heart attack?"

"I didn't mean to scare you." Matro moved toward my desk and sat on the chair, his typical smirk absent for once. "I'm sorry about your father. Your mother got the call before I was able to locate him."

"He didn't kill himself," I said.

"I agree." He sighed. "Car and Orida are scouring your father's office for leads. We couldn't move in until the cops left."

"How did you know?"

"I know a lot of things," he murmured.

Maybe it was fatigue or the shock that pushed me to the edge. I jumped at Matro and directed all my anger at him. "And you didn't bother to save him? You couldn't even warn me?" I wrapped my fingers around his thick neck and squeezed.

Matro didn't fight back, although he did pry my hands from his neck. "There are many things I wish I could prevent, but I can't. Our enemies continue to grow in number, and we are not as strong as they are here in your world."

"Stop throwing riddles at me." I wiggled free from his grasp and collapsed on my bed. "Why are these things happening to me?"

"You are not yet able to see the bigger picture, my friend." Matro followed me to the bed.

"I'm tired. I'm freakin' angry and lost. Can't you tell me *anything?*"

"Believe me, I know what you are feeling. I lost so much in the war." The sorrow in his voice made me pause. "I'm still mourning my family, as I mourn for your loss and Shannon's."

I shuddered at an incoming spasm and squared my shoulders, but when Matro laid his big palm on my back, the pressure instantly disappeared. More tears threatened to spill, and I buried my face in my hands.

Matro sat beside me. "I'm sorry this had to happen. With each passing day, their strength grows greater. I'm afraid that time is running out. We must leave soon."

I lifted my face to look at him. "Who's 'we'?" I asked.

"All of us."

The faint scent of rain drifted in from the window. It comforted me until I heard a muffled noise from across the hallway. My heart skipped, and I shot out of bed and ran to my parents' bedroom. Before I could open the door, I heard a familiar voice

"I'm sorry you're grieving again, Cynthia."

Matro was right on my heels when I burst in, expecting the worst. I was surprised to find my mother and Detherina looking up at me.

"What's going on here?" I looked at my mom, at Detherina, and then back at Mom. "Can you see her?"

Mom nodded and sniffed.

"Then somebody'd better start talking!" I shouted.

272

Alpha

It was clear that my mother and Detherina knew each other. I crossed my arms and waited for an explanation.

"Why don't we talk in the kitchen while I make breakfast?" Mom said, tightening her robe.

"I'm not hungry," I snapped.

There were footsteps behind me. "Let your mother do whatever she needs to cope," Matro whispered in my ear, "and you will listen like a good boy." He turned me around to face the door.

We descended the stairs in silence, Detherina holding my mother's hand. Once we reached the kitchen, Mom went straight to the fridge. She juggled eggs, sausages, bell peppers, mushrooms, and a carton of orange juice setting them on the counter. She sliced and diced the ingredients with precise movements, looking reluctant to have the conversation we all knew was coming.

Detherina settled in the breakfast nook while Matro moved to stand behind her. I followed my mother's obsessive movement with my eyes until, unable to rein in my mounting impatience, I blurted out a question that had been bothering me.

"How do you know each other?" I directed the question at Detherina.

The set of her jaw when she leveled her eyes at me told me that I might not like her answer. "You'd better sit down," she said.

I sat down, even though I resented the additional delay. "Tell me."

"You're the son of the true leader of Tranak, Brian. Your real name is Alpha," Detherina said. She glanced in my mother's direction.

I sprang from my chair. "Mom, what is she saying?"

"It's a long story," she murmured while attacking the bell peppers.

I turned back to Detherina. My vision had already been spinning from lack of sleep, and this crazy revelation made it even worse. "What do you mean I'm the son of the true leader of Tranak? My father was Gerald, and he just *died,* in case you weren't paying attention."

"I told you before that you would learn things that would come as a shock to you. Your real father is Drenton, the fallen leader of our realm."

How in the hell was it even possible? Was I some sort of rotten hot potato that everyone was just passing around? "Drenton?" I turned to my mother again. "What about Dad?"

This time, she stopped chopping and met my eyes. When she made a shaky gesture toward the breakfast table and sat down, I followed.

"I met your real father . . . " she paused and blew her nose. "We met when I was still studying at the university. I found him one night at the bus stop, near death. I helped him to my apartment and nursed him back to health."

"Wait. If he was an Aarmark, what was he doing here on Earth?"

Detherina answered, "We escaped here when we were being pursued by our enemies. At that time, they couldn't penetrate the Earth's atmosphere. The air was too thick and stifled them. Since they were more powerful than us and were killing everything and everyone in sight, we hid here until we could go back to fight."

I pressed my hands over my ears, refusing to believe their story. "No. I'm Dad's child. I have baby pictures with him." My shoulders grew tight and a powerful tremor rocked me. "Fuckkkkkkkk."

Detherina glided over and placed a hand on my shoulder. The instant her palm touched my body, the tics dissipated. Her touch was like a balm to my taut muscles.

Then my mother took my hand. "While I was pregnant with you, your father had to leave and help fight the war against Pratrim."

"And?" My eyes were suddenly blurry with tears. What had possessed her to keep this important detail from me? What gave anyone the right to withhold such vital information from me?

Detherina spoke again. "With your father's leadership and an alliance with another race, we were able to win that war. However, he took a blow to the head in battle, and he died."

I was getting sick to my stomach. "And I'm not supposed to know about this?"

"You are the heir to your father's throne. To keep you safe, the committee leaders decided to keep your existence a secret until the time came for you to lead our people."

"What about all the stuff you told me before? You said you're the Totren, a queen of some sort. Is all that a lie, too?"

"I would be next in line if there were no heir. You are the hope of our people. That is why we did whatever we could to keep you safe and away from the watchful eyes of the Ergans and the leaders of Pratrim."

"You risked Shannon's life to protect me?" I backed my chair away as another wave of spasms hit me. Clasping my hands behind my back, I tried to stop the tics from coming full blast. "Why have you kept us in the dark?"

"Putting a child in harm's way is the most painful thing a mother can do, and I would not have risked her if there were any other way. But we had to convince our enemies that I am the new leader of Tranak, which meant putting her in a vulnerable position."

I stared at Detherina in disbelief that she had made my Shannon a sacrificial lamb on my behalf. "No. This will stop now."

"Is that an order?" Detherina asked.

"What do you mean?" I leaned on the counter while my knees shook. "This is madness," I whispered to myself.

"You reached maturity today, which explains the headaches and keener hearing. Your eyesight will improve in a few days. Once you get to Tranak, you will be endowed with all the gifts we possess. Then you will take the seat of your ancestors."

"I don't believe you."

"Come with me, and I will prove it."

Like a petulant child, I muttered under my breath and followed her with reluctance.

Detherina led me to the bathroom and snapped her fingers. The lights turned on by themselves. "Look at your body in the mirror." She stepped aside.

When I lifted my shirt and turned around, I discovered the same markings I had seen on Shannon's neck. "What the hell? How come I'm just seeing this now?"

"Matro tells me that you don't spend much time looking at yourself in the mirror. The mark has been there all along, but it was not as pronounced until now."

"You mean my parents could see it?" The marks were in red, running across the nape of my neck and down to my tailbone. There were inscriptions in a language I didn't recognize.

Detherina nodded.

"The others?"

"Humans can't see the marking unless you allow them to do. Yours is bigger than most, being the mark of the true successor to the throne."

I pulled my shirt back down. "What does that inscription mean?"

"It is your name. Your father asked the assembly to name you Alpha when he learned your mother was having a boy. However, Cynthia wanted you to have a normal childhood, so she gave you a common human name."

"Did my father know about all of this? Gerald, I mean. Not Drenton."

"That is for your mother to answer."

Detherina led me back to the kitchen.

"What about Shannon?" I asked her.

"She will return with me to Tranak on her birthday. There, the stain bestowed on her by Axhatas will be purged."

"When is her birthday?" I asked. Funny, in all the time we'd spent together, I'd never thought to ask.

"In four days."

I slumped to the floor under the weight of this revelation. "What about Dad? Where did he fit in?"

Mom dropped to the floor next to me and cradled me in her arms. "He knew I was carrying somebody else's child when he married me, and he loved you like his own. He wanted you to have a normal childhood and refused to expose you to your father's people until we could no longer prevent it. We planned to tell you about your heritage together. He wanted to be here with you when you faced this."

Tears spilled from my eyes, and this time, I didn't try to hide my grief. Together, Mom and I cried for the loss of a great man who had been the only father I'd known.

"Was everything a lie?"

"A lie told often enough becomes the truth. We did this for your safety and the safety of the people you will lead." Detherina closed her eyes.

"I'm sorry that you had to find out this way, baby," Mom sobbed.

"Did you know this was coming?"

She hesitated. "I feared it might be. When you started getting into fights, I knew some kind of change was coming."

I looked at her and was reminded of that night she locked herself in the bathroom. "Was all this the reason Dad grounded me?"

"He was hoping that if we were able to limit your association with the Aarmarks, your transition would slow down. I'm so sorry we kept you in the dark."

I nodded. It wasn't an easy pill to swallow, but it wasn't her fault that my destiny was taking a mean detour. Everything I knew and believed in had changed with the snap of a finger.

"Detherina, I have one request," Mom said. "Brian gets to stay here until after he graduates. That was Gerald's wish, too."

Detherina turned to Matro. "You think you can handle the situation here until then?"

Matro gave me a hard look, and then nodded. "The boy is a natural. With a bit more training, he might be better than Drenton. He was able to wound Axhatas. That is not beginner's luck."

"Well then, we will get all the full-bloods here to help guard Alpha. You will be with him at all times."

Matro smirked. "Haven't I been up till now?"

It was time for me to speak up. "Wait, what? You mean you've been watching me my whole life?"

"Never a dull moment with you, kid." He laughed.

"Do Mark and Darryl know anything about my real identity?"

"No, it would have been too risky. They are human, which was enough to keep you safe. Your Tourette's made it a bit easier to hide you. With a human affliction, the spawns of Pratrim wouldn't suspect you at all."

All the suffering I'd endured had wound up being my saving grace. Well hello, irony.

"What happens to Kevin? Is he a part of this?"

"He was manipulated by Axhatas, I'm afraid, but he will not be a concern now. Say the word, and we'll take care of him for you."

That took me aback. "We're not murderers, you hear me? We're not killing humans, ever. You do your thing in Tranak, but we will go with human morality here."

Matro bowed his head. "As you wish."

Mom took my hand. "We're going to bury your father as soon as they release his body. I'm sorry you had to find out this way."

"I'm not leaving without you."

"I can't come with you, baby boy. There is no room for me in your father's world."

I shook my head. "There is no way I am going to leave you by yourself."

"I've been preparing myself from the moment I found out I was pregnant with you. The memory of you and Drenton and Gerald will always be with me, so I will never be alone."

All of a sudden, the revelations of the day became too much to bear. I felt my muscles tighten without warning, and all I could manage was to cling to my mom before the room spun out of control.

Then everything went dark.

"Curly? Are you okay?" Shannon's voice roused me.

I opened my eyes and found her staring down at me with a worried frown. We were in my room, curled up on my bed together. "What happened?"

"Your mom called me. She told me that you passed out after you found out about your dad. Oh, Brian. I'm so sorry." Shannon wrapped her arms around me and cried into my shoulder. "This is so unfair. Both of our fathers."

Still a bit disoriented, I hugged her close and tried to get my bearings. There were no words I could offer that would make any of this better.

After a while, her sobbing stopped. "I'm so sorry. I don't know how it could be true."

I sat up next to her. "I'm sure Dad didn't kill himself."

"If he didn't . . . who did?"

"I don't know, but I'll be damned if I don't find out." I would stop at nothing to avenge my dad's death, even if he wasn't my biological father.

Shannon nodded and fell silent for a moment. Then she said, "Would you like something to eat?"

My stomach growled on cue, but I shook my head. Instead, I took the remote from the nightstand and started flipping through the channels until I found the news. No matter what I was going through, I hadn't forgotten my dreams. I was determined to prevent the deaths I'd seen in my nightmare.

The news anchor began addressing recent earthquake predictions and recommendations made by geologists. While several coastal states were mentioned, the California Earthquake Prediction Evaluation Council had determined that no great risk existed in California. I remembered my vision of a long bridge collapsing, and I knew. *San Francisco!*

I dialed 9-1-1 on my cell phone and didn't bother letting the woman who answered finish her greeting. "I want to report that a huge earthquake will hit San Francisco. You have to warn everyone. People are going to die."

"Sir, we do not take prank calls lightly. I suggest you hang up now. Do not contact us as a joke again, or you will be subject to arrest." Then I heard a click, and the sound of the dial tone followed.

"She hung up on me," I muttered to myself.

"Curly, what's going on? What earthquake are you talking about?" Shannon yanked at my arm.

"Nothing. I just panicked when I saw the news." How could I tell her about my dreams? Would she even believe me?

"I've been having some strange dreams," she said out of nowhere.

I gaped at her. "What kind of dreams?"

Her expression turned guilty. "The night before the dance, I dreamt that someone killed your dad. I didn't really think too much about it when I woke up, but then I heard the news this morning."

"You dreamed about my dad?"

Shannon nodded.

"Who killed him? What did it look like?"

"I couldn't see clearly. There was this figure in a dark robe. All I remembered seeing was the hands—"

"What hands? What did it do to him?"

"It pushed something inside your dad's mouth. It wasn't really a hand, more like claws. That's all I could remember when I woke up."

"Fuccccckkkkk!" The word was out of my mouth before I could stop myself.

"What do we do now?" Shannon ran a shaky hand across her forehead, and her eyes were filled with fear.

Rightful Heir

Monday morning rolled in like a thick, sunless haze. Mom contacted my school first thing to tell them I'd be absent for the week. I didn't mind not going to classes, but I was worried about Shannon. After a quick phone call to Mark and Darryl, I'd established them as her guards, and I knew that Car and Orida would be on hand to assist. I wouldn't take chances with Shannon's life.

As usual, Mark honked the horn when he arrived, not at all concerned that he was waking up the entire neighborhood. I raced out of the house to stop him.

"Dude, can the honking, will you?" I hissed when I stuck my head inside the passenger window.

"Oh, sorry," he said, raking his fingers through his hair.

Despite his apology, I knew he'd do it again tomorrow.

Darryl looked up from his cell phone. "Are you okay, Bri?"

"Yeah," I said with a shrug. "Have to help my mom make arrangements."

"Don't worry. We'll keep an eye on Shannon." Mark flashed a thumb's up. "Car will be waiting by the entrance."

I debated whether tell them about my mind-boggling revelations from the night before, but I decided to hold off. Mark and Darryl had been dragged into this mess deep enough.

"Thanks guys. I'll text later."

Shannon came out looking bedraggled, which was a first. Yet she smiled when she spotted me and said, "I'll call you."

Darryl switched to the backseat and let Shannon take the front.

"Take good care of her," I said, closing the car door.

Darryl and Mark saluted.

"We'll come by after school," Mark said and revved the engine.

I waved them off, feeling a bit strange about being away from Shannon all day. I glanced at her house before turning back to mine. Once I did, though, I stumbled backward. Graffiti similar to what I'd seen at school was splashed across the front of my house. The same three circles were linked together, with a three-pronged spear running through them. The design was spread over the entire house in bold, red ink.

There were a few other symbols that I didn't recognize, as well. I looked behind me, but none of the people on the street gave any reaction. This must be meant for my eyes only.

Rushing back inside the house, I passed my mom, who was talking on the phone, and ran to my bedroom. I rubbed Matro's calling card, and he soon materialized. "I saw the markings out there," he said, sounding distressed.

"I don't understand what they mean," I said while I pulled

out my chair and powered up my laptop.

"They are telling us that they know about you. If we don't get back to Tranak and finish what we started—"

"You mean they're giving you an ultimatum?" I interrupted.

"They are talking to you, now. They work better here than we ever could, and they are manipulating not just minds, but the elements as well."

"You mean they will keep hurting the people around us?"

"That earthquake might be prevented if we go soon." Matro sighed.

I threw my hands in the air. The fate of too many people lay on my shoulders. After living a dull, normal life, how was I supposed to cope? The whole situation was insane. There was a host of creatures after me, and somehow I was expected to lead a group of people who had lied to me for years.

"The lies were meant to protect you," Matro replied to my thoughts in a hushed voice.

"If you expect me to believe anything you say in the future, you'd better not keep me in the dark anymore."

"That is the plan."

"What about my dad? Did Car find anything?"

"Yes. He died of an overdose."

"He wouldn't kill himself."

"He didn't. There were marks on his neck that indicate it was a forced suicide. However, the traces are not visible to human eyes."

Too much death and too much information—my brain was short-circuiting. Without giving it much thought, I rummaged inside the desk drawer for my medication. My Tourette's could take only so much, and I'd do more good if I were able to stay conscious.

"The blackouts are caused by your ongoing transition," Matro said.

"When will it be over?"

"The final phase will begin once you reach Tranak."

Darn it.

Matro watched me pop the pill but said nothing. Within the next thirty minutes, I felt my muscles relax, and the wild thumping inside my chest slowed down to normal.

"I'm going to drive Mom to the funeral parlor. Are you going to tag along?" I retrieved my jeans from the top of the hamper and marched to the bathroom.

"I'm always with you," Matro replied.

I stopped in my tracks and pivoted on my heel. "Just like my own bodyguard?"

"More like a personal trainer," he retorted. "We have called on all those of royal blood to help us out until we can get you safely to Tranak."

"What can they do?"

"They will help guard you."

"What about Shannon?"

"She'll be protected as well." Matro sighed. "Look, this is real. You're very important to us, to our people. We need you to lead us like your father once did."

"Isn't that a tall order for someone who wasn't prepared for it?"

"Feel the power in your veins. Your tics will diminish by the day. Already you are able to hear things a mile away, even if you haven't realized it yet. You can see things that a normal human doesn't. It's been there all along."

"How could I not notice any of that?"

"You didn't talk about the things you saw to other children, but every night, you would tell Cynthia and Gerald. Afterwards, I'd wipe your memory clean for the next day. Alpha, this is your destiny."

"Jesus, is my name really Alpha?"

"The one and only in Tranak."

"So even my own name was a lie," I muttered.

"We did it to—"

"Cut the crap. Whether you agree with me or not, this deception wasn't fair to me or Shannon."

"It was not our decision. Your father gave the orders. We were only doing what he asked of us."

I considered this for a moment. "What was my father like?"

"Exactly like you. Tall, serious, and strong."

"In other words, boring?"

"Never. Your father was a friend to everyone. He died saving my family from an attack. I vowed to protect you with my life in return."

"Don't you want more for yourself?"

Matro's face hardened. "The only thing I want now is revenge, but that is a conversation we'll save for another day."

The rest of the day passed by in a blur. I'd had no idea of the amount of energy it took to make decisions like choosing a casket, flowers, readings, viewing hours, and the burial. A simple service would have been easier to arrange, but Dad's family needed closure, and he had a lot of friends and colleagues who wanted to pay their respects.

I just wanted it to be quick and painless for my mother. The process was killing her. It wasn't fair that she was going through so much. Dad had been her best friend, and I knew that they'd loved each other deeply.

Detective Sander phoned the next day. As I'd expected, they

were closing the investigation and labeling his death a suicide. This didn't sit well with me, but no one would believe me if I told them the truth. So I kept my mouth shut.

I hated funerals. If there'd been any way I could have skipped it, I would have run and hidden. But my mom needed me so I sat in the front pew next to her and Dad's brother, Uncle Ray, while Dr. Singer, my doctor and Dad's best buddy, gave the eulogy.

The cemetery was packed with friends, distant relatives, clients, and Dad's co-workers. I wasn't surprised by the huge turnout. Dad had been a beloved doctor in the practice he'd established. He had made many friends throughout his life, and it was fitting that everyone should pay their last respects to such a good man. It was a relief to hear that most of them agreed that Dad wouldn't have given himself an intentional overdose.

It was around noontime when we reached his final resting place. Shannon hadn't strayed too far from me all day, flanked by Mark, Darryl, and Car. A lot of kids from school showed up, which in and of itself was a shock. Detherina was on hand, and so were Orida and Matro. There were many new faces I didn't recognize.

Judging from the scent in the air, I figured the Ergans were present, too. Just when they were lowering the mahogany casket into the ground, I caught a glimpse of four figures in the distance, robed in black. When I spied Matro go rigid, I knew that he was aware of their presence, too. He gave Car a warning look.

The weather in the past few days had turned chilly, and an unexpected rain shower began just as we were ready to leave the burial site. The downpour dispersed the crowd, the people scrambling back to their cars. Dad's brother and I ushered Mom to the waiting limousine, while Shannon followed in another car with Elizabeth, Mark, and Darryl.

"Uncle Ray, can you take Mom to the reception while I take care of some business?"

His eyebrows rode up, just like my father's used to do. "Sure, kid. Don't take long."

Before I could close the car door, I heard the screech of Car's motorcycle. Matro and the rest went running flat-out, but only I could see.

"Mom, I'll follow shortly." I waved the driver off, ignoring her protests. With the heavy rain, it was hard to determine in which direction Car and the others had gone. I followed my nose, palmed the dagger inside my blazer pocket, and made sure that I had the kordag Car had given me.

"Right behind you," Matro said, tossing something to me.

"What's this?" I looked at the small black stick in my hand.

"You'll soon find out."

While we ran through the thick bushes that lined the cemetery grounds, we discovered the paved path that led to the dense mountain that bordered the property. I could hear shrieks and the heavy clash of metal in the distance.

Then a whirring sounded right next to me before I had a chance to react, and a vacuum sucked us inside a cannus, where we found Car.

"Being invisible is our best weapon against them at the moment," he explained. Car was heavily armed, a holster that held different weapons zigzagged across his chest. "You can't fight them until you know how to incapacitate them."

"Who were those guys in dark robes?" I asked, shoving the dagger back into my pocket.

"One of them is Axhatas. The others are clan leaders. It's a mystery how fast they were able to regroup. It is worrisome, too, because there are so many of them."

With a mighty swing of his hand, Matro threw his kordag, which struck one of the Ergans. Gooey yellow liquid squirted from its body before it fell onto the muddy ground. To my amazement, the weapon worked like a boomerang, spinning back to Matro the moment it had hit its target.

"The kordag thinks the way you do," he explained, and then he went for another Ergan.

Feeling like a character in a comic book, I clutched my weapon and leapt out of the cannus.

"Damn boy, why do you have to make everything difficult for us?" Matro jumped out after me, while Car continued his killing spree from the cannus.

"Behind you!" Matro shouted when one Ergan nearly got me by the leg.

I pressed on the middle of the handle, and the reumdag stretched to its full size. The handle molded itself to the shape of my hand while the Ergan and I were still circling each other. The reumdag worked the way I remembered, except this time there was more energy in its twirl and I felt the power in my veins.

"Come on, doggy. Come and get me," I said, beckoning the creature closer.

"It's not a dog, for crying out loud!" Car hollered from afar.

Gnashing its teeth, the Ergan jumped up, but I pushed it back down with the blunt end of my weapon. It dropped to the ground, whimpering. "This is for my dad," I said, then struck the damn thing. True to its function, the reumdag melted the creature. Then I spun to help Matro, and we began operating like a fearsome duo, annihilating all the Ergans closest to us.

Car's cannus came roaring back. "Hop in," he called out to

us. We jumped in, and Car continued to maneuver it without effort.

"Where are the others?" I asked when we shifted in the direction of the funeral reception.

"They're cleaning up. The clan leaders don't dissolve, so they need to be burned."

"What happened to Axhatas?"

"He's a smart bastard. He knows when to fight and when to run. We're at full force here, and he's not going to get to you."

"Cool." My palm relaxed on the reumdag, and it suddenly shrank to pocket-knife size. "Whoa, this is amazing." I replaced it in my breast pocket.

"Don't forget this." Matro produced a small, square box.

"What is it?"

"I believe it is the perfect time to give this to Shannon."

Matro vanished before I could ask what he meant. When I took a peek inside the box, I found the necklace Dad had given me and flinched. Had Dad seen this coming?

People were streaming into the reception hall when the cannus dissipated around me. I glanced around the parking lot to check if anyone was paying attention, but the rain had everyone busy hurrying for shelter.

I joined Mom inside. After receiving a flood of sympathies and handshakes, I was able to slip away and find a quiet spot with Shannon. Madame Elizabeth and Gilbert were nearby talking to my mom and Uncle Ray, while Mark and Darryl were circling the buffet table like hungry wolves.

"Hey." I sat down next to Shannon. From the corner of my eye, I could see Matro standing guard.

"Hey. How are you doing, Curly?"

She looked lovely today. Her white blouse had a frilly

neckline and made her beautiful face stand out like a pearl inside a shell.

"As good as can be expected under the circumstances." I took her hand and pressed the black box into it.

"What is this?" she asked, her eyes widening.

"Happy eighteenth birthday, Shannon," I murmured.

"You knew?"

I nodded.

"I didn't want to say anything. It didn't feel like the right time to celebrate." Then she opened the box and gaped. "Oh my God, this is beautiful."

I took the pendant from the box. "Here, let me help you with it."

Shannon turned and lifted her hair, and her scent drifted around me. "Does it have a special meaning?" she asked.

Dad hadn't explained that part, so I found myself giving it a meaning of my own. "We'll never be apart."

Shannon turned around after I secured the necklace. "How does it look?"

"Perfect as always," I said, but I was looking at her face.

"I'm having a little get-together tonight. Mom wanted me to invite you, but I wasn't sure you'd want to come. Can you get away for an hour?"

I thought about it. If Detherina intended to whisk her away tomorrow, I wanted a chance to say a proper goodbye. In the short time I'd known Shannon, my world had shifted to revolve around her alone. If this was love, then I might die of a broken heart before I could find out if she felt the same way.

My Prodian

Mom opted to stay home that night, which was
understandable. She needed some time to mourn in private after
the grueling days following Dad's death. For safety's sake,
Matro left two Binarians with her to stand guard, and if anything
were to happen, we could be there in an instant.

Dressed in my cleanest jeans and a plaid shirt, I walked
across our lawn to Shannon's. The front door opened the moment
I reached the porch, and Gilbert greeted me with a bow.

"None of that, Gilbert. We're cool."

Gilbert reddened but inclined his head. "As you wish, sire."

"No titles, either. It's Brian."

When I got inside, Mark and Darryl were already seated on
the sofa with heaping plates of food.

"You're late," Mark said before he shoved more food in his
mouth.

"Where's Shannon?"

"We haven't seen her." Darryl swallowed fast, then whispered, "Who are these people?"

I looked around me. Some of them I'd seen during the funeral earlier, but there were unfamiliar faces, too. The men and women both wore the same type of clothes as Detherina and Matro, except theirs had more color. My guess was that these people were from Tranak. A few wore an air of supremacy that suggested they were the royalty Matro had mentioned earlier. They tracked my movements with interest, whispering among themselves. For once in my life, I didn't feel nervous about being under a microscope. They all nodded in my direction, some bowing their heads to me as Gilbert had done. That would take some getting used to.

"Okay, what's with the bowing?" Darryl asked through mouthful of food.

"Long story. I'll fill you guys in tomorrow. Let me find Shannon first."

I walked past the throngs of mingling guests, which parted like the Red Sea to let me through, and found Shannon in the kitchen with Detherina, Matro, and Car. She looked up at me with tears in her eyes.

"Is it true?" she asked.

My eyes drifted down to her hand. She was holding a dagger similar to the one that had been given to me, except hers had a half-moon shape. Just like the kordag, it contained a strange yellow liquid.

I stopped in my tracks and looked to Detherina for confirmation. She nodded. It looked like this was the moment of truth.

"Yes," I said.

"Why didn't you say anything?" She closed the gap between us, and Car shifted uncomfortably in the corner.

"Can we speak in private?"

Shannon nodded.

To the rest of the assembled group, I gave my first official order. "No one follows us."

Since the whole house was filled with guests, some even spilling into the backyard, the porch was the only private place we could talk. I took her elbow and escorted her out the front door.

The night was cool. Thanks to the rain earlier, the fresh scent of the wet grass tickled my nose. I also noticed that the stink of the Ergans was absent. I brushed off the steps before I invited Shannon to sit next to me. She still held on to the dagger and was brushing her finger along the blade.

The sight made me wince. My kind, sweet Shannon shouldn't be dealing with this. "They told me when I found Detherina—er, your mother—talking to my mom. Everything happened so fast, and we haven't had the chance to talk."

Shannon stared ahead. "That was some news. All this time, I've been living a lie. Now, I have a *new* mother who I've just met."

I tripped over my words as I tried to form a clear question. "How do you feel about Detherina?"

She shrugged. "I don't know her at all. Ask me again later. It's just weird. But it makes sense now why I never felt a real connection between Elizabeth and me."

"I'm so sorry. We're in the same boat. It blows, I know."

Shannon sighed. "It is what is. Let's get out of here?" She pulled at my hand.

"You're ditching your own party?"

"Why not? Aside from Larry and Moe, I don't know the rest of the people in there."

I hesitated for a moment. It was a dilemma. I was the one who needed protection, if they were telling the truth this time. Did I care about that? Not really. Well, not at the moment. I wanted to get away, too, and escape the scent of death and Shannon's looming departure.

Whatever happened tonight, I would make sure that Shannon got to celebrate her birthday like a normal human teenager. After all, eighteen was a big deal. It was a moment we waited for all our lives.

"Fine. Let's go." I jumped up and pulled Shannon to her feet.

"Should we tell them we're leaving?" she whispered.

"Why don't we live on the edge for a change? No babysitter, just the two of us."

I coaxed her into my car and got the engine started, not turning on the lights until the car left the driveway. Then I floored the gas. At the sound, the front door of the house swung open and people came rushing out, but I saw Matro in the rear view window ordering them not to follow us.

"Watch where you're going!" Shannon pointed back to the road.

"Don't worry. It'll be fine." I glanced sideways and gave her a wink. "I'm going to stop by the store to grab something, and then we can go to the Observatory."

"It's late. Don't they close off the roads to traffic after dark?"

"I've lived here long enough to know my way around. Trust me."

We stopped at the local nearby grocery store, and I hurried in. When I got back to the car, Shannon eyed the brown bag, which I stashed in the backseat.

"What's in it?" she asked, shifting to look over her shoulder.

I slapped her hand playfully and waggled a finger at her. "It's a surprise. You have to wait."

We lapsed into silence that lasted the rest of the way to the observatory. The area around Griffith Park was dark, visitors long gone at this time of day. The lights from the dome served as our guide while we drove up the deserted road. We passed a few vehicles on the road, most likely local residents. When we reached the dark spot where Mark, Darryl, and I always left our vehicles, I parked the car.

I took Matro's calling card and made sure that my reumdag was hidden inside my jacket. "Better hide your dagger. I don't think the rangers would be happy about a teenager running around with a weapon."

"Oh, yeah." Shannon tucked the weapon handle-first into the waistband of her jeans. I got the grocery bag from the backseat, and we headed down the path I'd hiked many times in the past, using my cell phone's flashlight app to light our way.

The spot I had in mind was about a fifteen-foot drop from road level. No one would suspect we were there if we kept our voices down. Since it was dark, I had to rely on my memory to get us there. I turned off the light once we were clear of the bushes. The pale glow of the moon, along with my new enhanced vision, was enough for me to see what I was doing.

Shannon settled in while I rummaged inside the bag. I produced a small cupcake and stuck a candle in the middle. "I hope you like chocolate."

"Curly, you didn't have to!" Shannon said, but I could tell that my surprise had made her happy.

"I wanted to." Next, I retrieved a bottle of apple cider and two plastic glasses. After I poured out a glass for each of us, I found the matches and lit the candle, and then sang happy birthday to her, although it was off-key.

When my off-key serenade was done, Shannon closed her eyes for a brief moment and then blew out the candle.

"Did you make a wish?" I asked.

"Yeah. I hope this one comes true." Her tone was wistful.

I raised my plastic cup in a toast. "Here's to us. Happy birthday, Shannon." After I'd chugged down the cider, I looked up at the night sky, feeling content.

Shannon broke into my reverie. "Why don't we eat the cupcake?" She moved closer to me until our shoulders were touching. "You take the first bite."

She held it up to my face, and I took a huge bite, smiling like an idiot while I chewed.

"Oh, you're such a dork. You have icing all over your face." Shannon leaned forward, but instead of wiping my mouth with a napkin, she covered my lips with hers.

Time froze. I couldn't move and didn't dare close my eyes in case it was just a dream.

"You said you wouldn't kiss me until I asked you," she murmured. "Well, this is me, asking you."

If I hadn't been sitting down, I would've fallen over. Shannon was asking me to kiss her. I stared at her, not sure what to do next. *Do I pull her closer? Do I lean forward? What in the hell is the right way to kiss?*

"Curly? Is something wrong?" Uncertainty crept into her eyes.

"I don't know the first thing about kissing," I admitted.

"There's no right or wrong. From what I remember, you kiss just fine." She smiled, closed her eyes, and lifted her face to me.

With nervous fingers, I reached out to cup her chin and then lowered my lips to hers.

Her lips were soft and icing-sweet, and I let her set the pace, exploring her mouth while my whole body ached for more.

My hands seemed to know just where they wanted to go. I let my fingers glide over her back, feeling the softness of her body pressed against me. Shannon clasped her hands behind my neck with a happy little murmur, and I started to relax, my heartbeat echoing in my ears.

When we finally surfaced for air, I was sure that Shannon' satisfied expression mirrored mine.

"Why me?" I asked once I remembered how to speak.

Shannon shook her head at me and smiled. "You are a cute boy with a kind heart, and you are good to me. Why *not* you?"

"Does this mean we are . . . well, you know . . . " *Damn! How do I say it?*

"What?"

"I want you and I to be, you know . . . crap. This is difficult, Shannon." I traced my finger along the curve of her neck.

"I don't know what you're saying, Brian."

"I want to kiss you again. And I want you to be my girlfriend." I gave her another kiss before she had a chance to answer.

She gave my shoulder a little push. "Of course I want to be your girlfriend. All you had to do was ask." This time, Shannon's kiss was slow, steady, and mind-blowing.

A swishing sound came from close by. It took a few seconds for me to understand what was going on, but Shannon had jumped to her feet before I could react. Without hesitation, she aimed her dagger and flung it at our unseen attacker. There was a thud, followed by silence. Her dagger swung back to her, and she caught it like a pro.

"Wait here." She glanced upward and narrowed her eyes, glancing left to right as if she were tracking something.

"Shannon, no." I sensed danger on all sides, and I pulled my weapon from my pocket. The reumdag extended to its full size as several Ergans appeared before us, gnashing their teeth.

"We're made for this," she said as we stood back to back while three Ergans circled around us.

Alpha, it wasn't easy finding you. We're going to finish this here or on the other side. You're going to pay for what you've done to us. The unspoken sentiment drifted in the acrid air.

Those words were meant to scare me, but they failed to do more than fuel my rage. "No. I'm going to make you pay for what you did to my father and my people. This is just the beginning."

They rushed us at once, but instinct guided me. I struck out, and an Ergan fell to the ground with a loud thump, allowing me to give the final blow before I turned to face the next challenger. Out of the corner of my eye, I could see Shannon going for the kill, and her movements surprised me. She jumped up, somersaulted in the air, and then jumped onto the back of the creature before plunging the dagger into its hide.

Stunned at her display of agility and courage, I let down my guard, and another creature lunged at me, catching me by the shoulder. Its claws dug deep into my skin. The sting was agonizing, making me stumble backward. I was saved by Shannon's swift reaction. She flung her dagger at our party crasher, killing it in an instant.

My mouth gaped while she wiped off the grime from the blade on her jeans, as if she had been doing this all her life. Then she ran to me and began examining my injury.

"Brian, are you okay?" she asked, trying to get a good look

at the damage to my shoulder.

"It's nothing." I waved her off, downplaying the pain from the deep gash.

"Don't move. Let me see," she scolded in a gentle voice. She took out a small bottle of the concoction she'd used on me before and poured out some onto my wound.

Her movements seemed so precise and automatic that I started to wonder. Had she been hiding knowledge of fighting from me all along?

A dart of pain distracted me. I hissed at the sudden sting when the liquid seeped into the cut and penetrated the affected muscle. I closed my eyes while I waited out the momentary discomfort, and when I opened them again, the deep gash was already closing up.

"Good as new." Shannon grinned and pocketed the bottle.

"Thank you." I rotated my arm and it did feel as good as new. "Wow."

"You're welcome," she said, looking quite smug.

"What was that about?" I asked, still floored by her fighting skills.

"Which part?"

"The acrobatics and ninja moves. Since when have you been able to do that?"

Her eyes sparkled. "Detherina—I mean, my mother— mentioned something about that. She said that since I reached maturity today, I would know what to do when the need arose."

"What does that mean?"

"I think I was destined to be your Prodian."

I opened my mouth, but then shut it again. What could I say?

I had been given the exact opposite of the truth. The plan to keep us safe had worked, but that didn't mean I liked it.

Shannon, my beautiful girlfriend, was now *my* Prodian. I was overjoyed that this meant we'd be together, but I couldn't help cursing fate for twisting our destinies into this deadly game.

"Come here," I said, returning my weapon to my pocket.

"Yes, Alpha." Shannon tucked her dagger back inside her waistband. When she walked into my arms, it felt so right.

"You knew about that, too?"

She looked up at me with a smile. "Yeah, but I still prefer Curly, if you don't mind."

"Not at all. As long as you don't mind me calling you 'babe'." I kissed her forehead.

"Babe." It sounded like she was testing out the word. "Hmm, I like it."

"So what's next for us?" After another quick kiss to her lips, I led her back to our earlier spot. I sat down and pulled Shannon into my lap, wrapping my arms around her.

"I leave tomorrow," she said.

Although I'd known about her impending departure, this reminder still hurt.

"I don't think I can handle being away from you."

"It's only temporary. Dethe– er, *Mother* said you'll be following me right after graduation." She shifted around and straddled my waist, making a shudder run through me. "I'm going to miss you."

"Not as much as I'm going to miss you." I kissed her mouth and tried to ignore how my body was reacting to her proximity.

"Okay, party's over," Matro said, appearing out of nowhere.

I kept my hands around Shannon, and she buried her face in the crook of my neck, giggling.

"I thought I gave you an order?"

Matro chuckled, hovering over us. "You're still in training.

Until we reach Tranak, I'm running the show here."

"We'll see about that, won't we? For now, why don't you take off?"

His eyes flickered. "Sure thing, but not because you're ordering it. I'm just a nice guy giving you a little time to regroup before you get an earful from Detherina." Matro promptly disappeared, but the lingering sound of his laughter echoed in the quiet night.

Shannon jumped to her feet. "My mother sounds like a terror."

"Oh, you can say that again." I took her hand and let her pull me up. We gathered our trash and headed to the car. Before I opened the car door, I pulled her in for a long hug. "I'm not sure what I'm going to do without you around."

"Half a year will pass before we know it. Besides, you have a lot to learn before you get there. Imagine, you'll be leading a group you hadn't even heard of a year ago." Shannon stood on tiptoe to kiss me.

For now, I would bask in the glory that I, the freak with a tic, was holding the prettiest girl on the face of the earth. Soon I would lead a realm of unimaginable beings on the path to safety and happiness. What more could a teenager ask for? If nothing else, it would make a great superhero story. I just had to make it out alive if I wanted the chance to write it.

Thank you for your purchase. Please log on to Amazon.com, Barnesandnoble.com or Goodreads.com and leave a review for this title. I would love to hear from you.

Sneak Peek from
Path of the Guardian,
the second book in
The Prodian Journey series
by Lorenz Font

Chapter 1 - Graduation Day

"Baby boy, aren't you going to finish your Mickey Mouse waffles?" Mom called out from the kitchen.

Standing in front of the mirror, I rolled my eyes and checked my reflection once more before dashing down the stairs. Some things never changed. For special occasions or whenever I was sick, my mother made those waffles. They'd been my favorite breakfast, sure, but that was ten years ago.

"Mom, I ate two already."

"Okay . . . fine." I heard the clattering of dishes and was certain she wasn't too happy about having leftovers.

"Come on. We're going to be late." I kissed her on the cheek, and she turned around with tears in her eyes. "What's wrong?"

"Oh, nothing." She tried shooing me away.

"You can't be crying for no reason."

"I wish your Dad could have been here today. He would've

loved to see you graduate."

"I miss him, too." I pulled her into my arms, feeling the gravity of my father's absence today more than ever. He would've been so proud of me.

She let me go and dabbed her eyes dry with a tea towel. "You have everything you need?"

I held up my blue cap and gown for her inspection, but it was my outfit that caught her attention. "Shorts and T-shirt for graduation? Back in my day, we dressed in our Sunday best."

Chuckling, I gave her a mock salute. "That was *eons* ago, Mom."

She playfully pinched my arm. "You look like you just got out of bed."

"No one's going to see my clothes underneath this heavy drapery. Let's go. I don't want to be late."

We hurried out of the house and into my car under the supervision of some of the fiercest warriors from Tranak. They had been watching over us since I turned eighteen, which was the official date my leadership began in their universe.

Unbelievable, yes. Since that day, I hadn't been able to wrap my mind around the events of the year that followed. I'd come a long way indeed, from an outcast freak-with-a-tic to the leader of a parallel world I'd never known existed. Mom had struck a deal with Detherina, the interim ruler of Tranak, so I could stay with her until graduation day. It was fine with me. In all honesty, I wasn't ready to be a leader and leave everything I'd ever known behind.

Mom's request might have delayed the inevitable, but it pushed my other dilemma to the forefront. I missed Shannon McKesson.

Shannon had been whisked away after we celebrated her

eighteenth birthday. The stain given to her by Axhatas, a prominent leader of our rivals from Pratrim, couldn't be treated here on earth. She was better off where antidotes were available to her. With the promise that she would be protected and guarded by our best warriors, I'd agreed to let her go without me.

Fighters Matro and Carionis escorted my car while I drove my mother to the Greek Theater. Matro led the way inside a cannus, the preferred mode of transport in Tranak that was invisible to human eyes, and Carionis rode his motorcycle behind us. This had been the protocol ever since I'd reached my Aarmark maturity. I had to be guarded by an armed male or female wherever I went for my protection.

Good thing I wasn't going on a date. Having armed bodyguards would be a total buzz kill. If Shannon were still around, hanging out would have been a big production with a bunch of colorful creatures following us around everywhere.

When we arrived, the venue was humming with activity. Cars were lined up outside, and security was trying to direct traffic. The colorful balloons, flowers, and leis added to the electric atmosphere, and I felt a small shiver of excitement. I spotted Mark Stanton and Darryl Martin, my best buddies, hanging by the entrance. They waved at me.

Even before I opened my car door, Krug, a hulking male with long, platinum blond hair, was waiting outside. "Go on and knock them dead," he said and took over parking the car for me.

I quickly donned my blue gown while Car escorted my mom to my side. "We'll be around. You have some toys with you?" he whispered.

"I never leave home without them." The dagger belonging to my Aarmark father, Drenton, was tucked into my waistband while the reumdag, my favorite weapon, rested inside my pocket.

Although Matro didn't expect an ambush, we always practiced caution.

Axhatas had escaped during our last clash, and the Ergans had eased off, no doubt needing to regroup after they discovered they were after the wrong person.

My real father had planned the deception, and Detherina had executed it to the letter, even though it meant jeopardizing her own child. My Shannon had been made to appear to be the next heir to the throne, focusing our enemies' attention on her. The ploy had worked, and it had given me time to reach my prime without constant threats to my safety. Being diagnosed with Tourette's shielded me from suspicion, as well. After all, no one would ever suspect that the person with such an obvious weakness would be the leader of an entire realm.

I never thought I'd find a reason to be grateful for all the years of suffering from constant twitching and embarrassing verbal tics.

However, the ongoing war had become much more personal for me when my human father was killed.

"Bro, they're about to start," Darryl said, gesturing at me to hurry.

I gave Car a silent order to stay by my mother's side. He nodded.

"I'll see you in a bit, Mom." I kissed her on the cheek and then joined my friends.

The three of us went to find our spots in the procession line, prodded along by anxious teachers and parents. Once "Pomp and Circumstance" began to play, we marched in alphabetical order down the main aisle and took our seats. Good thing Darryl was in front of me. The ceremony wouldn't be as boring with someone to talk to. Although life had changed, I still felt self-conscious around other kids. My tics had disappeared as soon as I hit my Aarmark maturity seven months ago. I didn't miss the spasms and jerking at all. It was a relief to be free from my Tourette's symptoms, the F bombs in particular. Now, I wished more than ever that Shannon could see me, just a normal guy for once.

Darryl threw a balled up piece of paper at me, and I caught it just before it hit me on the forehead. "Dude, you're spacing out again."

"Just enjoying the sunshine. I heard they don't get much heat up there." *Up there* meant Tranak. Right after our graduation celebration, I'd be leaving everything I knew and loved, including my mother.

I looked around the sea of proud faces, wishing with all my heart that Shannon could be there. It wasn't the same without her.

The commencement exercises began. Special awards were handed out, the speeches were given, and then the diplomas were distributed. Since most of the academic awards had been given at a special ceremony two nights earlier, the program didn't take long. I'd received two awards. Not too shabby for a guy who hadn't given the year as much effort as he'd hoped.

The principal called out my name. "Brian Morrison."

I followed the line of kids who were eager to get their ticket to freedom. As soon as I received the rolled parchment tied with blue ribbon, I turned around and waved it in my mother's direction.

Back in my seat, I waited with the rest of the students for the graduation proclamation, when we removed our caps and threw them in the air while our Alma Mater played in the background.

I caught one of the flying caps and then clapped Darryl on

the back. "We did it, bro."

"Sure did." His smile turned somber. I'd be MIA for a long time, and our plan to go to the same college wasn't going to happen.

Mark was waiting for us about seven rows behind, wearing a big grin on his face. "Freedom!" he said as soon as we got within hearing distance.

"I thought this day would never come," I said.

Darryl whipped out his cell phone. "How about a group picture?"

Our families tracked us down, and Car took pictures of us with our parents. A feeling of sadness swept over me again. I understood my responsibilities, but a part of me wasn't ready to let go of my human life.

The ceremony was followed by a luncheon at my house at Mom's insistence. I was in no hurry for it to end, but I knew I was pushing the time, judging by the impatient glances Matro had been throwing my way. He'd been sticking to me like glue but hadn't said much. He seemed to understand the weight being placed on my shoulders.

"Let's play one last time," Mark suggested after our third trip to the buffet table.

"Yeah," Darryl said, although he didn't sound enthused.

We played *Call of Duty* three times before Matro entered my room.

"Alpha, it's time."

The name had yet to grow on me. I stared at my friends, feeling a growing lump in my throat. "I guess this is it."

Mark nodded, and Darryl sniffed.

"I would say email us, but I know you can't." Mark extended his fist toward me.

I bumped it with mine. "I'll be back before you guys know it. Remember, I'm still your best man."

"And I'm chopped liver?" Darryl pulled us both into a group hug.

Matro coughed from the doorway. "We have to get going," he said.

"Remember, I'm going to sneak out if I can," I whispered to my friends.

"I heard that!" Matro's muffled voice sounded reproachful.

Saying goodbye to my mother was the toughest. Her tears poured like a flowing river. I stood and held her for a long time, wishing she could come with me.

"I love you, baby boy."

"I love you, Mom."

Her hug tightened. "I'm going to miss you."

"You know I'll be back to visit."

She nodded. "I know. Promise me that you'll take good care of yourself."

"I promise. Take care of yourself, too."

It was painful to think it would be a long time before I saw her again. I hated leaving her on her own. She had already lost her husband, and her son was abandoning her, too. My only consolation was that several fierce warriors had been assigned to guard her 24-7. They would ensure her safety and give me some peace of mind.

Mom answered with a sob, but eventually let me go and offered me a small smile. "Go make us proud."

I watched her climb the stairs before I turned to Matro. "I'm ready."

He nodded. Instead of taking the cannus as I thought we would, Matro steered me toward the center of my living room.

"What are we doing?" I asked, feeling an increasing vibration around me.

"We're going to take a wild ride." Matro's eyes twinkled, and he pulled me to stand in front of him. "Ready?"

"Do I have a choice?"

His laughter filled the room while he traced his thumb through the air, creating a rectangular pattern. The room started to vibrate, and my stomach churned. As the vibration on the floor increased, so did my nervousness. My Aarmark maturity hadn't prepared me for space travel. A door appeared before us, solid and daunting. Before I could step back, Matro opened it and shoved me into a black void, then followed close behind.

I screamed like a little girl when I fell into the abyss. My head throbbed and my vision spun, but I kept my eyes open, not wanting to miss my first inter-realm trip. Rays of white, green, and neon yellow flashed before my eyes, blinding me. After a few minutes, the sensation of falling stopped, and we zipped along a tunnel bathed in deep red light.

Matro kept his eyes closed, his face serene during our entire journey, but I was unable to relax. I lost track of time, distracted by the spasms that radiated from my neck down to my feet.

The sensations diminished, and I found myself standing on solid ground, my heart thudding in my ears. The air smelled clean, almost sanitized, with none of the smog inherent to Los Angeles. As dark as it was, my eyesight adjusted at once, and I was able to see everything clear as day.

Matro's usual robe had been replaced with armor the color of liquid silver and looked like a second skin. It covered him from his neck all the way down to his feet. His face had lines of pale blue running from his temples down to the edge of his chin.

"Why do you look like that? Did I miss something?"

"This is what we Aarmarks look like here in Tranak. The shield replaces the clothes humans wear on earth. Do you dig yours?"

I looked down at my body and discovered that just like Matro, my whole body was covered by a similar shell. "Mirror, I need a mirror."

With a flip of his hand, Matro produced a small rectangular reflector. I didn't miss the smirk on his face.

"Jesus Christ, this is how I look?" I stared at my face, noting that my usual dull blond hair had been replaced by long, silver locks. My face also had markings—two silver lines that crossed the bridge of my nose and ran underneath my eyes.

"Yes. And I must add, you are your father's spitting image."

"That's a good thing, right?"

"Yes, but it also is a dead giveaway. Our enemies would recognize you from a mile away."

That didn't sound promising. "So you're telling me I'm a sitting duck?"

Matro patted my shoulder. "Not if your guards can help it. Anyone trying to get to you will have to deal with them first." He gestured toward an imposing portal that was guarded by two figures clad in black armor. "Shall we?"

Rather than comforting me, his assurance gave me pause. Should I be honored that my subjects were willing to lay down their lives on my behalf? It was a strange idea to grasp.

My apprehension doubled the moment I stepped out of the gate into my new world, and without warning, stumbled upon the biggest crowd I'd ever laid eyes on.

"Welcome, Your Grace," Matro said with a grin. "Your people await you."

About the Author

A professional daydreamer, Lorenz Font discovered her love of writing after reading a celebrated novel that inspired one idea after another. Since being published in 2013, she has been conspiring, butting heads, and enjoying her spare time with vampires, angels, samurais, and other creatures she has created in her head.

Her perfect day consists of writing and lounging on her garage couch (a.k.a. the office) with a glass of her favorite cabernet while listening to her ever-growing music collection. She finds writing urban fantasy exhilarating and places an intense focus on angst and the redemption of flawed characters. Her fascination with romantic twists is a mainstay in all her stories.

Lorenz lives in Southern California with her supportive family and three demanding dogs.